BOLD CROSSINGS

LANCE ELLIOT OSBORNE

HOPE YOU ENJOY
THE ADVENTURE!

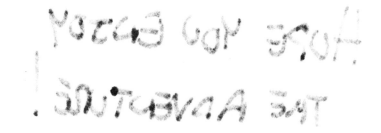

Hope you enjoy the adventure! LEO (handwritten, mirrored)

ISBN: 978-1-66780-633-4

To Katherine, Ian, Cali, Sabrina, Olivia, and Aiden...my band, my People.

And in memory of my Penatʉka sister, Juanita Pahdopony.

The prairie on the southern plains was a boundless, treacherous sea. The great rivers of Tejas eased and tumbled through it, buffalo and other beasts consumed it, and the peoples of many lands—drawn to all its untamed bounty—made bold crossings.

PROLOGUE

Deep Roots Beneath the Walls

WHEN THEY ARRIVED, I WATCH THEM PARK
along the fence line near the gate. Young and old, wearing their
Sunday best, stretched as they climbed out of their cars and
squinted into the dappled Texas sunlight. After nearly 200
years of hatred and distrust, this day had been a long time
coming. The adults quickly found comfort among their own but
the children were curious ... more social. For some, the racial
compass barely moves even after centuries. For the young,
there is no compass.

This is a historically segregated cemetery: slave graves
are outside the back fence, Hispanic graves are crowded in
their own area, and the Anglo graves are in the largest section
shaded by big oaks. The fourth group of visitors this morning
are Comanche, most traveling from Lawton. Their ancestors
hadn't marked graves in this fertile river bend, not like the
others, yet they're around us—unseen but represented.

I'd arrived early. As the dew rose with the sun, before anyone would see my homage or judge my actions, I set a shiny hand-forged horseshoe on the ground against Malcolm's headstone and scattered Blackfoot daisies over the fence for Wᵾkᵾbuu. Now it was time to give my speech. The cemetery was quiet. That just made me more nervous...

"I've practiced this speech about a million times. My wife says I give it in my sleep. All that practice and I'm still not sure I will make it through the whole thing. I guess that's because it's not really my speech; it's yours.

"For me, this all started with a few photos, a settler boy's journal and the tape-recorded reminiscences of an old Comanche woman. They changed my life.

"This morning, here in this sacred place, each of you will have a decision to make as to how this day will end. Will it change your lives? Will we work and eat together or walk away on the same separate paths we've walked for centuries?

"Regardless of how we enter this life, regardless of the color of our skin, the language our ancestors spoke, the way we worship, or the way we view the land that we live on, we all share one certainty: our end. Therefore, it seems appropriate that we start here, here at the common end, the resting place of your ancestors. Death, you see, is the great equalizer. But do we have to wait for death to be tolerant of each other, to make peace? Do we have to wait for death to know that we share hopes, desires, and ambitions just as we share sorrow, grief, and heartbreak?

"Why do we wait? Why do we choose to let death rule our lives like this? Imagine the abundant richness of lives well shared. Imagine

the power of common interests, concerted
efforts, and a collage of creative endeavor.
Aren't we choosing to live less than a whole life
when we insist on exclusion, when we cut
ourselves off by choosing hatred or disdain?

"After so many years, in this sacred
place, can we break through past choices that
have limited our lives? In this sacred place, can
we choose to be more inclusive, to break down
walls that divide us, to listen to those who we
have traditionally pushed away? In this sacred
place, is it time to recognize the value inherent
in every person, and in so doing, find more
value in ourselves?

"Since humans first roamed the earth
our motivations have driven our behavior.
Despite culture, creed, or philosophy our
motivations are the same: to live, love, and
thrive. Our point-of-view colors our reality, not
our inherent human qualities. One man's
farmland could be another's favorite place to
hunt; it is still soil. A woman's child could be
her investment in the tribe's future or a legacy
to carry a family name from across the sea; the
child is still a son or daughter.

"We are more than branches in family
trees. At the far end of our roots, we are distant
cousins with every other human on the planet.
Most of you have ancestors buried in this great
bend in the river. Surely, that lessens the
distance between you. Surely, your ancestral
roots in this fertile soil bind you in a way that
makes you stronger together than apart.

"I close with this thought from Reverend
Martin Luther King Jr.: 'He or she who is
devoid of the power to forgive is devoid of the
power to love. There is some good in the worst
of us and some evil in the best of us. When we

9

discover this, we are less prone to hate our enemies.'

"My friends, your next steps are entirely up to you. When you're ready, our forewoman will have her team help us finish opening the spaces in the fence and build the new stiles over the walls. And when we are done, we can dine together here at this table as one family in honor of your ancestors and, most importantly, with hope for future generations and their power to love."

ONE

Dark Dreams

DECEMBER 26, 1829 – COVINGTON COUNTY, Mississippi. Ma gave me this book-o'-pages for Christmas. I don't know how I'll ever fill it. There ain't that much in my head.

Ma says I need the writing practice. Maybe. She says when a man writes, his soul is in the ink. There ain't a lick of sense to that, but I don't cross her on it. She says the Lord guides my hand. I don't see that neither. They're my hands—cuts, callouses, dirt and all. Mostly they just hurt from farming every day. Why would the Lord want that?

Had one heck of a dream last night.

I was down in a box-shaped hole. Dirt piled up around me, smelling black and moist. I hate dirt. I ain't touched, I swear it, but my dreams come on strong and this one was bumfuzzling, to be sure. I raised out of that dark place and found myself walking in a village. No sign of a living thing, 'cept for a light coming from the blacksmith shop. My name was on the wall of the shop in big white letters, all straight like they's on the cover of a book saying, "Malcolm M. Hornsby."

I was born for smithing. Crave doin' it most every day I work this darn farm. A blacksmith don't feed the stock, don't shovel manure all day, don't mend fences, and ain't got a thing to do with no farm dirt. If I was looking for my soul, I'd more likely find it bending a red-hot rod of iron to my will than in writing words, but in my dream everything was muddled. My hammers, tongs, the anvil—them things was all there, but I couldn't touch 'em. My hands wouldn't move. I was cold, stiff, and floating above it all, lonelier than I ever been.

Then, for a minute, there was a young girl in the shop with me. I couldn't see her face, but I could hear her crying, quiet, like when they're burying folk. She sounded a lot like Ottilee Jameson, a girl I fancy from down the road. Can't swear by it, though. Then the lamps dimmed and, sure enough, I was back in that hole in the ground pushing black dirt out of my face as fast as I could.

My pa woke me. Though I dreaded his words, it was good to hear his voice, good to know I wasn't really, well, you know, passed on or something. Pa whispered, "Malcolm, get yourself out of that bed and tend to the hogs, boy. Can't sell 'em hungry. Then get back in here for your breakfast. We've a full day before us. Won't be long now, you going to wake up in another country." I sat up in the bed I share with my little brothers and wondered which is worse: slopping hogs or bad dreams.

Tarnation! How's a man gonna make a choice like that?

I DON'T KNOW MY AGE FOR SURE IN YOUR years. The way of Taiboo to write everything on paper was not the way for us. We walked on the land in flesh, but we lived in memories. I do know this. I am older now than anything or anyone I have ever loved. I am still a healer among the People, but behind my back they laugh at the old ways. Today, here in Lawton, they call me the Winter Woman, but before I had a name given by my father.

You say that others here remember little of the long-ago days. I remember much. My visions have always been strong. My stories come easy. I remember often as a young woman I would not sleep well because of my dreams. One morning after such a night, the pink sky held me. The smoke, fog, and smells comforted me. Father said it was a seer's dream. He stomped his foot and nodded as if to say, "Daughter, this is a sign."

In the dream, I rode hard, at first among all the Penatɨka, the elders, warriors, and children. Older horses pulled supplies. Dogs ran beside us. Our dust was thick. People and animals faded in and out of the pink darkness, but soon they disappeared and I rode with the dying sun to my shoulder in the cool night air, alone, away from our Great Clear River.

"My little brave bird," said Father, "yours was a dream of a kaheeka, one who would tell stories ... perhaps a healer of the people ... and a good wife." I shook my head, but just a little so Father wouldn't see. The dream frightened me. Being a wife frightened me more.

I pulled the buffalo robe tighter around my shoulders and watched our morning fire, let its warmth and light cover me, let the dusty dream swirl and dance like the smoke until it vanished into the red sky. Only then did I speak. "Father, little birds do not tell stories."

"Perhaps, Wɨkɨbuu ... you have not listened. When you listen, you will hear what others cannot and you will be a kaheeka."

So since you have asked, I will tell you these stories. I will paint with the cedar smoke and the memories it brings. So you know who I am. So you know the People.

DECEMBER 29 – TRAIL TO VICKSBURG. HARD day. Worse than most. At least we are nearing the end of this. I blame it on my pa. It's his fault we's moving these young'uns to a most dangerous place. When I think of it, I start to boil. Find it calming to write about it in a poem. Maybe that's what Ma meant before about my soul in the ink?

For one-hundred miles, we's forced to roam
Carry a baby brother on my back
Family slog beside me all the way from home
Boots near pulled off by mud deep black

For one-hundred miles, we smell wild meadows
The damp muck of forest floors
Crossed tree limbs rub and bellow
Night winds whistle through absent tent doors

For one-hundred miles, we wear scratchy wool shawls
No match for the razor frost
Little brothers hide their faces when they bawl
All feeling in their skin is lost

For one-hundred miles, we walk on half-frozen peat
From Covington to Vicksburg, Missisip
Seven days and six nights with a schedule to keep
A steamboat to catch, no time to let slip

For one-hundred miles like so many 'round us
We Hornsby's on a westerly tack

Can't see the gain 'cept a strong reason to cuss
Fighting thoughts to turn and head back.

We must be quite a sight on them trails. The oldest of us children is my high-handed brother at fourteen, the youngest my baby sister just shy of one year—between them four more brothers including me.

For most of today, Pa was nowhere in sight. He and Uncle Moses-Smith rode ahead hoping to hurry us along. Ma drove the wagon. Mattie, our house slave next to her held the baby wrapped in so many blankets it was hard to tell where she was in the bundle. Two mules pulled, two dogs followed. Our male slaves, my friend named Tom and his pa, trudged along with us five boys, every one of us muddy to the knee.

We wasn't the only frozen shadows on the road neither. The closer we got to Vicksburg, the heavier and noisier the traffic. There was rough, mean-faced drovers with their herds of cattle, sheep, or hogs. These sun-dark men smelled awful, spit tobacco, and swore up a storm. They was cracking their whips so, it sounded like guns in a hunting party.

This is one terrible winter for traveling by foot, but Pa's urge to move is stronger than the elements. He wants to see around the next bend so bad it's driving all the family. Not me. I wanted to stay home, to have a trade that would take me away from farm work, but Pa won't listen. He says, "We're moving to Texas, son. Them high falutin' dreams of yours will wait."

Behind us, we left belongings that didn't fit in the wagon and those Pa wouldn't sell at harbor-town cut rates. We left places we knew and good people we trusted. We left favorite horses, good hunting, and productive soil. I don't like to talk about it, but we left our granddad and the graves of our two dear young brothers, too.

Then there's this girl who lives in the big house down the road. Ottilee. She has eyes so warm when she fixes them on me, my legs melt like cheap brass bars. Her dad has the gotta-go fever too, but her ma just had another baby and it nearly killed her, so she won't travel for a while.

Pa said there was more fertile land at a better price than any ever dreamt. Sure, he said there'd be hardships, dozens, but also opportunities to test a man's fortitude. "Fortitude" must be a big word to impress Ma. He held up his fist like a man in a penny opera and said soon we'd be in "pure adventure on the edge of the Texas frontier." I never tried that word "fortitude" on Ottilee Jameson. Didn't even get to say a proper goodbye.

I hate Texas already.

SOME MEMORIES ARE VISIONS, FLASHES OF color or magic. Some, the strong ones, have sounds, smells, and touch. Some bring deep feelings of love, fear, or heartache. All these visions are for kaheeka, but as I am in my winter years, they can leave me breathless.

I remember feeling so small as the earth trembled. It smelled of churned-up soil and trampled bluestem ekasonipu. I closed my eyes and listened to the sounds of our buffalo and the warriors' horses. The wind blew across my bare skin and I shuddered. It was the last hunt without heavier buckskin on my feet, without a blanket. Kwihne, the coldest season, was almost here.

I had run over many hills that morning. My legs were tired, feet sore, moccasins covered in dust. It was my first hunt so close to my father and brother. Before, I had worked with the older women and girls from farther behind, gathering the spoils at a slower pace. Now in my thirteenth full season I was old enough to take the skin on my own and learn the ways of a Penatɨka wife, but I was alone and a stone's throw from hundreds of frightened giants. The bulls' dark wooly coats bounced and jostled on their necks as they galloped. At the top of their shoulders, they were two hands taller than my father.

In the hunt, I wanted to be brave like my older brother, but was told to sit and wait for my father's signal. It took too much time. Time to think of the horns. Time to think of the hooves of full-grown buffalo bulls—sharp and dangerous. I worried, "What if I make a mistake?"

I heard a familiar sound: a small, subtle command to a horse somewhere among the buffalo. I looked over the ridge just in time to see my brother charging an enormous bull only a hundred paces away.

Wowoki was tall and sinewy. He rarely wore a shirt, except on the coldest of days. The other girls said he was tuibitsi, handsome, but to me, he was just an older brother. He would always play too roughly, brag too much, and take too many chances. Worst of all, he called me Huutsúu Kwanaru, Stinky Bird, instead of the name given to me.

Wowoki, Barking Dog, was in his fifteenth full season and nearly a warrior. He seemed to have no fear. He rode as well as any. He would stand in place with a rifle or bow and take a charging enemy with one shot, then yell at the dead or dying for having dared attack. Most of all, my brother hated all that was Taiboo, those with white skin.

On this day in the hunt, I watched him calmly lift his rifle with both hands while riding his horse at full speed among the great wooly beasts. Before I saw the smoke from his gun and heard the shot, before I saw the bull skid and roll in a cloud of dust, I knew my brother would take the kill. He rarely failed.

Wowoki gave out a loud, celebratory whoop and looked in my direction, but my father had been very clear that I should wait for his signal. My brother yelled again and waved his rifle. I looked for my father but couldn't see him over the grassy hills.

I knew Wowoki would make fun of me. Worse, he may grow angry. His anger was like a fire, burning anyone too close. I spoke in silence to the wind and dark clouds. "Why should I wait? After all, I am trusted to skin on my own. I don't know if I want to be a wife, but until I am, I will learn as I please." I slipped my beads under my shirt and set the skinning knife made of Taiboo steel between my teeth. I looked for my father one more time.

There was no sign of him.

DECEMBER 30. TRAIL IS CHANGING NOW.
Almost there. The oaks and cypress look like they's wearing long gowns of moss. As we came 'round a bend in the trail, we saw Pa and Uncle Moses in a clearing waving us forward. Pa yelled at us. "We've a boat to catch, Hornsbys!"

Ma flicked the reins with a "Get-up, mule!" and the rest ducked their heads a little lower into the freezing wind and moved their feet one more step ahead, then another. All 'cept me. I was bent with the weight of my sleepy little brother over my shoulder. I stopped to look back in the direction I thought was Covington County, back home, back to Ottilee.

That's when my older brother, Billy, yelled at me. "Come on, Mal, you bookweevil. Ain't time for your regrets." I straightened right up to make myself as tall as possible and whispered under my breath so my ma wouldn't hear, "Tarnation!"

I knew I ought to heed my brother, but I fought it. I took a few steps back down the trail toward our farm. It would be a long walk with just a little brother for company. That was when Daniel groaned a little, so I stopped just to be sure he was right.

I glanced back over my shoulder and watched my family moving on without me, a lonesome sight. I whispered to Danny that we'd better think on this a bit. Reckon my looking after him and Ma is above the rest.

I POPPED UP AND RAN, AVOIDING BOTH THE
buffalo and prairie dog holes scattered in the tall grass, but
once I neared the bull, fatigue and fear clouded my judgment. I
circled the giant and moved toward his belly. I did not see my
father's frantic waving. My brother had spotted another bull
and was giving chase in the dust. When I realized my mistake,
I froze, stared into the eye of the hulking animal and noticed
the sound of his heavy breath. He shouldn't be breathing. The
bull moaned, bellowed and kicked his legs in an attempt to
stand.

I heard a loud crack when the bull's hoof caught the
top of my head. I remember dropping to my knees and the
feeling of warm blood running down my face. Everything spun
around me: the buffalo, the clouds, the hills, even my dog who
circled and barked at the big bull. They all seemed to spin in
silence. I saw my father racing toward me, but strangely did
not hear the hooves of his horse or the sound of his rifle when
the gun flashed and the restless bull slumped in death.

As the sky drew darker, I heard my brother calling me
by my given name, "Wukubuu! Wukubuu!" I lifted my head to
look for him. It was hard to focus but I am sure I saw a red
buffalo calf with a quarter-moon scar just above his eye,
staring at me. I reached for the charm around my neck and
rubbed the smooth wooden beads.

All went dark and silent.

JANUARY 2, 1830 – VICKSBURG. GOT A LOT TO
write on this new year. Spent a cold night in a stranger's barn
with my brothers and our horses while Ma, Pa, and the baby
slept in a boarding house. Then this morning, had to walk
sideways to see around the crate in my arms and avoid patches
of ice on the gangplank at the boat. Guess it all piled up on me
enough to bring out the devil words: "Darn, why don't we just
stay here? Goin' to Texas is already hell."

I glanced up at Ma at the far end of the upper deck. If she'd heard them words she'd be after me with a switch. Luckily, she and our house slave, Miss Mattie was busy with baby Diana and corralling my brothers, else them boys would've wrestled their way into the river, that's certain.

The port at Vicksburg was a busy, noisy place, even in this terrible weather. Boats and rafts of all sizes bobbed on the river as far as I could see. Why, with a good head of speed, I could have jumped from one craft to another and ended up on the other side, a half-mile 'cross. The docks was crawling with slaves, cargo movers, crews, passengers, and folks in city or country clothes saying goodbyes or welcomes. The air smelled of river water, burning wood, hot oil, and cooking. I reckon my Ottilee would call it "a ladle of life's stew." I just love the way she talks. Ma says Ottilee can sure turn a word for her age.

Then darn if I didn't slip on ice the next step. As hard as I tried, I couldn't get my footing. Folks on the upper deck laughed at me in my short muddy trousers dancing a jig. I'm sure my eyes was as big as saucers. The crate was bouncing. I was slipping and stepping as if rolling a log on water. There was a couple of girls on the deck; might have been my age. They 'bout giggled themselves into the heaves.

Lucky that Tom jumped to the gangplank and caught the crate just as I neared the edge. Of course, he had to shoot off his smart mouth. "Whoa there, Malcolm! Ma Hornsby have yer hide if yeh drop this crate in that big water." Couldn't let him best me in front of them strangers so I said, "Tom Walker, you don't wipe that laughing grin off your face, I'll have your hide."

Darned if he didn't put me right in my place. "What yeh gonna do, hit me with one of yeh books?" We laughed aloud. Then I remembered and reached into my coat pocket to check that my book and a stack of pamphlets was still safe. They were.

We pushed and shoved with the other lower deckers to get on board. That's how it is when you can't afford a berth above. I'd just as soon stay down with Tom. As we snaked our way along through travelers' belongings, cotton bales, and hogshead barrels, I whispered to him, "What yeh reading now?" Tom looked around. "I ain't. Couldn't really hide it on the trail. What yeh got? I seen yeh with yer head in something." I opened up my coat. "I got Robinson Crusoe outta Ma's crate. Yeh can have it when I'm done. I hear there's blacks in it."

Tom asked if I was sure he could read all the words. I reminded him quietly that I had taught him everything Ma taught me. He smarted back that he ain't gotta read so much as me, and then he asked why I was at it so often. I had to think on my answer for a bit. "Guess it helps me forget what I don't like and dream 'bout what I do." Tom looked me straight in the eyes, something I never seen him do with anyone else. Then he asked, how many books I figured I was gonna need to read?

Tom has a way of challenging me like no one else; it's like we're playing checkers, even when we ain't. I told him I wasn't sure. "Wouldn't it be something to read all the books there is? You suppose a man could do that?" Tom just shrugged and shook his head, so I asked about Pa.

Tom smiled. "Yeah, I seen'm box yer brother Billy's ears and give 'm first watch on yer family belongings down here. Pa Hornsby say all these boats full of thieves and hustlers, say he don't even trust the captains. Ain't that something?"

I wasn't listening much. I was looking forward to Billy getting his due.

DREAMS IN FEVER OR WITH A HEAD WOUND can take the dreamer down a frightening path, all alone. Wowoki told me later that I stood and stared at the big bull, then laid back down and curled up like a newborn. All I remembered was the dream. Smoke billowed from the bull's nose and mouth. His eyes were like little fires and everything he looked at was burning. I needed to run from that bull, needed to get away from the burning grass, but I froze there to that place, my feet part of the prairie, my hair tied to the grass.

I could hear my father's voice but could not see him in the growing smoke. I tried to cough the smoke out of my lungs but it hurt my head. My brother yelled at me to move, his voice loud like a tʉmakupa, a mountain lion's, roar.

The big bull turned toward me and I had never felt so alone. He scraped at the grass with his front hooves. Then in the smoky sunlight, a huge warrior stepped in front of the bull. I could not see his face, but it was easier to breathe in the coolness of his shadow.

I laid down in his arms and was safe.

SURE ENOUGH, AS WE ROUNDED ANOTHER stack of tobacco barrels we heard someone playing Yankee Doodle on a penny whistle: my brother, William Watts Hornsby. He's a year older and a half-foot taller than me when he stretches full up. His eyes is dark blue and serious. Had a man's beard for a year now. Mostly, he loves to boss me. "Listen Bookweevil, unlike you, I'm already a man and next in command of this here family, should anything ever happen to Pa."

I hate when he talks about Pa like that.

Billy was nowhere in sight, but we heard the penny whistle and I yelled after it. "Billy! Billy Hornsby, if Pa put you on watch, you'd better get your backside over here!" The whistling grew more distant and I shook my head. "Don't do this again." Tom laughed at me, knowing I'd had fallen into one of Billy's traps. The whistling stopped, and we heard my brother's voice. "Hey, flat-headed little brother, I'll tell Pa that you took the watch! Much obliged to you, Bookweevil!" Then he laughed his way up the stairs to the fancier deck.

I kicked one of them crates and threw my hat. "Hellfire!" Tom laughed at me. "Mal, your old mop of black hair is stickin' out in every direction." I told him he was one to talk with that wool on his head. "Tom, I'm stuck. I can't leave. Pa will have my hide. Damn Billy and damn Texas!" Tom stopped laughing and whispered, "Quiet, Mal. Yeh pa hear such things, he liable to whip yeh. Yeh ma's liable to take a bar soap to yeh teeth."

I stuck my hands deep into my trouser pockets as I have a habit of doing when I need to think. In my right pocket, I found my silver-dollar-sized clock gear and gave it a rub. Tom was right. My pa is following a stubborn dream that won't go away: more farmland, more room to grow his family, and all at a rock-bottom price with no high falutin' soft-handed rich men looking down at us. When Pa and Ottilee's father speak of cotton and land in Texas, they get a wild look in their eyes as if they were starving for it, and nothing or nobody would get in their way. It's a restless fever, and that fever had me rubbing my good-luck charm to a shine.

WHEN I WAS JUST A BABY, AGAINST CUSTOM, my father named me. I was born in his favorite camp area, in a wide, fertile bend of the Great Clear River. His hunts were productive after my birth. His love for María, my mother, was strong, but in the first warm season, I grew sick. My neck and face blotted with red spots. I would not eat. My ahpu worried he would lose his precious child. He carefully painted his face and best horse and rode hard through the night to the west, to the mountain they called Father of the Great Clear River.

As the sun rose, from the top of the mountain he could see the river and its valley snaking through the rugged hills. He sat at the edge of the great canyon above the water, burned cedar, and sang, under the spell of the mountain until he fell to sleep.

A loud buzzing woke him. He opened his eyes and saw a tiny hummingbird. She had a shiny green back, her wings were a blur, and beneath her chin were red spots. She bravely defended the Ekapo flowers from other hummingbirds and butterflies. Father lay on his back as still as death and watched this brave little bird until she ate her fill and flew to the next bush.

This was a sign.

He hurried his horse back to camp to find I had grown stronger in the night, the spots nearly gone. I was eating again. I would live, and though naming was something that usually occurred after several seasons, I would be Tupaapi's Wʉkʉbuu, his hummingbird. "This strong little girl," he whispered, "will lead the People."

JANUARY 3 – MISSISSIPPI RIVER. GOT A GOOD lantern in my little corner of our cabin. Trying to write some before Ma makes me douse it. I've read and studied all I can about this place called Texas. Talking about it with my father has been a harder proposition. As we packed the wagon back home, I tried.

Reuben Hornsby is known throughout the county for his serious nature. It's no different when he speaks to me. "Mal, I'm expectin' a lot of help from you and your big brother, hear? You might not have time for so many of your books."

I told him I knew what he needed. I asked if I don't always do my share. Pa heard the unsaid in my voice and pushed me for it. "Son, you got somethin' on your mind, you best get on with it before we freeze to this spot and the packing stays half done. What's eating at you?"

I couldn't look directly at those hard eyes. He pushed again. "Maybe you're too smart for your own good, Malcolm.

It's tying up your tongue. A man has to be practical too, you know. Especially where we're headed." I kicked mud off the wagon wheel. Pa sighed, banged the side of the wagon with his fist, "Tarnation!" He turned for the door. "Boy, you're wasting my time and there ain't no time to waste. You let me know when you think you're man enough to ask whatever it is."

That's when I turned and yelled at Pa's back without thinking. It was one word he never heard much, "No! I mean, Pa, why? Why we goin' anyway? To Texas? It has got to be the most backwards place around. It ain't even a part of our country."

Pa stopped but didn't turn. I knew better but couldn't quiet myself. "And why ain't we bringing Grandpa Moses? How's he gonna make it without us? What are we gonna do against them injuns, with Ma, the boys, and baby Diana to look after? What do we know about injuns? Billy said we's to swear an oath to Mexico or somethin' and say we's catholic."

Pa was losing his temper but I kept on with my fool mouth. "Is that true, Pa? Ma ain't gonna do that, is she? Why I reckon she'd as soon court the devil as declare an oath to some Italian potentate." Then he exploded. "Malcolm Hornsby, watch your words!" Pa turned and stared me down with steel blue eyes. Even in that icy cold, I 'bout melted.

He practically growled the words out. "Son, get your head outta them books and machines, and start learning our business. There are a dozen solid reasons for doin' this, and doin' it in Texas. Besides, family is always family."

Then he opened the door and with a few heavy steps, left me to stew. I wanted to run down and hide in the Jameson's barn, but I didn't. I reached into my coat pocket and pulled out a small stack of pamphlets, careful to keep the wind from blowing the lot of 'em across Mississip. I thumbed through the stack until I found what I was after. I held tight to the edges of the creased and yellowed pamphlet and read the cover:

TRANSLATION

OF THE

LAWS, ORDERS, AND CONTRACTS

ON

COLONIZATION,

FROM JANUARY, 1821, UP TO THIS TIME

IN VIRTUE OF WHICH

COL. STEPHEN F. AUSTIN

HAS INTRODUCED AND SETTLED FOREIGN
EMIGRANTS IN

TEXAS

In the margin of the pamphlet cover, one of the
previous owners had hand-written a list: Cherokee, Shawnee,
Karankawas, Tonkawas, Wacos, and Tawakonis. Someone else
had added another tribe's name in larger letters and underlined
it several times: "Comanch."

AS I GREW, I HEARD THE STORIES OF THE
People, the N~~u~~m~~u~~n~~uu~~, and of my band, the Penat~~u~~ka—the
honeyeaters, known as the quick-to-sting. The N~~u~~m~~u~~n~~uu~~ are of
the Shoshone in the north. We separated from the mother tribe
and traveled south, many full seasons before I was born. The
migration was long and difficult, many died, but it brought our
People closer to the horse and buffalo, the animals at the center
of our power.

We did not claim the land, as the Taiboo do now. We
fought to survive and keep anyone uncooperative out of our
hunting, trading, and living places.

My father would say, "This place and all it offers is ours—as is the air we breathe—if only we are brave enough to keep it." Taiboo were the same as any other tribe of people who threatened us. If they entered our lands, they must become kin, captives, trading partners, or face our fearless warriors who wish to dominate all enemies.

It is not our way to speak of the dead, but it is only to teach you.

In a raid, my father captured my mother to teach her Taiboo father a lesson and to expand his own family...elevate his status. My father was originally of the Kwaharʉ band, the antelope people. He and his sister were taken into the Penatʉka as orphaned children. He was eager to prove his place among his adoptive kin.

Father says that in the beginning, my mother was different from other captives and his first wife. She didn't understand the language. She didn't know her place. The work was hard, the days long, and the living harsh, but she never cried, never complained.

Before her capture, Mother spent most of her childhood on her father's ranchería or in the permanent camp that they called San Antonio de Béjar. Her life was safe, predictable, and settled, but Penatʉka are always on the move. There was always something new for her to learn. There was always work to do. Though some of the other women acted jealous, some vengeful, Father insisted they treat her well.

When times were good for the band, the women were more giving. They taught her how to be Nʉmʉnʉʉ, showed her the ways of the Penatʉka. Eventually Father fell in love with this fair-haired beauty with green eyes, and she fell in love with the quiet warrior. Ordinarily, he would have to bring gifts of many horses to the bride's father. For her hand, he didn't give up a single horse but, as he told it to me, he did give up his heart. Soon, there was a baby on the way.

As I grew, my mother taught me her language. To her, hummingbird was "colibri." We did everything together: took long walks to gather food, prepared hides, washed in the rivers and streams. We picked handfuls of flowers for making colored paints. We worked and learned the ways of the People together, but the Taiboo pox took her before my seventh full season. The pox took many; including my father's first wife, Wowoki's mother. We mustn't speak their names.

The pox took the young and the old, but the Penatɨka are fighters. Our band renewed itself and grew. I grew too, but I carried my sadness for a long while. I tried to remember her. My father would rarely speak of it, but once he said, "Look in the quiet water, my little bird. The one you miss is there in your eyes. Her charm is around your neck. She is always with you. Look for the signs."

There were no signs.

Year after year, I rubbed these wooden beads and the cross while the memory of my mother faded. My father's words were no help. Could this be why my brother was always so angry? Perhaps the Taiboo brought this death of mothers to us both.

I was angry too.

JANUARY 3. PAST MIDNIGHT, CAN'T SLEEP. Everything and everyone on this boat seems to make noise. I've eased out of the cabin and into the saloon. Men here stay up all night gambling and gaming. Ma would have my hide if she knew where I'm sitting. I reckon it's as good as time as any to tell more about the day.

I was with Tom on the lower deck this morning, sitting quiet, caught up in my own thoughts, when the whole place started rattling. Then a thunderous rhythm began as the engine played music to my ears and the ship's steam whistle blew open like a big startled goose. The deckers rushed about to make final preparations. I reached into my coat pocket for a worn-out pamphlet: Robert Fulton's "Travel Revolution." I held it up as a divining rod to show me the way to the steam building up in them boilers.

I glanced in Tom's direction. He knew, if I was a moth, that engine was the flame. He shivered, grabbed one of our dogs, and pulled him over for a wrestle, dismissing me with, "Oh, go on wit yeh, I'd just soon sit here. These dogs better company anyhow." I felt bad for leaving him and tried to make up for it. "Grab one of them blankets, Tom. You ain't got a thread on you" but Tom took it wrong and shook his head. "Oh, just get, Malcolm Hornsby, take that mop of hair and get."

I walked around the next stack of barrels and there was the beautiful, dangerous boiler of the steamboat Pocahontas. It was a big black metal cylinder—tall as a man—nearly half the length of the boat, and a beehive of activity. My hands shook as I thumbed through the pamphlet for the diagram showing how the boiler turned water and wood into power. The crew pumps fresh water into the boiler. Wood burns beneath the cylinder to heat the water until it turns into steam. The steam runs through long pipes and pushes the pistons turning the gigantic wheel on one side of the boat. The wheel is fitted with large wooden blades that dip in and pull at the river.

It's dangerous. Everyone in Mississippi who's paid a lick of attention knows there's been thousands killed or maimed in explosions. I reckon most feel the speed and ease of travel worth the risks. It was like a big drum calling me, despite the dangers.

Like most steamboats, the Pocahontas skims across the top of the water. In Vicksburg, I heard boat captains bragging they could "navigate a large puddle," but how will her shallow draw do in the ocean down south? No one was asking. Better just to look further ahead I reckon. Maybe we all have a fever of some kind.

I watched them lucky engineers and firemen, their faces, beards and clothes covered in black soot. They was sweating in the cold, throwing one log after another into the furnace and pumping water into the boiler. I tilted my head back and closed my eyes to smell the wood, oil, and smoke. I listened to the drumming sounds of the cranks, valves, and rods. With a shudder that shot up through my legs, we was underway.

The big ship eased out into the muddy river. I stepped out on deck and watched as the Black leadsman dropped his rope and weights to measure the depth of the river. He called out to the pilot above in the wheelhouse. "Quarter twain! Half twain now! Mark twain, there!" The Pocahontas was on course at a safe depth of twelve feet.

SHALL I FINISH THE STORY OF THE BUFFALO calf? On this hunt, we were two night's travel from the big bend in the Great Clear River—from my mother's final resting place. In my darkness, I also dreamed of my mother. Father said I was smiling and this gave him hope. For just a moment, I saw her clearly, her gentle smile. Then the dream changed. My mother was gone. I heard singing and voices. My head ached.

I woke as someone wiped the blood from my face with water. It felt good and tasted sweet as it ran into my dry mouth. I opened my eyes but what I saw was blurry. My father sang beside me. Wowoki sang softly too, but in his voice I heard something different, something I had never heard from him before: fear.

He whispered, "Wʉkʉbuu, you must wake. Wʉkʉbuu, wake! I'm sorry; it is my fault, I…" Father reached for him and firmly squeezed his shoulder. A warrior did not apologize, certainly not to a little girl. Wowoki's tone changed, "You should have waited … Wʉkʉbuu … as father told you." I noticed he still hadn't called me by the other, hurtful name.

Father returned to his singing. I felt his strong, callused hands on my arm. I could sense his rocking. I longed to feel my mother's touch. I longed to see around me, but all was hazy. Then dark again.

I don't know how much time passed. I could smell the cedar smoke and taste the prickly-poppy tea as someone dabbed my lips with a soaked cloth. I heard my paha's voice and her medicine song, and I remembered the red calf with the scar. Perhaps he was a sign from my mother. I tried to sit up. The earth spun. My father spoke softly but his words ran together. I reached for my charm and rubbed the beads. It was no use. The darkness, the dizziness was too strong. I crumpled back into the grass and fell into a sleep I had not asked for. Was this the suhu mupitsi, the owl of death coming for me? I would fight him, even in my sleep.

Again, I awoke enough to hear my father's voice as he dipped the cloth in the tea and wet my lips. In his song, I heard the strain of his many worries. His eyesight was fading. This season's hunt had not gone well. More Taiboo were entering the Comanchería every day. Word had come from the other bands to the north that along the Arkansas River, the People and our allies the Kiowa battled for the first time with Taiboo soldiers.

The blanket that made up our empire and enabled our freedom to live and roam was starting to fray. For the Penatuka, changes were coming—too subtle to notice perhaps—but they were coming, rising rivers from a distant storm.

JANUARY 6. MA'S A HARD-WORKING WOMAN but ain't bent by it. When she stands, she stands straight and proud. Makes her seem taller, more formidable, especially when insisting that one of us boys recite the scriptures or wash behind our ears. Anger her and she'll knock the back of your head so hard you'll see stars. Charm her and she'll bake you the best biscuits in the south.

She comes from North Carolina farming, one of seven children, tobacco their main crop. Farmin' is mostly a man's place, but Ma made it a point to understand the way everything worked. Her pa said she asked too many questions. Ma says she worked extra chores to earn money for books to read, and I believe her, seeing how she insists we learn it too.

At the dinner table Pa would say, "Yep, she's the smartest woman I ever met. Don't know why she married me." Ma would look down and shake her head but everybody knew she was smiling. Sometimes, Pa would say it different, especially when sitting with my grandpa and uncles drinking whiskey or cider. He might say, "Ain't you smart enough to know your place?" Ma would look hard at him, like he was one of her kids and she was about to leather him for letting a devil word slip. If he were clever, Pa would cover his tracks using us children, "Look out, Hornsbys, she's got her Scottish up." Then he'd make scary eyes at us around the table. We'd laugh, but Pa was always extra nice to Ma afterwards. Once, he even made a middle-of-the-day trip from the fields just to bring her flowers and sit inside with her a spell.

If there was one thing that made my ma a bear, it was protecting us children. She'd known the heartache of losing two children. In moving away from Mississip, we was leaving behind the graves of my little brothers, Elisha and Leonard, who both died from diphtheria. Their deaths put a gray cloud over her most every day. When I think about my baby brothers, I can't help but remember Ma crying while burning candles and waving them over them little bodies.

The birth of my other brothers and little sister Diana helped some. Still, Ma takes all the blame for them earlier losses and no amount of talk will ease her. She is single-minded about our health and safety. That's Ma's fever.

Looking at her today in the ladies' cabin, surrounded by my younger brothers and sister, she had her eyes closed tight and she was swaying back and forth, holding Mattie's hand while they sang a hymn. "I to the hills will lift mine eyes, from whence doth come mine aid. My safety cometh from the Lord, who heaven and earth hath made." She sings them Scottish psalms when life seems against her. You can hear a bit of the old country in her speech too; like a kitten's purr, her "R's" rolling just a little.

I stepped next to my three younger brothers and mussed their blond hair. Then I forced myself to look Ma straight in the eyes. They's darker like Billy's and full-on angel or tyrant, depending on the moment. I tried to say the right words. "Ma, it's going to be okay. I was just down inspecting our boiler and engines. They look in top shape and the finest men are workin' them. We're gonna be happier than a hog in house slop all the way, I promise you. Miss Mattie, this beats riding in that darned old wagon with us children walking, don't it? Heck they got indoor privies on every deck."

Mattie tried to smile as she rocked Diana. Ma kept singing under her breath, but I sensed she was listening. "I'll check on the boiler every half-hour or so, if you wish it, Ma. Won't sleep a wink from here to Texas; I'll swear to it." Ma didn't open her eyes. She reached for my hand, pulled me closer, and spoke low so only I could hear. "Mal, I fear Texas will be the death of me and my children, but the lord is working through your father and we will follow his path. With all my heart, I believe this son, or praise the almighty, you and I would not be on this dreadful boat going to this dreadful place. You hear?" She squeezed my hand. "Malcolm, next to our lord, you are my rock. I swear I could not live without your kind heart. With you by my side, I shall tolerate this journey."

I whispered low so the strangers around us wouldn't hear. "I love you, Ma."

I CAN TELL WHEN MY FATHER WAKES FROM A dark dream. I have seen him in the mornings staring into the distance for answers that escape him. Rarely does he speak of such things, but once, breathing hard from the struggle the night brought him, he shared his thoughts.

33

Only a short time after my accident, he joined us at Muutsi's fire and he was not his usual quiet self. "I did not sleep well, Wukubuu. It was another night of visions and animals on their hind legs. They crawled from small caves, growled and moaned as if their animal spirits were trapped inside. Some had the face of Taiboo with dark eyes and hair like buffalo. They crawled, showed their teeth, and hissed at me like kwasinaboo. They filled our teepee with their sounds. There was no place to run, no air to breathe.

"Then one stood above all the others and they hid in fear. He was a wasápe, a bear with a Taiboo man's face. He smelled of kwitapu but worse. He spit a dark vile fluid and howled. He reached for me with his long black claws and I could not fight him; my hands and feet were bound. He pulled me by my hair. Then he saw you, Wukubuu. His eyes grew wide and his nose flared to take in your smell. He dropped me and walked toward you with hate in his eyes. I struggled to stop him, to stand in his way, and I found the strength to bite his great hairy arm, but his smell and taste were awful... I fear this spirit will darken many of my nights."

Father's dream frightened me too. Seeing it in my mind, I wished to be close to a young warrior in our band, to feel protected by his strong arms, but those thoughts also angered me. It was as if I was two spirits, weak and strong. What I lacked in strength I could make up for with magic and cleverness. After all, the fox is small but does not fear the bear. I did not need a warrior to save me, but to fight dark dreams on my own was lonely.

The only thing worse than a dream of darkness is not minding the signs. My accident with the numu kutsu, then my father's dream.

I missed the signs.

TWO

Rivers Make Their Own Paths

JANUARY 7. TODAY ME AND TOM LEANED ON
the rail and watched my younger brothers on the shore
throwing mud at each other. Little Danny was getting the
worst.

Tom stretched and moaned. He and the other slaves
been sleeping on the boiler deck for several nights. I noticed
something else: Tom's stomach was putting up a racket. I
asked if he'd eaten lately. He pressed his hand into his belly to
stop the growling and talked over it. "My pa shared what Ma
Hornsby sent down with others that ain't as lucky. He's out
fetching more vittles now. We sharin' de one stove with
everyone on this deck."

I looked down at my feet, too embarrassed to speak.

The Pocahontas was tied at a wood station along the
Louisiana side. Dozens of smaller boats and rafts passed us,
heading down river. Black deck hands sang and loaded wood
and water onto her boiler deck from the shore.

Harper's Creek and de roaring river

That, my dear, will live forever

Then we'll go to de Indian Nation

All I want in this creation

Is a pretty wife and a big plantation.

Along the shore, cabin passengers—men in suit coats, some in buckskin, and women in bonnets or hats—stretched or sat on the solid earth. Some strolled under small black umbrellas. Pa, Uncle Moses-Smith, and Billy sat on the bank, bareheaded. The two brothers smoked their pipes, the smoke swirling around their heads. They looked like twins in them dark coats, with nearly matching black beards. I noticed their faces had tanned to a dark caramel brown 'cept for the tops of their heads.

I looked down at Tom's arms next to mine on the rail. They were nearly the same color. Then I said somethin' awful half-witted. "Tom, why ain't your skin the color of your pa's? He's dark as the night." Tom peered at me from under his hat as if I'd grown a carrot for a nose, and then he let me have it. "Yeh got a nerve. I ain't askin' you about yer ghostly white behind. Or why you and your three little brothers have different hair? Why yeh big brother have such a beard and all you got is three whiskers to your name?"

I couldn't blame him one bit for saying them things, but he went on with words I'd never heard from him. "Don't want to be like my pa. Mal, I don't want to be a slave all ma life. We's like brothers, you 'n' me. What if the time come to, well, you know, sell me to someone else? Maybe you and I goes off on our own together. We could start our own farmin'."

I asked him what had got into his head and assured him that there ain't gonna be no selling. Then he turned his back on me and asked the hardest question. "How you know? You not gonna make the choice, time come." I reached to put my hand on his shoulder, but I didn't. Instead, I tried to change the subject. "I heard if you fall and drown in this river and you is lucky enough to get fished out, they put you over a barrel and press the river water right out you."

Tom pointed to the boys and asked, "What if yeh drownin' from mud in yeh hat?" We watched my towheaded siblings—Josephus, seven years, Reuben Jr. five, and Daniel three—stuff mud in the little one's hat. Then if that little scoundrel didn't go and place the hat squarely on top of his blonde mop, mud dripping down his face. Then the other boys pounded Danny's hat down on top of his ears. It was just what we needed to change the subject.

Joe is growing fast; his hair is darkening and his ankles always show below his hand-me-down trousers. Reub is happy to have his little brother to play with and tease. Little Danny—who seems to eat more than the rest of the family combined—loves to make his brothers laugh.

Ma says the younger boys are devilish but she forgives 'em. "I can't blame you boys for your mischief," she says. "Your uncle is to blame for that, Lord save us." My uncle Moses-Smith is eleven years younger than Pa, and a quiet man, but he tells funny stories and slips us molasses candy when Ma ain't looking. There is humor and patience in him. He ain't hard in temper or voice like Pa. He'll look me square in the eye and give me the kind of smile that says, I know who you are and I'm proud of you.

They both come from Grandpa Moses Hornsby, a cranky old man to most, but not to me. Grandpa loves to tell stories of the wars. He loves when I ask him questions about the weapons and how they've changed. When he's done talking, he messes up my hair and says, "My little gimcrack, you ain't meant for farming. You meant for a whole lot more."

When I heard Grandpa Moses was too old to travel to Texas, I ran straight to the barn to hide my cryin'. On the day we were to leave, grandpa gave me this shiny clock gear the size of a silver dollar. He grasped the back of my neck with his rough old hands and whispered in my ear, "Boy, rub this and I'll be right there in Texas with you, and keep at them books. I don't understand 'em, but tarnation, there's bound to be somethin' good in all yer rumination. Just remember, no matter how far away you are, family is always family." Then I seen that grandpa was crying a little too.

On the deck, Tom put his arm right next to mine as if to compare the colors and he says. "He ain't my real pa." I didn't look up, didn't move. I let Tom leave his line in the water as long as he needed, then he finished. "Way he tell it, when I was a baby my ma died. He took me in. Your pa bought him shortly after and he beg that I come in de bargain. Now, all he talk 'bout when we on our own is whether your pa keep us together. He always look sad them times. I don't want to be sold off, Mal. Dis my place. You my family. Heck we more brothers than you and Billy."

I tried to sound sure but looked straight ahead and hoped I was right. "Tom, my pa would never let that happen. Besides, one day you gonna come smithin' with me." Tom grabbed my arm and looked it over. "Mal, where does a man's skin end anyway?" I told him I ain't thought that out, but I will. Then I grabbed his other arm, wrestled him a bit and said, "I do know this, family is always family."

THE WIND TESTED THE STRENGTH OF THE poles in my paha's teepee. I stood and tested the steadiness of my legs. The scar on my head was still very tender. My hand fell to the thin leather strip around my neck and down to the new elk-bone pendant. Wowoki did not admit to the gift but I recognized his handiwork: a carved buffalo calf.

My paha, Muutsi, was growing impatient waiting for help with the winter camp work. She let the inside fire burn down in hopes of urging me from bed and she was outside complaining in her squeaky voice, loud enough for most to hear in the camp. "If she wants the morning meal, Tupaapi's daughter must get out of bed and work. What warrior will want such a lazy wife?" When I stepped out and into the early morning sunlight, Dog hurried over and licked my leg. The cold twisting wind flipped my hair across my face as I answered her, "Good morning, my paha. I am surprised to see you here. All I heard outside was a terrible wind."

Muutsi mumbled and shuffled in her permanent stoop to stir the buffalo, berries, and tallow that stewed in a black iron kettle. The delightful smell reached my nose and jolted me fully awake.

The seasons had pressed Muutsi down so that she was not much taller than me. She wore her long winter hide dress, a hat of grey fox fur and moccasins. The skin on her exposed hands and face was brown and leathery, reminding me of an old boar. Her dark squinty eyes held little light. She had outlived two husbands, and would be without someone to hunt for her, were it not for my father, but she had powers. Muutsi was a healer.

She doted after Tupaapi more like a mother than an older sister. She endured his silences. He endured her firmness. They shared their grief over losing spouses. I began to regret my harsh words and thoughts and said to her. "Sister of my father, I am ready to work and eat. Perhaps we could even practice mixing some of the winter potions." Without turning to face me, Muutsi held up a hide bag of combs and pointed a crooked finger at a large pile of buffalo wool and horse tail. "Your father needs rope and halters, not potions."

I looked to my father's teepee. He was sitting outside by his fire with Isawura, a young warrior friend of Wowoki's. Perhaps they were talking business in their soft trading voices. I raised my hand hello. My father raised his hand to me.

Isawura, broad chested and serious, stared, pointed at me and spoke to Tupaapi. Father pointed toward his own head and nodded as if he was reporting on my injury. I felt the heat of anger on my neck and face. This was no business of Isawura's, even though he was of marrying age and his rare smiles interested me…a little. I spoke firmly without raising my voice, "When does a healer, a Kaheeka, stop making rope!"

Muutsi shook the bag. "When the Kaheeka is old enough to know exactly what the People need and not complain about it."

The buffalo wool and horsehair was raw, dirty, and matted. I would have to wash, separate, and comb it all out before the spinning. It would mean days of working my fingers until the muscles could no longer hold the comb. Though it was valuable work, I had no taste for it, but I was hungry, so I grabbed the combs from the bag and pulled my blanket tightly around me. Muutsi brought me a bowl of the stewed meat and mumbled her way back to the fire.

By midday, our camp was busy. Many warriors, including my brother, were hunting or scouting, leaving the women, children, and elders to the duller tasks. I jealously watched my aunt run back and forth to a nearby teepee—lucky to have some new excitement in her day. Pɨ-na petɨ had stopped her own work only an hour before to ready herself for giving birth. In an ever-tightening buckskin dress with a bright red blanket over her shoulders, she nervously waddled in and out of her teepee with the older woman.

I stared at the dirty tangled wool, wishing it away, longing for the powers my aunt had, when someone's shadow passed over me. It was Muutsi, pointing to Pɨ-na petɨ's teepee. "Come child. I will not be with the Penatɨka forever." It wouldn't have mattered if my aunt had asked me to pick up buffalo chips; anything was better than sitting there all-day combing hair. Then it dawned on me exactly what Muutsi was asking. "You want me to help with bringing the baby? Now? What will I do?"

Muutsi grabbed my arm and pulled me toward Pɨ-na petɨ's teepee. "Time to learn."

These words would change my path.

JANUARY 14. SAUNTERING DOWN MISSISSIP
for twelve days now. Made seven stops for wood. No wonder
the riverbanks are littered with tree stumps. Today, I spent
hours on the boiler deck watching the crew. Took off my boots
and socks, and felt the engine's heartbeat through the deck 'till
I got too darn cold. I wish with all my heart to work someday
with machines like these, with men like these, away from farm
life and worrying sick over the weather. The slow rhythm of
the boat and the river put a calming over me. I bet there ain't a
river like this in all of Texas.

The long trip is wearing on the other passengers. The
men are drinking heavier, arguing louder. Fights is regular.
When we heard we'd be in the famous city of New Orleans in a
little over a week, most everyone on the boat was excited, 'cept
my ma. Though Billy has no patience for it, I respect ma's
intuition; something she calls an dara Sealladh—the second
sight. When Ma says the old words, Pa makes scary eyes and
says, "Run children, your ma's a Scottish witch!"

Billy always kicks the dirt and scoffs, "There's no such
a thing. That's just a bunch of old Gaelic hogwash." It ain't.
Ma sees deeper than most folk. When she's worried, there's
good reasons you can't deny. She told Pa we's gonna have five
calves come spring and Pa built a new calf pen just in time. She
warned Billy about that wagon wheel in her dream and he
ended up broke-down in the creek trying to fish his hat
out…funniest thing I seen.

Today we all listened as the captain of the Pocahontas,
in his white linen suit, finished his lecture. "Ladies and
gentlemen, New-Or-Linz is the third largest city in our great
country." He waved his hands as if conjuring the famous city
right there on the deck. "Her port serves over seven hundred
steamboats durin' cotton-shippin' season, which obviously is
upon us. English is just one of many languages y'all hear in de
city. It's only right I warn yeh: in New-Or-Linz, de free black
outnumber slave black by a parcel. Why some even run their
own businesses. Ladies, I'm afraid their churches is primarily
of papal faith, and for all of you, my friends, please hear me
carefully: this city, I do love her so, but in this busy season she

is full of miscreants, hustlers, and thieves. Please, I beg of yeh, be on yer guard at all times. Keep to yourselves, and lord help you, do not allow a stranger to lend you a hand or lead you in any way."

My ma glared at Pa and Uncle as she wrapped her arms around her youngest and pulled them away from the other passengers. The Crescent City was no place for her babies. She had sensed it; the captain had just confirmed it.

Ma has the an dara Sealladh sure enough.

LET'S FINISH THE STORY OF Pᵾ-NA PETᵾ'S baby. The birth of a child to the People is like Taiboo finding gold rock in the ground. A new warrior is a promise of more horses, more food, and more power.

I helped my aunt soften the earthen floor of the teepee with water I carried from the stream. We dug two holes. Muutsi explained that one of the holes was for heating water with hot stones. The other would be for the bloody skin that protected the baby inside the mother.

While I brought stones and more wood for the fire, my aunt pounded a stake into the ground on each side of the expectant mother's bed. Once done, Muutsi sent me to gather sagebrush branches to place over the hot stones and under Pᵾ-na petᵾ's bedding. These would help the new mother heal. I also brought red cedar to burn for a blessing. Pᵾ-na petᵾ stared, winced, and looked away. She was only two years older than I was. This was her first child. Occasionally, she moaned from a wave of pain.

Muutsi sang an old lullaby, "Kima habiikwa, kima habiikwa, puibᵾᵾtᵾ come to bed, come to bed, sleepy-eyed." I couldn't remember ever hearing my aunt sing, especially so sweet and softly. Then she gave us directions. "Pᵾ-na petᵾ, lay down and open your legs. Niece, sharpen the knife." I didn't move. "For the rope of life, child." I still had no idea what she was talking about. "Connects baby and mother. We must cut it to complete birth." It was all so confusing, so wondrous, as if I were inside some secret band of powerful women, warrior women, who performed magic and used medicines to defeat evil.

The hours passed. Pʉ-na petʉ was brave. She would double over with the pain and try not to scream. Then, Pʉ-na petʉ yelled for all the camp to hear. "Is this the baby?" Muutsi quickly motioned me to sit near Pʉ-na petʉ's head. "Give her the bark to bite. Yes. Good. Now, Pʉ-na petʉ, grab the stakes and squeeze them with all your strength."

Pʉ-na petʉ did exactly as directed. Another wave of pain hit her and she moaned through her clenched teeth. I stroked her hair and joined my aunt in singing the soft song, "Kima habiikwa, kima habiikwa." The fire was warm; steam rose from the hot stones. All three of us were wet from sweat. The young mother screamed and tried to look between her legs where she felt the pressure.

This was all so strange: the noises, the heat, and the excitement. I tried to focus by wiping the sweat from my eyes and singing louder.

JANUARY 17. PORT NEW ORLEANS TODAY. MA sent Pa and Uncle Moses-Smith ahead on a mission: her children were not to walk, eat, or sleep anywhere near a place of sin and corruption. She'd seen enough drinking and gambling on this boat to plague her for the rest of her days, and she'd prefer to order her breakfast in her native tongue. Pa didn't turn or nod. He was workin' to read some fancy writing on a card. I saw it too.

Hôtel des Étrangers, Rue de Chartres

Près de la Cathédrale Saint-Louis

Uncle scanned the skyline, smiled, and pointed east at the bell-shaped dome on a church building near the river. "Do our best, Sister Sarah. See you under the clock at that there big church in an hour." Ma spoke like a judge to a no-account. "See that you do, brother. As the lord is my witness, I will not stand alone with these children in this city for long. If I must, I will commandeer a boat and we shall meet you down river at the murderous sea."

When we stepped from the Pocahontas onto the dock, Mattie carried Diana and checked on her often. Little sis had slept poorly the last couple of days and was awful cranky. Ma kept feeling her arms and legs for a fever.

Tom and his pa stayed behind. Wearing paper badges from the mayor's office to show they belonged to city visitors, they'll sleep and eat on the ship near our belongings until departure. Pa paid ten dollars a badge though he was cussing under his breath about it.

Once off the steamboat, Ma looked back and sighed in relief, but as she turned to face the city, I seen her stiffen. In every direction, there were noisy, smelly wharves full of blacks loading and unloading cargo of all kinds—including newly arrived slaves. Fishermen was unloading their catches—throwing fish, and crabs, and God knows what else. Beyond the wharves were markets with vendors selling strange foods and merchandise. There was yelling and carrying on. Wagons rattled. Steamships moaned and shrilled. It was deafening.

Ma grabbed my littlest brothers by the hand, held her chin up and stepped into the melee with a command for us. "William, Malcolm, keep a close eye on your brother Joe. The devil's in this place, I feel it." I reached for Joe and into my own pocket for my shiny clock gear. Ma's sense of this strange city was enough to urge me a little rub for Grandpa's luck.

We navigated carefully along wooden walkways and busy streets lined with beautiful new houses in the area they call French Quarter. Whole blocks was empty, newly cleared or partly demolished. Ma said it was runaway fires and fierce gulf storms, and then she whispered, "Most likely the work of our lord."

MUUTSI STOPPED SINGING AND SMILED. "THE head! Be strong, child, we are nearly there." Pʉ-na petʉ yelled but this time it tapered off into a long exhalation of relief. Muutsi yelled for all the camp to know. "The baby is here. A boy! You have given us a warrior!"

I stood to see but too quickly; it made me dizzy. I leaned against a pole for balance and saw that the baby was a bloody mess, his hair matted. My aunt tied off, cut, and carefully placed the cord in a leather pouch. The baby was gasping a little for air. Muutsi calmly turned him over and patted him on his back until he spit up a little and cried. It was a wonderful sound but I did not feel well.

"Should I get the father?" I asked, eager for fresh air. Aunt acted as if I'd suggested a great dishonor then she looked at me more closely. "No, this is not the time for a man near the mother or the baby. You look pale, niece. Is it your head again? Step out but come back quick. I need help to wash her son."

I stepped out of the teepee as the sun sank low in the sky. The air had grown colder. It refreshed me. Dog circled and wagged his tail. All around me, the camp was alive with activity, work and play. It was a good day for the Penatʉka, and now we were stronger by one more.

After we washed the baby, we wrapped him tightly in the softest hide and placed him beside his mother to drink from her breast. Once Muutsi was sure the infant was eating well, she grabbed the leather pouch containing the rope of life and motioned for me to join her outside.

I shuddered now in the growing coolness. Muutsi looked at me, through me, as if she was seeing some magic that was new to her. "Wukubuu, you glow like the setting sun. The medicine is strong within you."

We walked a short distance to the nearest oak and hung the cord on a limb. If no wild animal or strong wind disturbed it before the cord dissolved, it would be a sign that this baby, this warrior, would live a long and prosperous life. As we turned to reenter the camp we met Tupaapi and the new father, who acted disinterested. Tupaapi spoke for him. "Sister, have I a new friend? A child, a warrior? And you look for signs with the rope of life, yes?"

Muutsi nodded. The new father whooped with joy. He jumped, spun, and skipped off to tell the other men in the camp. Tupaapi touched Muutsi's arm, nodded his head, and smiled for a moment. He put his hand on my shoulder. "Daughter, we need to talk." I glanced up into his dark eyes, but they held no clues as to why he was summoning me.

THE STREETS WERE LINED WITH RUN-DOWN hotels, dark nooks and alleys, gaming houses, small theatres, and smelly smoky taverns. Restaurants, butcher shops, cafés, and bakeries spread food smells of all kinds. Strange music and foreign tongues drifted by our ears. I swear I heard the steel-against-steel of a sword fight as we crossed Conti Street. Me and Billy wanted badly to explore but Ma kept us ducklings in a tight group.

After a walk of a dozen blocks or so, we stepped into a grassy square and saw Pa and Uncle waving from under the big clock in the cathedral. It was a grand building and I imagined the tools they used to build it.

Once we made our way to the hotel, we was in for a surprise. The man at the front desk was tall, black, and dressed in a dark purple suit coat and matching bow tie. It was the first purple suit I'd ever seen. The man's teeth were bright and straight, his smile confident. "Bonjour Monsieur, comment allez-vous? Bienvenue à l'hôtel des Étrangers! Je suis votre hôte, Monsieur Dumas." Ma turned to Pa with a glare. Pa stepped forward. "Maybe we ought to talk to your master. He speaks English, don't he?"

I looked around the lobby at its soft furniture, fancy glass lamps, and rugs that looked thick enough to sleep on. A black woman near Mattie's age dusted the lamps like a bee working her way from one flower to the next. A large painting of an officer from the revolutionary war hung over the fireplace, and against another wall stood the tallest clock I ever seen. Heck, it was taller than Billy, even taller than our purple-suited host.

The fancy man smiled again. He held out his arms as if he would hug the whole lot of us Hornsbys. "Je suis un homme libre, Monsieur, et le propriétaire. Comment puis-je vous faire." The housekeeper cleared her throat—plainly a signal. The man looked at her, bowed, and said, "I am your host, monsieur. We have cared for the General Marquis de Lafayette. He pointed to the large painting of the officer above the mantel. I am sure we can make you feel as comfortable as possible, yes?"

Pa looked at Ma for some level of approval. She stared right back. Pa set a tight roll of paper money on the counter. "Them is Vicksburg bank notes. They's sound as a bell." Monsieur Dumas looked unconcerned. Pa continued. "We'll be needing two rooms for three nights. We're on the Pocahontas, headed to Texas. Our captain said you'd oblige."

The tall man bowed. "Oui, Monsieur." Pa tilted his head like a puppy seeing a barn cat for the first time. Our host quickly counted and handed most of the money back to Pa. Then he rang a little brass bell. "We are at your service, monsieur. Please do not hesitate to make any request. Oui? Yes?"

Pa stared at the tall black man one more time, nodded his head, and touched the brim of his hat as a young uniformed black man about my age gathered up our bags and headed for the stairway.

Everyone was tired as they climbed behind, but me and Billy was itchin' to get out and explore this wonderful, terrible place on our own, so he quietly asked. "Pa, me and Malcolm are gonna go check on Tom and our belongings." Ma shook her head but Pa nodded. "All right boys, but stay out of trouble, ye hear?" He glanced at Ma, "And get back here quick. No fooling around."

We spoke in unison as we bounded back down the stairs, "Yes sir!"

MY FATHER'S TEEPEE WAS LARGER THAN most. Though not chief yet, he was a respected leader. His status in the band was growing. He had his sister and me to prepare hides and cook for him. Thanks to his riding skills and those of Wowoki, he owned a marɥa of valuable horses. Tupaapi was an exceptionally skilled trader. He possessed a keen eye for opportunity and a way of making everyone feel as though they were coming out ahead in a trade.

He sat and signaled to me to sit in front of him. This was a small honor and I was grateful after the long day. We sat quietly, no words for a few minutes; this was my father's way. I noticed a few more wrinkles in his tan face. His lips were thin; his nose wide and dignified. He squinted all the time now, struggling to see things more clearly.

Finally, he opened his eyes and spoke. "It is fitting that you learn the ways of your aunt, Wɥkɥbuu. Your responsibilities to your people and to our family will grow. Someday soon, you will have a family of your own." He had never spoken of such things. I looked down and focused on keeping my breathing quiet as he continued. "You are old enough, my daughter, to marry. Your brother has approved of my choice as well."

I jumped up but couldn't decide what to say next. I stomped my foot and turned my back on my father. Tupaapi slowly rose to his feet and stood silently. Finally, he touched my shoulder and spoke in his soft trading voice. "Wukubuu, I know you are different from the others. The Creator, in disguise as a wolf, once promised the first Numu tenahpu that he would have a mate. The man was alone and eager for a mate but afraid for a different reason. He said to the Creator, 'How do I learn to share this place and its abundance with another?' The Creator said, 'You do not. Her heart is better than yours is. In many ways, she will be the master. If you are lucky, she will share this place with you.'"

I did not answer. We both stood quiet and still until my father spoke again. "Daughter, you will be the master. You are old enough. I gave my word this morning."

I didn't dare look up at my father. I couldn't let him see my fear and anger. I ducked out and ran from my father's tent. I was sorry for the disrespect but I needed the air. Muutsi watched me run past. She looked down and shook her head—a sign she felt my anger.

Isawura was to be my husband.

ME AND BILLY HAD NEVER SEEN A SLAVE auction. We figured it could be the most entertainment two men from the sticks could have. Besides, we'd only be a few blocks from the hotel. Torches lit up the crowd around us as they jostled for the best view. We found a seat in the back.

Right away, I learned what darkness there was in this affair. A tall bear of a man, round and red-faced with blood-shot eyes squeezed by us to go around the crowd. I watched him scribble his name in the bidders' ledger, pay his dollar, and spit tobacco in the dirt beside the trader's table. Then, of all things, he came and sat on the bench right beside me.

Dirty hair hung about his face and shoulders. On account of his girth, every breath was difficult and raspy. His sideburns, red in the torch glow, puffed out from his fat cheeks. From neck to toe, he wore sweat and tobacco-stained buckskin. In his belt, he carried two pistols, in a scabbard sewn onto his right boot, a large knife. His smell was the worst I'd smelled. Billy pretended to gag until I kicked his leg to stop.

The man caught me staring at his knife, so I thrust out my hand as not to insult. "Malcom Hornsby of Covington County, Mississip." He stared for a moment at my hand, not taking it, and then grumbled as he patted the knife, "Jacques Boucher. You got de reason for starin' boy, you'd best keep to yerself." I politely shook my head and told him I didn't mean no offense. Darn, if he didn't grab my arm and squeeze it hard, then push his face in mine. His breath was like a dead rat. "Listen boy. In Texas you would be shot for dis insult and no one would miss you none de same."

When he said "Texas" I meant to push for more detail, but Billy elbowed me in the ribs and shushed me. The auction was starting. Boucher let go of my arm and leaned even closer. I had to grit my teeth and try not to breathe through my nose. Then he whispered, "In Texas, I get all the land I want, all the slaves I need and soon, Jacques Boucher be rich from some Span-yard's land. He some duke, maybe a count, I dunno. He never set foot der."

That didn't sound right to me. In Missisip, a man's stake was protected by law. Stealing a man's horse or cow was an offense. Tryin' to take a man's land was worse. I started to ask another question when Billy elbowed me again. Boucher was paying me no mind anyway. He'd let go of my arm and turned his attention on the poor souls up front.

A tall Creole trader with caramel skin rang a bell. The traders and their freeman servants led forty men, women, and children out of a pen. They looked freshly washed and the men was clean-shaven. They wore clean clothes; the men wore hats and shoes, the women calico dresses and kerchiefs for their heads. Some of the men wore iron leggings, the chains ringing softly as they walked. The freemen led the men to one side of the auction platform, the women and children to the other—the tallest at the front of the row, then the next tallest and so on.

Once the slaves were in their positions, a black boy in his early teens and dressed in a plaid suit stepped forward and played a reel on the fiddle. The traders ordered the slaves to dance. I didn't like that—something 'bout it didn't seem right. All I could think about was my friend Tom. I reached in my pocket for my clock gear and rubbed a bit. I was awful glad Tom was nowhere near.

Once the dancin' was over, the bidders moved about them slaves as if they's buying horses. They made the children, women, and men hold up their heads and walk back and forth. They inspected their hands, arms, legs, and bodies. They made the slaves open their mouths and show their teeth. Jacques Boucher didn't inspect even one of 'em. He just sat. As the auctioneer worked the crowd in both French and English, the freemen pulled purchased slaves from the lines, some smiling because they were lucky enough to sell with a friend or loved one, some with eyes flashing anger, and many crying. Boucher waited silently through the whole auction, then stood and walked forward as the freemen returned the unsold to the pen.

Billy poked me. "Let's go, weevil, Pa's gonna have our hides," but something was telling me inside that even with the darkness, I needed to learn more of this. I pulled on Billy. "No, let's wait a bit, see what happens with that big smelly fella."

THE SPIRITS ARE ALL AROUND US. IN THE animals. In the plants. In the wind. On this day, the wind whispered to me. "Run, Wukubuu."

It was different back then, between a man and a woman. There was always a question of honor, to your father, to the Penatuka, to the People. For me it was exciting and terrifying. I had so many feelings and too many times, they were crossed.

I stood quietly as my father, Isawura and Wowoki walked among Isawura's prize horses. The horses whinnied, shivered, and nudged for more attention. The People were well skilled at taking horses from other tribes and the Taiboo, but our true strength was breeding the painted ones for endurance, speed, and size. We would trade off the stolen stock, but we rarely parted with the best of our bred horses and mules, not unless there was a great deal to gain as in a trade for a wife.

I saw Isawura look my way, and then continue the negotiation. He had lived through 18 full seasons and was a warrior of growing importance. He was not as tall as Wowoki but broad across the shoulders and exceptionally strong. When there was heavy lifting to do in the camps, Isawura was always in the middle of it. He and Wowoki were close, like brothers themselves, but I could not bring myself to know him. His face was broad, his eyes dark and distant. I could not read them and there was no giving.

The marriage was to take place after the next winter hunt. I would live in his teepee. I would be his first wife and as so, I would lead any other wives, but the thought of it darkened my spirit. I had no appetite for the firmness of it. My heart raced. I wanted to run.

Only two moons before, I began the life of a full-grown woman. Muutsi explained the blood between my legs as my tsihabukatu or being "on my moon." My body was changing in other ways as well: hair where it had not been and pitsi on my chest. I was learning the skills of a midwife too. I wanted to learn more. I needed more time; time to think. I felt trapped. I just wanted to run—run from all these men, from the camp, from the Penatuka and live with the beasts. At least they were free.

The wind whispered to me, "Run, Wukubuu."

I looked toward the hills where the sun rose and saw myself riding there. I saw myself standing before the men's council cave in defiance. I tapped my foot and rubbed my buffalo pendant. I looked at the pendant in the sun and noticed for the first time that my brother had carved a scar on the head of the young red bull, just above his eye. Had Wowoki dreamed of the same animal? Had I talked of him in one of my deep sleeps after the accident or was he real?

With so many nʉmʉ kutsu on the prairie, I could not hope to find the scarred calf again, and yet, I yearned to see him, talk to his spirit. If I could, I would go and find him. The wind whispered to me. "Run, Wʉkʉbuu," and I ran.

BOUCHER APPROACHED TWO TRADERS: THE tall Creole and a short white man with a deep scar across his chin. "Bonjour. Tu vas bien? You doing well?" I couldn't understand it all, but their voices were growing louder. The white trader pulled a small pistol from his belt. His boss made the point. "De auction is over, monsieur. We do not know of this reserved merchandise."

Boucher slowly reached for a wallet from inside his coat. "I have de resources, mon ami. Surely, yeh would not deny a veteran of de famous battle of Canal de Rodriguez, no?" The traders looked at each other. The taller one nodded. With torches in hand, they led Boucher into the dark behind the pen. Something was afoot and one look at my brother told me he wanted to see as much as me.

We stood in the shadows to watch. The trader opened a dark shed. We could hear the sounds of chains and murmurs of a strange language. I didn't have to understand them words to know they was full of fear and dread. I was feeling more and more that ma had been right about the devil being in this city.

In the torch light, we could see the trader point inside. "Dat one, she carry a baby inside. Two for one price. You pay addition for shackles and chains." Boucher pushed back in the negotiation. "I pay addition to feed de both of dem." The trader worked his side in perfect rhythm. "But de reward may be worth de trouble. Have a look."

Boucher pulled a young, pregnant girl to her feet from the shed. He looked her up and down in the torchlight, turning her slowly. She was tiny, but her belly pushed out against her threadbare cotton-sack dress. He forced his fingers beneath her lips to check her teeth like the others had done. Then, he pulled at her ear lobe and yelled, "Hey!" She cowered. Boucher laughed. "Well, she can eat and she can hear. Des just what I need. We gonna call yeh Martha."

Boucher turned and looked in our direction. I wasn't sure if he saw us or not, but that's when we high-tailed it, seen enough.

We didn't slow down until we neared the hotel. There were many dark corners and shadows. We was both a little spooked. Billy sensed my caution. "What is it, weevil?" I kept my voice low. "You figure Tom and his pa went through all that dressing up and dancin' before pa bought them?" Billy spoke quickly, as if he's erasing the idea from my head. "Nah, Pa bought Tom Elder off another man down in Forrest County. Your Tom come with the deal." Of course, I couldn't let one of his words go. "He ain't my Tom, Billy. He's my friend." Billy's voice went hard. "That'll have to change, Mal."

IT WAS WRONG TO TAKE MY FATHER'S HORSE without permission. It was also dangerous. My hair covered the scar but fits of dizziness still forced me to lie down occasionally. There was a storm in my head, and riding could be difficult. I regretted the decision as soon as I broke from the brush heading east toward the council cave, but I did not turn— the freedom was stronger than the fear.

The People used the hills to avoid enemies or the prairie's summer heat. Sometimes, my father would ride there alone to clear his thoughts. Perhaps I needed this medicine: to be alone with the horse and the hills.

The council cave was only for men to enter. I knew the crystal waters were only for the men's ceremonies, but they were at camp. Perhaps I could make a fire, fast, and ask my mother for guidance? By keeping the saddle-shaped mountain to my right and following the dry bed of Sweet Creek, I made it to the cave near mid-day.

The entrance was a towering hole in the rock cliff. The skies had clouded over, and little bits of snow danced in the breeze. I sat on the mustang, staring into the great darkness. When I pulled at the rope and softly heeled the horse to move him closer, he stood his ground, stamped a hoof, and complained.

We were not alone.

Perhaps it was a bear, mountain lion, or wolf. Whatever it was, the unseen was large enough to scare the horse. I stared hard into the darkness, listened, tried to smell a scent, looked around for telltale scat. It was safer to know your enemy than to turn your back on him, but there were no more signs. I leaned forward and patted the horse's neck. "Tami, little brother, you have done well," and as I turned him and eased him back toward the camp, I whispered, "I felt it too."

I was flying again, wind whipping through my hair. The stallion's movement through the cold air and light snow brought a clearness to my thoughts, gave me time to consider why I had run. Marriage is part of Penatʉka life, is it not? I have always known the day would come, but why does it feel wrong? I must be strong. I must convince my father that this is not my path.

I would speak directly to him in the morning. I needed to see his eyes as we spoke. As the sun rose the following day, I found my father sitting at his fire smoking his pipe, just as he did every morning. He waved me over but showed no other emotion. I approached his fire and lowered my head but did not speak.

I listened to the fire crack and hiss for what seemed endless moments until I stood and faced him. "Father, I..." He raised his hand and spoke softly, firmly. "You will have more time, daughter."

JANUARY 18. CAN'T GET BACK TO SLEEP SO writing a bit. Earlier tonight, there was a loud knock at our door. Pa and Moses-Smith was sharing one bed. Billy, me, and Josephus shared the other. We was all fast asleep when Mattie yelled from outside the door, "Master Hornsby, the baby's bad sick." Pa and Uncle shot out of bed and pulled on their trousers. Billy and me did the same. Josephus slept through it all. In our socks, we followed Mattie to the women and children's room down the hall.

Reuben Jr. and Daniel slept soundly in one of the beds. Ma sat in the other corner in the flickering light of the lamp. She rocked Diana in her arms and hummed a hymn. Every few rocks, she stopped to dip a washcloth into the water bowl on the dresser and touch the baby's head and cheeks. Pa spoke softly, "Ma, we're here."

Ma looked up, her face tired and eyes wet. Her voice was distant, lost a little. "She won't sleep at all. I thought she was just growing or bringing in a tooth. She woke us up complaining something awful. Got a fever now, seems to be climbing. And, Pa, she won't eat." Ma shook her head and spoke quietly. "I won't lose another baby, Lord. Do not ask me to live through that, please."

Pa took over. He whispered but did so with a firmness that all heard and none would cross. "Mattie, you and Moses-Smith carry those two young'n's back to our room and bed them down with Josephus. They need to sleep. Billy, you get downstairs and find Mr. Dumas. Tell him what we're fightin' up here. Mal, go with your uncle and bring our boots and shirts."

Billy was first out the door. He ran right into Mr. Dumas who was ready to help. "Monsieur Hornsby, we heard the footsteps. For whatever you need, all our resources are yours."

Within minutes, more help arrived. Both men were in black suits and perfectly tied bowties as if they'd been waiting for our urgent request. Dr. Ducatel, his mouth covered in a thick black moustache, didn't say much. He looked at the other man, puckered his lips, nodded slightly and raised his eyebrows as he checked on the sick baby girl in his arms. The other man was slim, had short grey hair on the sides of his baldhead, and a grey moustache and goatee. He introduced himself with a bit of a bow as, "Monsieur Louis Joseph Dufilho, the pharmacist."

The doctor spoke gently, "Madame, she is likely to have de swamp sickness, de ague, which generally does not show itself this time of year, but the temperature has been so, haut et bas, so up and down." I seen Monsieur Dufilho look away as if fightin' his thoughts until Dr. Ducatel carefully placed Diana in his arms. The pharmacist stared at her for a moment as if she were his own. His eyes began to water as he eased her into Mattie's arms and whispered, "Mercí." He wiped his eyes and turned to Ma and Pa. "Madame, Monsieur, she is a strong little girl. I have medicine from the bark of a tree in South America; des is de quinine. I will give her a dose now and leave you with more for the rest of your voyage."

Pa reached for his coin bag in his pocket. The doctor reached to stop him. "No, no, your host, Monsieur Dumas, has already taken care of des. You have no further debt to either of us." Ma wiped her eyes, took Diana from Mattie's arms, and kissed her on the forehead. "She's still so hot." Dr. Ducatel smiled. "Keep her cool with the water as you are doing, but don't let her chill. This will reduce the fever by the morning."

Monsieur Dufilho shook Pa's hand but stared at the floor as he stepped out of the room. Dr. Ducatel lingered. "We understand your concern, Madame, Monsieur, quite well. My colleague and his wife have recently lost a son much younger than your fillé." He looked toward the door and his friend in the hallway. "There is no medicine for this particular pain. I pray this will not be your fate. Bonne nuit."

THREE

Journeys Rough and Gentle

IF EVER A MAN COULD BE A MOUNTAIN,
Isawɨra was that man. I was still unsure if my path was that of
a wife, but I did enjoy Isawɨra's company on occasion.

When the sun disappeared, it hid behind the red
mountains far to the west of us where the Great Clear River
begins. I had seen these red mountains once, perhaps in a
dream when I was much younger. I remember how they rose
into the sky, quiet, strong, difficult to navigate. Though his
name meant wolf bear, to me, Isawɨra was the sun mountain.

He would never speak of it, but he was close to the
hawk that hunted the sun-filled sky. When he hunted, the hawk
would hunt with him. If Isawɨra was out of sight, the hawk
would cry for him. Many of the People had dogs. Isawɨra had
hawks.

I remember he watched for when Wowoki was not near
my fire. He would visit and taste my cooking. I had heard that
he could eat a great deal. Perhaps this is where he got his name,

but when he was with me, he ate very little. He spoke even less. I would have to pry the words from him as we use big limbs to move rocks in a stream, and often the words were more grunts than talking. I would say, "Isawɯra how is the food tonight? Does it please you?" He would answer, "Hmm." If I urged him on and reminded him that Wowoki eats somewhere else, he nodded but took no more food. I would tease him. "How do you grow so big and strong without eating?" He just shook his head.

If my food was not working, I knew one way to get him interested. "Should I tell you a story?" His eyes lit up. He did not smile. I'd never seen him smile, but his eyes flashed a happiness—I'm sure of it. "Hmm. Wɯkɯbuu." It felt funny to hear him say my name. I think it may have been the first time. I felt the heat in my cheeks and hoped he did not see it in the firelight. What story do I tell him? I could think of nothing. My mouth would not speak.

JANUARY 20. SPENT THREE WHOLE DAYS IN New Orleans. Diana is eating as well as ever. I even tickled a laugh out of her. Mr. Dumas and his housekeeper checked in on the baby several times, refusing Pa's tryin' to repay them each time. Ma was happy to attend Sunday services this morning at a Presbyterian church that Uncle Moses-Smith found while exploring the city; the first city church she'd attended since she was a little girl in North Carolina. She was surprised to see blacks in the pews but in too good a mood to question the ways of this strange and giving city.

Now the Pocahontas, with us Hornsbys on board, is winding its way down the Mississip again. I have to go. Ma's not sitting well with being back on this boat.

New Orleans was an adventure I'm sure I'll remember for a very long time. Wonder what's next.

HE WAS PATIENT. MOUNTAINS OFTEN ARE.
Then I had it. "I know!" I jumped up from the fire. This was a
standing story. Isawura watched as I paced back and forth,
conjuring the characters out of the fire…

>*"As you know, Coyote is occasionally*
>*helpful to the People, but most of the time he*
>*tricks others for what he wants. This is the story*
>*of Badger tricking Coyote instead.*

>*"Coyote was walking along one day*
>*when he came across the Badger. "Hello,*
>*Huuna. You look hungry. Will you join me in*
>*getting something to eat?"*

>*"Kutseena, what do you propose?" said*
>*the Badger.*

>*"You go to the prairie dog camp and*
>*pretend you are dead. I will follow and say to*
>*the prairie dogs, 'Our enemy is dead. Let us*
>*dance in his honor.'"*

>*"Kutseena, I cannot see how that will*
>*feed me."*

>*"Huuna, trust me. We will eat well, I*
>*promise."*

>*So, the Badger went to the prairie dog*
>*camp and pretended he was dead. Soon the*
>*Coyote came to their camp and spoke. "Look*
>*brothers and sisters, our enemy Huuna is dead!*
>*We should dance in his honor."*

>*The prairie dogs knew no better. They*
>*came out of their holes and followed the*
>*Coyote's words. "We will now stand in a circle*
>*around Huuna and dance the death dance with*
>*our eyes closed."*

>*As the prairie dogs danced with their*
>*eyes closed, Coyote killed several of them until*
>*one prairie dog opened his eyes and warned the*

others. All those who had survived ran back to their holes.

Badger stood and helped build a fire and they began cooking the prairie dogs, but once the meat was ready, Coyote challenged Badger. "This meat smells so good. I have an idea, Huuna. Let's compete to see who gets the best meat. We will race around this hill and the first one back to the fire gets to choose the best meat."

Badger shook his head. "Everyone knows that I walk and run with more difficulty than you. This is not a fair contest. You will obviously win." Coyote rubbed his chin. "I will tie a rock to one of my legs and give you a head start. Is that fair?"

"Yes," yelled Badger, and he took off running around the hill. As promised, Coyote tied a rock to his foot and began to follow, but soon he cut the rope and ran much faster. What Coyote did not know was that Badger had hidden in the brush only a short distance from the start. He watched Coyote pass by and then ran back to the fire in the opposite direction— easily beating Coyote to the food.

Badger pulled the best meat from the fire and walked up the hill to feast.

When Coyote arrived at the fire, he was out of breath and even hungrier than before. He spoke aloud. "Foolish Badger, I ran so fast I didn't even see you on the trail. Now, I will eat all of the good meat and you shall be all the hungrier" but as he looked through the coals, he could find nothing but the boniest prairie dogs. All the good meat was gone.

Badger walked down the hill nibbling on a bone. "Kʉtseena, you look puzzled."

*Coyote saw the bone and knew
something had not gone as planned. "Badger,
have you eaten all of the best meat?"*

*"Of course, I won the race. In fact, I
have been here a very long time waiting for you.
I was beginning to worry that you would not
return and would go hungry, but I have left you
at least a little to eat."*

*Coyote sulked. He shook his head and
blew his breath through his nose, and as Badger
returned to his home, he heard Coyote howling
into the night sky and thought to himself, "I
have tricked the trickster."*

Our fire had burned down a bit, but in the light, I saw
Isawura smile just a little. He nodded his head. "Good story,
Wʉkʉbuu. It has made me hungry."

I smiled a little too as I gave the sun mountain more
food.

JANUARY 27. DIANA CELEBRATED HER FIRST
birthday today while we was on the roughest of waters. Only
one year old and she's traveled over eight hundred miles by
wagon, horse, and steamboat…survived a bout of malaria. We
were determined to celebrate.

In Scottish tradition, Ma buttered the baby's nose,
saying, "The devil cannot take hold of a greased-nosed child."
We each gave her one gentle smack on the bottom. Diana
thought that was funny and laughed at every sibling. Pa lifted
her once above his head and then held her face to face for a
Welsh blessing.

"I will walk with yeh across distant paths.

Flowers and dreams will bless our journey.

Into your eyes, I will gaze an' holdin' your hand,

I will walk with yeh whatever may come.

Bydded inni gerdded mewn heddwch.

May we walk in peace."

Diana pulled Pa's beard. Then she smiled and giggled at her big family and the fellow passengers who had nothin' better to do than join in. That little half-pint put a smile on a lot of folks today, through the worst of it. This poem is for my wee Diana.

I swear to you misters

Nothin's better than little sisters

Laughs light up a room

Give the biggest kisses

And if I had some

She'd be pullin on my whiskers

I couldn't help but wonder what Texas would be like for baby Diana. How will one so little survive in such a difficult place?

WE DO MOST EVERYTHING WITH OUR HANDS, the People. We tan the hides that we use for our clothes and blankets. We stretch hides over frames to make drums and rattles. We use porcupine needles and claws from small animals to sew the leather we use for shelter. Our warriors make shields from the thick necks of buffalo bulls, and war bonnets with hides and large feathers.

With our hands, we fight, we heal, and we love. Our hands had to be strong. The skin was tough and rough to the touch from all the work, but I remember even now the first time Isawura touched my hand. It was by accident, I think.

We walked along the river to find winter flowers for dying hides and the sun was very bright so we kept our eyes to the ground. I did not see the tree branch in front of me, Isawura grabbed my hand and pulled me back just in time, the blow would have been right on my tender scarred head.

I smiled up at him and thanked him. He did not let go. He held it in his large hand and looked at it as if examining a precious flower or baby animal. I felt my cheeks flush again but I did not pull away.

FEBRUARY 5. FINALLY ON SOLID GROUND.
This morning, the Pocahontas eased her way into traffic at the mouth of the Brazos River. Nearly every one of us passengers stood along the rails at her bow pushing to get the best view of the little community of Velasco and this place called Texas.

From the upper deck, I could see the village: one wooden house surrounded by hundreds of tents of all shapes and sizes, wagons, horses, mules, and people—people everywhere. There have been many stories told on the ship about this port. Dozens of families arriving every day from the United States, Mexico, and Europe. Mexican authorities is struggling to control the flow of us immigrants.

As the captain of the Pocahontas steered her into place for docking, a smaller keel-style boat forced its way in front of us. It was all our pilot could do to keep from running over the smaller boat or crashing into the dock. He blew his whistle, but those in the keelboat ignored it while a young officer directed the men at the oars. The men looked rough. They hadn't shaved in days. Their uniforms was tattered and soiled. When two of them stood to help dock the boat, Moses-Smith pointed out they's wearing leg irons and chained together.

Billy asked if they was soldiers or prisoners. Moses-Smith suggested they were both, but that didn't make a lick of sense. How can a man be a prisoner and a soldier? Does he guard himself? I asked my uncle what kind of place is this Mexico. He took a long puff on his pipe and answered, "Seems it's a place where they force the lowest of men into soldiering just so they can have an army."

Once we were able to tie up to the dock, we passengers headed down the narrow plank, carrying our lives on our shoulders. Sure enough, the Mexican soldiers from the small boat stood right before us to have their leg irons removed. They was blocking our way. It was embarrassing especially for the soldiers. Until crewmembers from our ship pushed through the crowd, we just stood there.

The young lieutenant in charge of the squad and his sergeant held their ground. They yelled at our crew and all of us in Spanish, and I could tell they weren't words to use around your mother or sister. An engineer from the steamboat, one of those soot-covered men I'd watch during the journey, raised his shovel in a threatening way. Darn if that lieutenant didn't pull his pistol from his belt and turn to his sergeant with words I couldn't make out. That sergeant grunted, raised his rifle and hit the engineer square in the head with the butt of it. Poor man. Blood flowed from his forehead and his knees buckled. The rest of the crew dragged him back to the boat. I rubbed my clock gear and whispered to Billy, "Welcome to Texas."

Billy whispered back that they ain't soldiers. "Most of 'em ain't even got guns. Pa get the land he wants, we ain't gonna see them around. All they doin' here is taking their share of what we got. They gonna leave the injun fighting to us."

Of course, I had to ask Billy what he knew about injuns and he had to show off by saying he knew plenty more than me and that I couldn't shoot a gun without endangering friend and family. I gave him a push and said he's sure good at shooting off his mouth! Moses-Smith stepped between us and told us to save our sap on account of our having a lot of work to get everything off this boat and into this new country.

Somewhere out there, our future is waiting for us and he reckoned we best go get it.

FOUR

Fighting Fires

KOHTOO WAPI IS WHAT A TAIBOO CALLS FIRE.
As with the strongest of stallions, fire can serve or destroy. I
remember a time when kohtoo wapi nearly took me and all the
People.

My paha stood silently as her brother studied and
squinted at the dark clouds in the western sky. In recent
seasons, I watched as he lost trust in his eyesight. Though he'd
been careful to tell no one, I knew by the way that he squeezed
his eyes to see. The wind swirled his long grey-streaked hair
across his face. He turned back to watch our first camp of the
rainy season. We had left winter camp in the big bend of the
Great Clear River only three days before. Two days of travel
had brought us here to a camp that was just beginning to look
complete.

In a grass-covered low place between two hills, our
families would tend to breeding their horses, prepare for the

season's trading and start new families. It was the time of marriage for the Penatɨka, a busy time.

Tupaapi turned again to face the wind and the oncoming storm. He tossed bits of grass into the air. It blew right back at him. Flashes of lightning streaked across the sky above and below the tall dark clouds. He was silent for so long, then he spoke to me. "Do you sense it, Wɨkɨbuu? This one is strong."

I didn't have time to answer. Someone approached on horseback from the camp. "Father? Let's go." It was Wowoki with Isawɨra riding just behind. They both carried their paaka and eetɨ. Wowoki leaned on his horse's neck. "We should hunt the old way today. In the trees, I am quicker with this bow than with the Taiboo rifle. Sister, join us. You may carry Isawɨra's kills."

My father did not turn his eyes from the storm, and I joined him in ignoring my brother. I was not interested in serving his or Isawɨra's wishes. Tupaapi tossed more grass, watched it blow back at him, and shook his head. "We will not hunt today." I hid my smile from my brother. He grew angrier. "Why? I have everything ready. The other warriors hunt. Huutsúu Kwanaru, bring the pitsaka to carry our kills. It is not good for warriors to waste the sun."

The thunder grew louder, closer. Brother's horse flicked his ears and tail, kicked and whinnied. Tupaapi tossed more grass; it blew back at him. He stared hard at the storm, willing it to change course or play itself out, then looked back at the camp once, twice, three times.

Wowoki dismounted and walked his nervous mustang up the rise. He turned his back on me and stood to face my father. "It is just a storm," he said. We are in the season of rain. It will pass and the tracking will be even better. The others will be ahead of us if we do not go now."

I glanced back to the camp. The wind blew over a half-built teepee. Children stopped their games of chase. The spirit of the storm was growing stronger. Great streams of light burst from the clouds and the sound shook us. Muutsi touched my arm. It was time to learn. She faced the storm and took three violent breaths, inhaling and exhaling as if someone was punching the wind out of her. She held the eagle feather up and watched the wind tickle the soft down at its base. Wowoki paced back and forth. "Well, what is it? Why are we waiting?"

Tupaapi glanced from his sister to the storm until she lowered the eagle feather and nodded. "Kohtoo wapi. We have little time." Tupaapi turned his back on the storm and spoke quietly to his son and Isawura, "This one moves fast. We are in his path. The other warriors will smell the smoke and they will come from the hunt, but too late I fear." Wowoki shook his head. "How do you know? It looks the same as any storm in this season."

Muutsi turned and walked quickly down the hill toward the camp as she warned, "He's coming right at us."

ONCE WE GOT OFF THE DOCKS, MOST OF OUR clan sat on crates in the shade and away from the howling wind. Pa was off at something with Tom and his father. Billy slept on a crate with baby Diana bundled up in his arms. I read to Uncle from the Translation of Laws pamphlet. I told him it said by Mexican law, he, Pa, and Billy would have to serve in the Mexican army. Moses-Smith puffed his pipe and said, "There ain't much chance of your pa allowing that."

I lowered my voice to whisper the next part in the pamphlet where it said there ain't to be no slaves. Moses-Smith pulled his pipe from his mouth, glanced around him and whispered back that my Pa would have to file some Mexican paper, that's all.

It was then I heard the mule, a squeaky wagon, and a loud familiar voice. That smelly beast of a man, Jacques Boucher from New Orleans, and his new girl was passing right by us. I tried to ease my hat down over my face, but it was too late. He pulled the mule's reigns to stop then spoke to his black. "Here dem boys I tells you about from the auction, Martha." Martha didn't move. I could see he'd shackled her feet and tied her hands to a ring in the floor of the wagon. She just stared out at the gulf.

Billy tipped his hat up to get a better view. Ma and Mattie pretended to mind the children. Moses-Smith extended his hand, though I seen his grimace once he's closer to the big man's smell. Boucher looked Uncle up and down, then me and Billy. Then he looked square at me and started in. "Boy, yeh seen the way men do de business of buying farm help, no?" I answered but I seen Billy eyeing me. "Yessir, I reckon."

Boucher spit then went on. "You got to buy de special ones from down in Africa and learn them right, no?" I didn't have an answer for him, so I just half-nodded. He didn't notice. He looked us over again and asked, "Where's yeh guns? You ain't tinkin' you just farmers gonna grow de cotton wit no worries, no cares? You boys soldiers now. You 'bout to fight one way or 'nother every day you livin' in Texas."

Moses-Smith glanced at my Ma, softly slapped Boucher's mule and spoke quiet. "Thank you for the sound advice, sir. We will surely keep it in mind as we acquaint ourselves to the ways here." Boucher tipped his hat to Ma as he passed. "Madame, welcome to de Texas." Ma was tired. She barely looked up and I'm glad. I don't like that man—he's all devil.

Ma would've known it too.

MY FATHER RAN DOWN THE HILL PAST MY aunt. I had never seen him move so fast, never seen him so alarmed. He yelled to us as he ran, "There, deeper into the prairie…across the stream; we must move now. I will see to the horses. The grass is not yet green enough to resist the fire. Go, go! Namʉsohitʉ!" Wowoki stuck out his chin. His cheeks flushed red. He mounted his horse and rode slowly past

Isawʉra who turned his horse to follow, neither in much of a hurry.

I had seen a Hueco girl once who had been caught by kohtoo wapi. Her hair was gone except for a few strands on the side of her head. Her arms and legs were so badly scarred that she could not bend them, and her face was without change; she could neither smile nor frown. She asked to touch my hair. Father said it was good magic so I let her, but I could not look at her while she did. She thanked me and as I turned for just a glance, I saw that she was crying. Kohtoo wapi takes everything away but the pain.

The People have a system, a way for everyone working together to break camp quickly, but in the face of fire, all was chaotic. Only the older warriors, women, and children were in the camp now and they were right in the path of the growing fire.

Women and children stripped the skins off teepees and lashed frame poles together. My father directed the elders and young women to herd the horses. An old, blind warrior wandered and yelled for help until someone took his hand and led him back to his family. The women wrapped still-hot cooking utensils in hairless skins, abandoning the morning breakfast.

The smoke moved fast. The wind swirled it around the camp. It stung our eyes and caused the youngest and oldest to choke and cough. Tupaapi rode back and forth trying to direct everyone through the haze but there were no landmarks, only smoke. He spotted me and yelled, "Daughter, you must make a signal from the hill over there! Take my rifle and fire a shot. Run now!"

FEBRUARY 5. SLEEPING ON THE EDGE OF THE village. The wind is blowing off the gulf and whipping straight through our canvas tents. Clouds are rolling across the full moon. The youngest of our clan is sleeping soundly as usual. Not me. All I seem able to do is listen to the wind and try to write by the moonlight flickering across our tent. Tom is snoring next to me. The journey has been hard on him. Tom, Tomas Elder, and Miss Mattie are no longer "slaves." Pa said according to the Mexican authorities they's now called "indentured servants for life."

My mind is racing through it all: sounds like, just to farm, we Hornsby men have to be soldiers, but we've never soldiered in our lives. The Mexican government forces their own, men who already had the worst of life, to be soldiers too. Them like Boucher, well, they look to do what they please with no care for nobody.

Tarnation!

Ma hadn't mentioned it, but all this seemed like signs to me, early warnings for what we's truly up against in this strange place. Maybe she just didn't want to speak of it.

I LIFTED THE HEAVY RIFLE AND HUNG THE powder bag over my neck, but the weight of my fear kept my legs from moving. I looked again in the direction my father had pointed. I could not see the hill. I turned and watched what I could of our band through the smoke. The panic was disturbing. There was usually such order.

The fire spirit spoke to me: Wʉkʉbuu, I am coming for you.

I ran.

The smoke stung my eyes and clawed at my throat. Dog raced behind me barking. My hair swirled around my face. The land began to rise beneath my feet. As I climbed, the air cleared a little. At thirty paces from its base, the hill lookout revealed a wide wall of flame racing, leaping across the prairie toward our camp.

This fire's spirit was dark. It danced, jumped, and roared, greedily consuming the yellow grass with its bright red teeth, leaving smoldering, smoking black ash behind. For the first time, I sensed its heat on my skin and heard its faint crackling sound like fresh meat on a fire. It was hard to breathe. It felt like I would fall into the flames.

I reached for my mother's cross and beads and rubbed them as I watched, forgetting the panic below. Dog's barking broke the spell. He had spotted a fiery runner climbing the hill just below us. Should I run again? I backed up the hill from the fire at my feet. Dog barked at the fire and me. Then I felt it, the weight of my father's gun in my hands.

With his usual contempt for having to deal with a girl, Wowoki had taught me well, but my fingers shook as I now followed the steps. First, open the frizzen and pour a small amount of powder into the pan; yes, that was it. Remember, not too much, not too little. Pull the hammer back to half-cocked, making sure the flint doesn't spark. Point the gun away from everything except the target—Wowoki had repeated this warning several times. Aim. Fully cock the hammer until it clicks, but don't touch the trigger yet.

I set the heavy weapon against my shoulder and pointed it at the roaring fire as if the lead ball might stop its rage. I pulled the trigger. The blast knocked me backwards and off my feet, but I held on to Father's gun. For a moment, I just sat. The dog licked my face and whimpered. The fire roared just below us, and the smoke covered us. I felt dizzy. There was no air in my breaths, just smoke.

I slung the rifle over my shoulder and crawled up the hill on my hands and knees. Dog followed. Our warning shot had worked. We fell in among the People as they rode or ran away in our direction, but I don't remember what happened after that. I'm told that I was out of breath. My head bounced loosely as I staggered, my legs weak beneath me. I don't remember Isawura reaching down from his horse and lifting me up to sit in front of him. I don't remember riding to the new campsite.

When I woke, I was beside my Aunt's fire. Though small, its sounds and heat brought troubling memories, a fear I didn't care for. Muutsi was building our teepee nearby. I stood slowly to help her, but discovered my father's rifle in my firm grip.

Many had watery eyes and coughs for several days and some had burns, but not a single man, woman, or child was taken by the kohtoo wapi. I helped Muutsi spread a salve made from the prickly ash shrub onto cuts and burns. Isawʉra came to check on me; he had small burns too, but he just grunted when I offered to treat them.

Many members of our band, especially the women and children, came and touched my arm to show respect. It felt strange, wonderful, and frightening all at once, as if their whole fate had been in my hands. I did not like the feeling, not completely. For many suns, I felt angry for not having my own time. I felt angry for many little things and could not explain it. I was sad without reason. Muutsi said it was the fire's dark spirit. She said it was a head sickness. She had seen this after a family death or in a warrior after a great battle. She made me tea many times in the day and assured me the darkness would pass.

It did not.

APRIL 27. TWELFTH BIRTHDAY BUT YOU wouldn't know it. Worked all day and every day since we arrived. Hardly had time to write. It's green here near the coast; suits our Mississip roots just fine, but there's a lot that don't.

Tall, thick grasses will cut your feet and legs. Oak, elm and other low trees seem to guard the streams with briars and poison ivy as their weapons. Worse there's plenty of nature here that'd kill you quick. Can't take a step without crossin' a snake, often as big as your arm. Gators lurk in most fresh waters. Clouds of mosquitoes block the light of rising and setting suns. They cover our skin with painful bites in seconds.

Ma has little tolerance for the heat, sand, fleas, and mosquitoes. With Mattie's help, she works furiously to keep us fed and safe, but by night she's exhausted and her back aches. One minute she's cold and the next feverish. Like Diana a few months back, she has a mild case of the ague. It's so common here, experienced settlers call it "the seasoning."

When Pa looks worried, Ma scolds him and sends him out of the house with a mission. She says this family is not growing any smaller. We need a place to settle and start our new life. "You and your brother are not going to find it watching over me. I've been through this sort of difficulty before. I will be fine I assure you. William and Malcolm are old enough to look after things. Now get!" Still, I worry and so does Pa. I see it on his face, especially when Ma is down with the worst. I don't think we could take losin' Ma.

Our house ain't much: a tiny picket where the logs point up and the bottom ends are buried in the soil. Don't even own the land beneath it; we're on the property of an established settler named Asa Mitchell.

Mitchell, his wife Charlotte, and their 15-year old son Nathan have been in Texas for eight years farming sugar and cotton and working cattle, but the poor-draining soil and weather have made for tough goin'. Still, like many of those who share in hardship, Mr. Mitchell was willing to give from what he had the most of, the land, and Pa sized him up as a man to trust.

Mr. Mitchell spoke slow, careful. "Well, we ain't no New Orleans here. Ain't no fancy hotels to take in strangers. Look after each other mostly. Pay what we can, trade or work to compensate. You're welcome here Mr. Hornsby for as long as you need." Pa asked how he and his family was getting on. Mr. Mitchell looked away, sad like, then sighed. "My wife is quite sick much of the time, sir. My son and I work a half-dozen jobs in addition to our own farming just to make do. Mr.

Hornsby, this land has an abundance, sir, I am sure of that, but I'm not sure if it's a Garden of Eden or the road to purgatory."

Pa just nodded. I seen he was thinking deep on it. Maybe he was wonderin' if his family might have been better off back in Mississip. Maybe he was changing his mind and we's headed home.

At least that's what I was hoping was in his head.

AFTER THE FIRE, MY FRIGHT DREAMS WERE much worse. Darkness in our heads is often worse than any darkness in front of our eyes. My visions grew. I will tell you of one dream that upset my paha the most.

> An old woman trailed behind our people as they moved camp. She made her camp right outside of theirs. The people lined up to bring her food and blankets. They wanted something in return. There were so many of them asking, pleading. It was the eagle medicine they wanted; medicine to take their pain, to free them of the ghosts, to bring them strength and honor, but she could not make the medicine. The eagle was yet to visit her. She tried other medicines from the otter fur, porcupine quills, and sage, but they did not give her power, only sadness.
>
> Then one night a Taiboo man who smelled of bad eggs came to her and held out his hand in silence. She asked him, "Are you the ghost of a dead one who led an evil life?"
>
> The man did not answer. Dark water dripped from his mouth like blood. He held out his hand as if to take her somewhere away, and she ran. She ran from the camp, away from the people she loved but could not save, but the

*smelly man turned into an owl and chased her,
his breath on her neck.*

*Ahead she saw a break in the earth, two
great cliffs that held a shiny ribbon of river
between them. The water would cleanse her. She
would fly down to the river and leave this ghost,
but as she leaped, her eagle wings did not grow
and she fell and fell.*

When I told her of this dream, my aunt rubbed her
hands together and pulled at her hair. She had burned the cedar
and sage for me. I had tasted so many of her teas that I had
forgotten the ingredients. With each bowl of tea, Muutsi would
describe what went into the magic and how to prepare it. I
knew she was healing and teaching at the same time but the
dreams continued.

In the middle of one night, she woke me. She was fully
dressed to be outside and had fed the fire in our teepee as if it
were day. "Niece, we go." I asked her where we would go on
such a cold night. She insisted. "Here is your blanket,
Wukubuu, and your hat. We go now."

AUGUST 14. BURNING HOT TODAY AND NOT A
bit of wind to ease it. Tom and me took the wagon south
toward the coastline and cut palm tree leaves to help repair the
thatched roof on the cabin.

The work was hard. We climbed the trees and held on
with our legs while sawing the limbs. The long pointy leaves
made our faces itch. Barbs lined the green limbs like shark's
teeth. The dogs sat below us and barked every time a limb fell.
As usual, Tom worked in silence. I swear, he'd never say a
word the rest of his life if weren't for me. I recollect our
conversation went like this:

"Tom, you sick? You ain't said more than a word since we set out."

"Thinkin'."

"Well, men have been known to think and talk at the same time. Of course, that ain't including my older brother."

Tom laughed. "Things gonna change."

"Yeah, like what?"

"Too many to name."

"Can you name me just one?"

Tom eased down his tree and sat against the trunk. I did the same, grabbed our canteen and handed it to Tom for the first drink.

"My pa say the work will get harder and the dangers deeper as we go west. He say in Mississip, we have a proper house, bed, a fire, and we's safe. In this place, we circled by everything hatin' us, with nothin' but canvas and our boots to protect us."

"Your pa said all that? I ain't never heard him string more than a handful of words in one breath."

"Said somethin' else."

"Yeah?"

"Said things gonna change fer us."

I didn't answer. I was thinkin' back on the conversation I had with Uncle Moses-Smith. We stretched out below the trees and closed our eyes to rest. The dogs did the same. In minutes, we woke in a cloud of tiny biting flies. We was swatting and swinging and the dogs was barking. On the ride back I asked Tom if he'd finished ol' Robinson Crusoe? In his usual way, he didn't go into much detail on the matter. Just a simple "Yup."

"Well it's just like in that book. Long as I have a roof, I'll see to it that you and your pa have one too."

"I know it."

"We made this right?"

"Guess so." He sat silently for a while, then, "Mal, yeh keep a big secret, right?

"I reckon."

"Mal, some day, I want a cabin and a farm my own. Pa says land is more valuable than gold to us. He says walking on soil that belong to you is the best feeling there can be in life, only most black men never get to feel that. I want to call a spread of dirt my own."

I answered without thinking on it much. "Well, that ain't so big. My pa rightly do that for you and your pa, give you a share to work. Let you choose the land too. What you figure, down close to a stream so there's plenty of fish?"

"No Mal, I was figurin' on somethin' different, somethin' that was all mine."

THE NIGHT WAS CLEAR AND THE WIND CALM. The stars and moon lit the land so we could see almost as well as in the day. Muutsi had a strange tone in her voice. She told me that my father had consented that after my marriage to Isawura and after I brought children, I could start taking on more responsibility as a medicine woman, but Muutsi must consent as well.

She stopped us on top of a hill away from the camp. "This I will not do until you have defeated the dark dreams. You still have the shadow of kohtoo wapi over you. I could give you my blessing. Your father could give you his blessing. All the people could give you the blessing. None can give you the power to defeat the ghosts—that is within only you!" She poked me so hard with her bony finger I had to step back to keep standing.

"You do not defeat ghosts with medicine. You defeat ghosts with courage. For the ghost uses fear as a weapon, and only fear. When you have your husband and children, when you are truly ready, you will go on your own into a night such as this, many nights alone. I cannot give you my blessing until you sleep without the ghosts of kohtoo wapi. Do you understand?"

Muutsi had already built a fire on the hilltop with two beds nearby. Because I was cold, the fire felt less of a threat and more like an old friend. Lying on my back, I watched the stars and imagined they were little fires sending their warmth as well. Soon my eyes could stay open no longer.

That night, I dreamed of two coyotes. They came to me on the hilltop. They circled me slowly, carefully, not as enemies who might attack but as friends who would test my courage, my honor, and me. They were there to guide me from the dark dreams, and if ghosts came to haunt us, we three would band together to defeat them.

I slept soundly until late morning. When I woke, Muutsi was gone and the fire had burned down. I had slept alone. No demons had taken me. No fire had chased me. The coyote would protect me.

Muutsi was pleased.

SEPTEMBER 10. OUR HOUSE ON MITCHELL'S land is small. You can practically reach the walls by standing in the middle. It has a dirt floor and no door, just a canvas-covered gap in the logs. There's no beds, just one hard bunk built into one wall. Ma doesn't have a stove or a fire inside, just a table and two chairs. At night, the house is crowded and noisy with Ma and the little ones.

The slaves, us older boys, Pa, and Uncle Moses-Smith sleep outside in our tents. The river provides fresh water, but it's no walk to take in the dark. The only place to relieve oneself is out in the bushes.

It's rough, but there's the occasional wonder. Last night, in our cramped little tent, Tom reached for my shoulder and gave it a shake. Then he shook harder. Then he pulled my hair. "Malcolm Hornsby, wake up!"

I shot straight up like a fish jumping for a fly, rubbed my eyes, and sneered at Tom when the first little light nearly hit me on the nose. Then there was another near Tom's ear, then more. Thousands of fireflies lit up our tent and all the others. They was moon bugs, all over the place like little flying lanterns. I watched them tiny lights flash on and off, near and far. Then I punched Tom in the arm and fell back into my bedroll. "That's for pullin' my hair, darn you."

He seemed set on talking. "Hey Mal, what yeh readin' now?" I answered but wanted to sleep. "I-van-hoe is the name." Tom asked. "Any blacks in that one?" I told him that it has a black knight in the story and he said he'd have a look when I was done.

I couldn't get back to sleep. I watched them moon bugs seems like for hours, and all I could think about was Ottilee. If she'd been here, she'd be giggling over them little lights and sayin' clever things.

The Jamesons can't get to Texas soon enough, I reckon.

MUUTSI'S LESSONS WERE SO MUCH LONGER than before. There was much to learn, I felt like my head would overflow with it all. As the days grew shorter, she would hurry through making medicines and teaching me how to use them. It was hard to keep up and frustrating when she would correct me.

The more I learned the more I felt my strength and power. My paha cautioned me to "walk on the earth with softer steps." That was her way of recommending I be more humble. She told me repeatedly that a medicine would only work if the sick person and I both believed as if a life depended on it. When I would indicate I was ready, she reminded me that I could not be a healer for the Penatɨka until I had married and had my own family.

I grew impatient and snapped at her. "Where are your husband and children?" As soon as the words left me, I regretted them. Muutsi looked as if I had stabbed her with a knife. She lowered her head and began to walk away. I pleaded for her to stop and forgive me.

She turned and spoke with her eyes closed and breathing very slowly as if calming a fire within her. "Niece, if you must know, I could not bring a child of my own to birth alive, though I tried many times. Soon, no warrior would have me as his. Now, to heal my broken heart, I bring every child for our people. I heal them when they are sick. I cook for your father, your brother, and you. Still there is always an emptiness inside of me that I cannot heal."

I stepped forward and held her arm. "Paha, please forgive me."

NOVEMBER 12. PA AND UNCLE MOSES-SMITH left today. As the sun came up, they sat on their horses with bedrolls and saddlebags. Seagulls circled and cackled above us in the rising wind. Pa gave us his usual list of chores. "Now, boys, don't let them give you no greenhorn prices for the wagon and look closely at them mules' teeth and hooves before you show your money. Your uncle and I will be in Matagorda for a week, maybe two."

Billy acted all grown up. He was nodding his head like an old mare. "You can count on me, Pa." Our father wasn't finished. "When you home, stay close to your ma. She's ailing more than she lets on."

Pa added one more chore after another to our list. "One axe and one adze is plenty for now, and sift through them nails to be sure they aren't tryin' to push nothing bent on you."

"Yessir." Billy looked our pa square in the eyes while he spoke. I hung back and stared at the large red ants scurrying 'round my boots. "Malcolm!" Pa's stern voice snapped me out of my trance. "You listenin' to me, boy?" I peeked up from under my hat and nodded.

"Your brother's in charge of this here outfit now." Billy smirked at me. "But you are to buy the rifle." Billy's eyes went wide. He turned and stepped closer to Pa's horse, but I could still hear him. "Pa, I can handle buying the gun. Old Bookweevil don't even like to shoot 'em."

The thing is I was already thinking it through. "Pa, you want a long barrel with a full stock, right? The Tennessee is shorter and that larger bore is for bigger game, but we can get more range outta the long. Of course, we want them new paper cartridges and I think it should be a breechloader, maybe—I gotta think on that a little. They's faster than the muzzle but the mechanisms wear out. Grandpa always talks 'bout the Ferguson being the best of the red-coat rifles."

Billy took off his hat and started hitting me on the head with it 'til uncle leaned over and caught him by the wrist. "Leave your brother be, Billy. He's got a head for these things." I just ignored my fool brother and walked toward the corral, weighing all the options as I collected my thoughts. They have this new firing mechanism called a cap. Beats a flint and pan light every time. We use that and the muzzle-loading we have ourselves a good reliable hunting weapon.

FIVE

The Most Unwanted Visitor

NOVEMBER 14. I NEVER MUCH CARED FOR shooting guns. The noise is terrible, and the result is always somethin' bleeding, but a grown man can't go far in a Mississip forest without one. There is too many life-taking dangers like bear, snake, or wildcat—and bad men out to rob the weaker. In Texas, all them reasons is a bushel-basket full of worse. It must take a special sort of man to look after a family in these parts, a man who can handle a gun in every way. I ain't sure that'll ever be me, but I know a thing or two about buying them. They are machines after all.

The clerk at the tent-covered general store was barely older than Billy, but he knew the ins and outs of firearms. I must've asked him a dozen questions about barrel and stock length, and the new paper cartridges. Most of the conversation was around them caps for spark instead of a flint and pan. I would have talked him plum out had it not been for Billy's constant interruptions and the regular, "Let's get this done and get, Bookweevil!"

When we's through, I was the one carrying the gun beneath my arm just like a grown man. I declare this made my brother twice the show off once we got to the stable. He lifted each of the mule's legs and carefully picked at hoof and shoe, and then he'd stick his chest out and sigh before opening his big mouth. "We ain't paying no greenhorn prices for these mules. We may have only been here a few months, but we ain't like them Easterners with their lily-white hands and no head for trading."

It got worse. He dropped the hoof and feigned disgust. "What you tryin' to pull here? These shoes are worn thinner than a lady's petticoat." The stable owner, an old man with a strong German accent, had a hard time hearing my brother. His eyesight wasn't the best either. "Vhat vas dat?" he shouted, more at the mule than directly at Billy. "Das is ein gutes maultier, gutes maultier."

Billy lifted one of the mules' lips and ran his fingers along the yellow teeth. "We ain't gettin' far if you can't speak English, mister." I swear his showing off wore me quick. I heard the blacksmith working out back of the stable. The pings of a hammer on steel were like the sirens of Ulysses. I picked up the rifle, and eased around the mules and away from that brother.

People think smithing is just about horses and hooves, but that ain't a quarter of it. Ain't no village can prosper without a good blacksmith to keep everyone in workin' weapons, traps, and tools, and keep their horses and mules from going lame. From brass, iron, steel, and tin, smithies build all sorts. Traps, chains, knives, axes, nails, awls, barrel hoops, hammers, and dozens of other necessities come from the smithy. Lord, I want a job like that something fierce. People look up to a good smithy. They need him.

I was disappointed to find this smithy's shop a mess. Hammers, chisels, bits of coal, iron and steel, horseshoes, empty bottles, and horse manure was everywhere in the oily dirt. The blacksmith, in his leather apron and gloves, had passed out in the grime. There was an empty whiskey bottle by his head, but at the anvil, working a fiery red horseshoe with the hammer and tongs, was a slim, dark-haired man with a thick beard.

He had removed his hat, coat, and top shirt and hung them neatly on a hook. The skin on his face and forearms was nearly black from days in the sun but the top of his head and upper arms was white and freckled. In his rawhide boots, he stepped over to his mule, and checked the size of the new shoe. By all accounts, I was sure I was looking at my first genuine Texas frontiersman, a Texian. Then I noticed somethin' familiar sticking out of the man's saddlebag, a small portable writing desk just like my ma's.

This was no ordinary frontiersman.

I DID NOT SEE ISAWᵾRA FOR MANY DAYS. Others in the camp, especially the warriors would look at me and smile as if they knew something I did not. Even Muutsi would look away from my eyes as if she hid some secret. I could get no signs from anyone in the camp.

Then on a bright sunny morning when I stepped out of my teepee, Isawᵾra was outside waiting for me and in his hands he held a paaka and eetᵾ, smaller than a warriors, but built for hunting just the same.

Isawᵾra said more words than I think I had ever heard him string together before. He said my father's rifle was not the weapon for me, that I was lucky it did not do more harm when I fired it. He said he had made the bow especially for me and set the arrows with the red bird feathers for good hunting.

He set the paaka and eetᵾ down at my feet and started to walk away, but I stopped him. "Sun Mountain, must I hunt alone with this gift?" Isawᵾra smiled bigger than I'd ever seen him smile before, but he said no more words. He just walked away.

I was beginning to think that perhaps I could be a wife and a healer for the People. After all, Muutsi had tried to do this. Though she is alone now, she started down this path.

I picked up the bow and pulled back on it. The line was strong. The bow bent smoothly. I would hunt well, but hopefully not alone.

"HOW DO YE?" ASKED THE STRANGER NOT turning, his voice rough like a rasp. I stood tall and answered clear. "Fine sir." He still hadn't looked at me. "Are you any good with mules?" The manner of his speech was slow and clear with a touch of German to it. It reminded me of a teacher I'd had in Mississip. That made me feel at ease. "I've been 'round horses in my time, sir, but am better with machines, tools, and such." The stranger turned his head, eyeing me. "In that case, would you help me with the bellows? That fire is starting to look like Herr Schmidt here—all played out."

I set the new rifle against the wall. While I was taking off my hat and jacket, my book fell from my pocket with a thud. I scooped it up and pumped the bellows for all I was worth. The coals in the furnace were soon glowing. Little pieces of red ash flew into the air. The stranger smiled and heated up the shoe. He asked me if I was a reader and I told him my Ma taught me. Then he said something funny before he introduced himself. He said, "That's good, that's right good. We need readers. The name's Josiah Pugh Wilbarger of Burnam's Station, soon to be of Bastrop." I just stared, seeing how I didn't understand much of what he was saying.

He caught on. "Sorry, you're new to Tejas ain't you? Bastrop's a little settlement just gettin' started by Mr. Austin about four days ride north by northwest. My family is still in the Burnam's ferry area. Me and this mule here come down for supplies and to lead some new citizens like you up north. Besides, supplies here is cheaper than paying the traders that come through off the Camino Real. How long you been in our little part of Mexico, son?"

Now that I had my bearings, I felt a little more comfortable. "Only a few months, sir. Sorry to bother you with it, but what exactly is a Camino Real?" Wilbarger smiled and nodded. "That's Spanish for the King's Highway. Questions are a sign of intelligence. Anyone ever tell you that?"

Maybe this man *was* a schoolteacher. He sure talked like it. Next thing he asked was what I like to read. I probably went on too long with my answer but no one had ever shown an interest like this. I think I said just a few words such as, "Oh, I read the usual—the Bible, of course, almanac, books my ma collected. Mostly I like readin' about machines, like steamboats, them steel plows, Whitney's gin, and guns, I reckon. Bought this new one today. My pa gave me the job. Said I had a mind for it."

Wilbarger dipped the hot horseshoe into the water. A loud hiss and cloud of steam cut me off, but only for a moment, so I kept at it. "Well, I read a lot. Gonna read every book there is. And, I reckon I'm gonna work with machines someday, for a living I mean. Mister, is there a place here in Texas for a man who is good with machines?"

That's when he looked a little perplexed as if he was struggling to answer, when he asked, "What's your name, son?" I extended my hand and introduced myself. Then he got a little serious. "Well, Master Malcolm, there ain't much in the way of machines in Texas. Guess slaves is the closest we come in these parts, but I believe we'll soon see improvements. Ain't no reason you can't be right in the middle of that, unless they pay a man a heap more for honest talkin'. Then I reckon you'll be a rich man."

I wasn't following Mr. Wilbarger, but I had my mind on something else when I asked if he "supposed I could sweep up a little 'round here? Drives me half-mad to see all this dirt." Then he just laughed.

Thought he was going to laugh into the next week.

THE DEAD MUST HAVE THEIR REST AND WE must move on, but I have heard many Taiboo speak of their lost ones as if they can bring them back...even if only in their dreams. I too wish I could bring my family back. I asked Muutsi many times to tell me of my mother's death. She finally surrendered, but she insisted it was only as part of my training.

She spoke of white-capped sores on my mother's skin. Of how death drained the blood from her lips. Of how father gently wrapped her body in a buffalo robe and placed it on his horse. He rode to the edge of the bend, above the land that would flood, buried her in a rocky crevice, and covered the place with stones. Then he gently twisted and tied two oak saplings to guard her resting place. In those days, we didn't place stones with words at a loved one's resting place, not like Taiboo, but deep in our hearts, we remembered just the same.

When he returned to camp, he burned all of María's possessions except one: her wooden beads and cross. He called me to his side and carefully placed the charm over my head. "Daughter, we have burned your mother's things to keep her from resenting the living. She would want you to have this charm as protection. You are old enough to care for such a gift, aren't you?" I remember holding the beads and rubbing the smooth wood.

Muutsi reminded me that later that day, my father cut off all his hair. When I saw it, I was frightened. He lifted me up into his arms, buried his nose in my hair and sang a death song in a soft whisper. This was long before the Taiboo came to our lands in such numbers, long before they began to bury so many of their lost ones in the ground.

I remember when my father heard from a small Hueco hunting party that white men were seen building square houses along the Great Clear River and exploring the Penatɨka's bountiful winter camp area in the bend. To see for himself, Father rode with Wowoki to the bend early the next morning.

What they found would change everything for the Penatɨka.

DECEMBER 1. PA AND UNCLE CAME HOME.
Said they'd seen all they needed to see of Matagorda. After they took a ferry southwest down the coastline and 'round a stretch of beach below the bay, they headed northeast to the small village. Pa said the ferry pilot was Italian and wore a funny striped cap. Uncle Moses loved to show us how the man introduced himself with a grand wave of his arm as "Comandante Santoro." They said he talked to his boat, a sloop he'd named Rosa, as if it were his wife. Moses had us in stitches telling us the story of that area with the commander's funny accent.

Uncle told us that one hundred and forty years back the French had landed there by accident with two hundred souls and little else. They didn't last long what with disease, Indian attack, and storms against them. Said their leader, LaSalle died at the hands of his own men in a mutiny and only a few children survived as Indian captives. Pa and our uncle heard that French ghosts haunted the land around there.

In town, Pa politely but firmly told the proprietor, Mr. Wightman, he'd be lookin' somewhere further, and Mr. Wightman sounded a bit desperate, "Isn't there anythin' you cared for, Mr. Hornsby?" Pa said there was one thing he couldn't get out of his head, that lovely rolling river over west. Mr. Wightman said the Spanish named it Colorado, though most folks never seen any red in her. As Pa and uncle road off, Mr. Wightman yelled after them, hoping for a last commission opportunity. "You need to find Mr. Stephen F. Austin, our empresario. He's got another colony goin' up north on this same river. Tell him I sent you, please!"

Then my Uncle told us a funny story. He said he looked around to ensure they's alone. Then he asked Pa, "Say, did you hear about Parson John from Matagorda? He was on his deathbed and with his dying breaths said to his wife, 'Give thy husband one last request, dear wife.' 'Of course, my dear,' said she. 'Six months after I die,' he said, 'I want you to marry Mr. Smith down the road and give him all this land.' 'But I thought you disliked that man,' she said. And with his final breath the parson said, 'I do!'"

As usual, Billy was hoggin' all of Pa's time. Why they hadn't even got off their horses from their long trip. "I made that German put new shoes on the mules, Pa. He was begrudging but I pushed 'em hard." I could tell Pa was only half-listening. "How's your ma been, son? You helped her with the boys, didn't you? I best check on her."

Billy didn't pay no mind. I swear he can talk more than an old mocking jay. He just kept on gabbing. "The wagon is practically new. Some family sold it back to 'em for a quarter of what they'd paid, then headed back to Alabama. Can't imagine people just givin' up like that. Can you, Pa? We ain't never doing that, not the Hornsbys."

MY FATHER AND BROTHER EMERGED FROM the tree line, dismounted at the river and walked along the bank leading their horses. Cardinals, jays, and vireo sang their songs to the morning sun. Up ahead, a water moccasin, a tuparokoo, slithered across the sand and into the river's edge. Then they saw them. Tracks from Taiboo boots and shoed horses crossing the broad stretch of a sand bar near the shore where the large snake swam. Tupaapi pulled at his hair with both hands and groaned. The Hueco were right.

Wowoki howled and chewed on his horse's rope. He pointed east and yelled, "Father, I will go now and destroy the Taiboo. I will humiliate and defeat every one of them." Tupaapi raised his hand and shook his head. "There is time enough, son. You are brave and show great honor, but the People need you as a leader, not a ghost."

It must have been hard for Father to be so calm. This was the land of many winters. This was the land where he fell in love with my mother, where I was born, and where his most beloved wife now rested. Only a morning ride to the east, the Taiboo were building a permanent camp with square shelters made of trees and stone.

Would they now flood this land and pile up like hundreds of floating sticks and limbs around it? Would they take food from the Penatɨka, starving our people? Would they take wood, making winters impossible to bear? Would they kill the buffalo?

The People had fought the Taiboo dozens of times and defeated them. The People had stolen their possessions and taken family members to make their own, but could they continue to defeat so many? My father breathed deeply to calm his thoughts then headed west—away from the Taiboo's permanent camp, away from the anger to a quiet place in the bend. Wowoki watched Father from enough distance to show respect.

Against our custom, the twisted young oaks near mother's grave marked the site. Father slid off his pinto and pulled Blackfoot Daisies from the ground nearby. Once he had a handful, he pushed through the brush between the oaks. Inside the thicket, he stood at the foot of his third wife's grave in a split in the rocks in the hillside. Beside the pile of stones, a half-dozen awonoo, armadillo pups, dark pink and oblivious, nosed through the thick leaves and grass for worms, grubs or ants.

Father told me that he laughed. I had never heard him laugh. Perhaps he was remembering his María. Perhaps she would have enjoyed such a sight; it is said she had a way of delighting in that which most Penatɨka took for granted.

Father said he scattered the daisies over the stones and would never visit again.

JANUARY 1, 1831. NOT THE SMARTEST WAY TO start the New Year. Went out on my own this morning. Pushed through cypress limbs and thorny vines into a small, bright green meadow by the river. A whitetail doe in the clearing hissed, thumped her hooves, and took off with a leap. Her fawn didn't follow. He crunched that sweet grass in his teeth as I eased closer, telling him all along he'd better go with his ma. Then I noticed the grass movin' behind him. Everything seemed to slow down. I saw the great-ridged back of the gator, the long snout, and the rows of teeth as he eased up the bank.

I didn't bring a gun.

I waved my hat in the air and yelled, "Tarnation! Get out of there! Run!" I'll be damned if that fawn didn't jump a foot off the ground and practically fly in his mom's direction. It was a sight. Then I checked the gator, seeing how I'd just sent his breakfast away. That ten-foot monster was coming right at me, mouth open, teeth bared, and those slit yellow eyes staring me down. My body shook. I turned to run but my boots slipped in the mud and I fell right to my hands and knees.

I could hear the breath of the beast behind me. I tried to yell and crawl away but couldn't get the sound out.

THE SUN'S WAKING SEASON IS MY FAVORITE. Everything is in bloom. There is so much promise in the signs. This was the time for my paha to gather many medicines. There were flowers for our dyes. The rains washed the land and fed the rivers. Many new foals were born to their horse mothers and to the People, making us stronger and happier. It was a busy time.

It was also a time for war and warriors. Isawura, Wowoki, and the other warriors rode further and raided more Taiboo camps. It was dangerous and Muutsi and I would spend time after each raid healing wounds and hearing the stories of bravery and honor. I did not always care to hear these stories. The warriors would brag of great bravery, but there was always someone's pain, fear, and suffering left untold.

I look back on these stories now and know they were not good signs. As a young girl, I knew only the People and their ways.

After one raid, the warriors brought home many cattle, horses, saddles, and scalps. Isawura came to me to help heal bad cuts on his foot and on one of his arms. He would not say how he had received the cuts, he did not say much at all, but I knew. In his eyes, I saw the misty look of a warrior who had been in battle, who had shown honor, but who now needed time to cleanse his dreams of the dark spirits.

It was as if the spring, our tahmaroi, was two seasons together: one of birth and promise and one of death, pain, and ghosts.

THE GUNSHOT WAS SO CLOSE IT RANG IN MY ears. Sparks and bits of the paper cartridge from the barrel burned my face. I looked up through the smoke to see my Uncle Moses-Smith standing there with the new rifle at his shoulder. Behind me, that dead gator lay flat out on his belly, bleeding from a smoking hole between his eyes.

Moses-Smith reached down to pull me to my feet and said the craziest thing. I could barely hear them over the ringing in my ears. "You racing that gator on all fours was awfully sportin' of you, Mal."

As we walked back toward the cabin, he said my ma was gonna lay a goose's egg when she seen me covered in mud. Then she'd tan my hide when she seen the gator. "You bought a decent gun, nephew. I believe it just saved your britches. Good thing, I hear that Mr. Jameson is writing letters to your Pa, asking about Texas. Wouldn't want that little Ottilee disappointed, would we?" Uncle Moses mussed my hair and laughed, but I didn't care about nothing but them last words. Not even an old mean gator was going to keep me from seeing my Ottilee again.

Tonight, after cleaning up and having dinner, I talked to my pa and uncle about meeting Wilbarger. They both looked at each other and nodded. Made me feel grown up. That is, until my ma grabbed me by the ear, spread salve on my burned face and sent me out to bed with a warning that if I set one foot out in this "god-forsaken country again without a weapon it ain't the gators that's gonna be my problem." On my way to the tent, I shuddered a bit at seeing the gator strung up in a tall oak.

I reached into my pocket, rubbed grandfather's clock gear and thanked him for looking after me.

THERE WERE SO MANY DAYS IN THE SPRING when the warriors were away catching or stealing horses. My brother, Wowoki, was especially good at both. They had many tricks they would use to bring home the wild ones. They would herd them into the canyons or deep ravines and catch them with ropes, or chase smaller groups until they were so tired they could run no longer. After a long rain, the warriors would wait by new ponds for the wild horses to drink themselves full and slow—making them easy to catch.

Isawura caught his share as well. I remember a bright morning after a raining night. The warriors must have chased a wild herd far from the camp for they had not returned, or perhaps they chose to seek shelter in the night's storm.

Word came round that they'd been spotted with dozens of captured horses nearing camp. Everyone stopped what he or she was doing and stood to watch their triumphant return. Isawura made a point of walking past Muutsi's teepee, leading more horses than any of the other warriors, including my brother. He looked taller and bigger than I ever remembered. He did not smile but I saw his eyes follow me to be sure I was watching. Maybe he looked for a sign of approval. It was hard to hide my pride for him, but I did my best to look disinterested until my brother pulled his usual tricks.

Wowoki heeled his horse to lead his captives quickly up between Isawura's horses and me. He yelled and whooped to be sure that I looked his way. He stuck out his chest and bumped Isawura's horse. The two of them pushed and shoved, forgetting me as they passed.

APRIL 4. SEEN MR. WILBARGER AGAIN TODAY. Me, Pa, and Moses-Smith found him loading supplies into his wagon. Over coffee in a tavern, we learned he'd farmed in Missouri, was married, and had been a schoolteacher in Matagorda. I knew it. He confirmed Pa's wariness regarding the coast too, assured us that Stephen F. Austin was upstanding, and that the Colorado River was the place to be. He even said there might be work surveying with him for Mr. Austin. That way, we'd see more than our fair share of the best land before anyone else.

Then his tone changed. The way he spoke in his calm and slow teacher's voice, it almost sounded like something good. I heard the warning words. I saw Moses-Smith stiffen. Pa heard them too. The words were Comanche, Waco, raids, stealing, settlers wounded, killed, giving up, and moving back to the States, but Pa heard something else first and that seemed to cancel it all out. He heard Wilbarger describe Austin's little colony as "good cotton land, thousands of acres for the taking, land that Mexico was practically giving away." Only catch was the best land was still in Comanche territory.

The Texian spoke plainly. Seemed the Mexican government was desperate to separate themselves from them savages, and us settlers would do the dirty work of it. Pa said in Mississip, the cost of an acre was a buck twenty-five or more. Wilbarger said in Austin's little colony, it was about 12 cents. He said Pa, as a married man who planned to farm and raise cattle, was eligible for a full league, 4,428 acres at the price of $531 paid over time and no cash required. Pa nearly jumped from his shoes.

Mr. Wilbarger offered to lead us north and introduce us to Mr. Austin. He said they could sure use good men like ourselves and that everyone's prosperity depended on it. Pa nodded. Moses-Smith shook Wilbarger's hand and held on long enough to ask a straight question. "I trust there are plenty more men like yourself where we're headed?"

Wilbarger smiled and answered carefully. "Well, there are more of the sort of men we need every day, I reckon. You and your nephews will be welcomed, and we'll do all we can to make the women folk feel at ease too." My uncle looked down and sighed slow and hard. "Sir, your words are a comfort, though I figure we just as well be clear on this, ain't gonna be nothin' easy about it."

THAT NIGHT THERE WAS A CELEBRATION IN our camp. We ate well, sang songs, and danced to honor the warriors for their skills and courage. I noticed that Isawura stepped away from the fire into the darkness of the camp and I followed, but away from the fire, the night's darkness had swallowed him up and I became a little frightened.

Then I heard his whisper, "Wukubuu." And from the darkness he reached to hold my arm. His hand was warm against my skin but I pulled away. He did not reach to hold my arm again but he asked a question I will never forget. "Wukubuu, if I am your Sun Mountain, what are you to me?"

At first I could not answer. I wanted to be sure of my words, but the words were not there. My silence filled the space between us like a loud flooding river threatening to take Isawura with it. He sighed and I heard him walk away, back into the darkness.

Would it have been so hard to have said something kind? I will never know.

APRIL 27. ANOTHER BIRTHDAY IN TEXAS. MA made me a cake and Pa let me go a half-day fishing with Tom and Nathan. We must have caught nearly every fish in that river; bass, cat, drum, and carp, you name it. Our stringer was full of fins and tails flapping in the water.

Seen a small side-wheeler make its way down the river too only it looked to be full of sick folks, most lying flat out on the decks. Just one or two of them on the boat was standing, taking care of the others. Nathan said he seen it once before: a whole village come down with either the smallpox, yellow fever, or cholera and everyone taken to New Orleans for doctoring, only most don't make it.

We seen what they was throwing off that boat into that river, we let all them fish go and walked home empty-handed.

I DID NOT SPEAK WITH MY SUN MOUNTAIN for many suns after that night. We avoided each other like angry bears, each afraid of the other and what might be said or done.

Muutsi gave me more work and some advice. As she handed me the hides, she reminded me, "Niece of mine, you know it can take many moons to work the most trade value into one hide. You may not always like the work but the time it takes does not darken the clouds for you. The work is expected. This is the same between a man and a woman. Busy yourself and enjoy the days without the dark clouds."

MAY 8. A HARDSHIP DAY. NATHAN DROPPED by and asked me and Billy to go fishing; said his ma was down bad with the fever. They had to wring the sweat out of her bed linen. When he helped his father lift his mother, she weighed nothing, and her skin was cold and clammy. His pa had practically pushed him out of the house after that. This was all Ma needed to hear. She and Mattie grabbed a few things and ran to the Mitchell cabin to help.

They were too late.

Ma came home all bent by it. She sat us down and told us Charlotte Mitchell had come all the way from Pennsylvania with her husband and son. She'd supported her family for eight years and in that time saw the Brazos River become the busiest shipping channel in Texas, her husband a leader in the area, and her son grown to be a fine young man. Nevertheless, she'd go no further. Ma said she looked so white and frail in her bed; you'd be hard-pressed to guess she'd fought so much to make it. Said she was one of god's angels now.

We helped bury Charlotte this afternoon, and then packed our things. Mr. Mitchell and Nathan came by just before dinner leading two mustangs, one golden tan, the other a spotted pinto. The elder waited a few steps back. Nathan handed the ropes to me and Billy and said these yearlings were his ma's favorites. She fed 'em sugar and such. Said they figured we'd get good use of 'em.

Billy stepped forward, took the halters and spoke low to say our Pa would want to pay for the horses. Nathan glanced back at his father, hung his head, and spoke so softly we could barely make it out. "My Pa…well, we can't have them around. You'd be doin' us a favor." Then Nathan turned and walked back toward his pa. They put their arms around each other and walked away, Nathan practically carrying his father along the trail.

THE PEOPLE WELCOME MORE NEWBORN SONS and daughters in the spring than in any other season, more colts and puppies too. Every year it was a time of new voices but also a time of loss. For every three new members of the band, one would die before the hot season. Pʉ-na petʉ's son grew strong.

I helped Muutsi with several more births as the flowers bloomed and the warriors hunted. Every time was an adventure, every mother brave and so trusting of my aunt's skills and knowledge. I began to feel nothing could defeat her magic and that I was learning this power too, until one of the births went badly.

The mother was older than most, one of several wives of a Penatʉka leader, but his favorite. While most of the mothers would show a strong face and move through the difficult dance as Muutsi instructed, this woman had a look of worry that no song, no sage smoke would lessen. She had tried to bring several children into this world; none had lived for more than a few months. She was small with narrow hips and she limped badly from a fall from her horse before she was even old enough to marry.

The baby was large in his mother, larger than most. Muutsi had worried the birth would be difficult. For weeks, she had given the expectant mother the root medicine to hurry the arrival. She waved the smoke over her. Nothing seemed to help.

When the time finally came, the mother was in great pain for two days before. The baby was slow in coming out. Muutsi did everything she could. We sang in the sage smoke from dark until dark. There was a lot of blood, too much blood. I could tell my aunt was worried. We must have tried every medicine and spell she had. Finally, the baby came but nothing my aunt could do would make him cry his first sounds of life.

His mother lived for only a couple days more, then she too went silent forever. Instead of gaining a warrior, the band had lost two members.

Muutsi spent three days away from the camp, sleeping upstream at quite a distance. My father, Wowoki, and I took turns checking on her, though we dare not stay for long. She was fighting the ghosts and needed all of her concentration for that difficult battle.

JUNE 9. WON'T BE WRITING AS MUCH FOR A week or two. Headed north. Left today at sunrise. Most of us quiet except my big brother, of course. He had to tell a joke, while the rest of us was still thinking on the Mitchells and their loss. "Hey Pa, what was that joke that grandpa used to tell every Christmas? You know the one, 'Kind sir, will you give me a loaf of bread for my wife and little ones?' and the stranger says. 'I won't take advantage of your destitution at Christmas. Keep your wife and little ones!'"

Lucky for us, Uncle Moses-Smith remembered one of grandpa's limericks. "William, a father once said to his son, 'The next time you make up a pun, go out in the yard and kick yourself hard, and I will begin when you're done.'" We all laughed, mostly at Billy's expense, but he didn't notice.

Me and Tom rode and talked quiet on the back of my new golden-colored mustang I'd named Jackson after the president. I told him about the latest book Ma had shared. He asked his same old question, "Got blacks in it?" I surprised him with the fact that it was writ by a lady. He said that maybe he wouldn't read that one. Then I told him about another book by some man named Billy Shakespeare. I can't make out a string of words in it. Tom shook his head and said "must be terrible hard if you can't crack it, Mal."

Then he spoke on something else we was all thinking. He asked if we was headed into the worst of it now? I snapped back quick about sticking together to let him know we's all right. I said the Hornsby family was on the move again, but no more walking, no more steamboats.

There were enough wagons, mules, and horses for everyone and all our belongings: Ma's books, our dogs, a small wooden beehive, chickens, our old cow, and a couple of breeder stock we'd traded for in Brazoria.

Unlike the trail to Vicksburg, this path wondered through some lonesome, treeless spots with tall grass and plenty of swamps. Along the trail, Ma, Mattie, and the younger children sang one of Ma's favorites.

"On Jordan's stormy banks I stand and cast a wishful eye
To Canaan's fair and happy land where my possessions lie.
I am bound for the Promised Land,
I'm bound for the Promised Land.
Oh, who will come and go with me,
I am bound for the Promised Land."

I WILL TELL YOU MORE OF THE MEDICINE story. There is sickness that I cannot heal, that no one can heal, and these powerful spirits bring ghosts to the heart of the living who remain.

My paha taught me well, and in helping her, I was able to see my path more clearly—these were the most important seasons of my life. In her lessons, she would speak at a fast pace and expect me to keep up. "Wukʉbuʉ, the Apache use crow feathers to ward off owls because the owl and crow are enemies, but I do not fear the owl like Apache, I do not believe owls are ghosts. How could they be so? Owls fly and live in trees. They hunt meat and kill quickly. They provide for their young. They talk boldly in the dark night like a warrior. This is no ghost, Wukʉbuu. It is not the owl I fear, it is Kwasinabóo, whose belly is always on the ground, who lays silently in wait for its victim, whose bite kills after a sun of pain and sickness."

Muutsi talked on and on as we walked among the high grasses and trees. At times, she would raise her voice as if daring Kwasinabóo from a dark place nearby. I could not tell if this was bravery or fear.

We hunted three things this day: red berry cedar, prickly ash, and milkweed. Muutsi used the red berry cedar to treat ghost sickness, dizziness, and pain in the head. She would dry and rub the leaves and sprinkle them on hot pecan coals to smoke the patient or use the smoke to urge ghosts to leave a teepee or camp.

She would make a powder, called fire medicine, of the prickly ash to treat fever, toothaches, and burns, but milkweed was for special healings. To my aunt, milkweed was one of three medicines that held the most power, powers beyond the understanding of all but very experienced medicine people. Applied to the body, a milkweed root paste would heal ghost sickness, bruises, bone breaks, and cramps. The paste would also help children with conditions of the throat.

Out of respect, to dig the milkweed root, Muutsi would only approach the plant from the west where the sun slept at night. She would drape a small strip of dark green cloth over the branches, then dig and separate the root from the limbs and leaves that she would scatter over the hole. It was these steps that she would entrust to me this day.

The path from the west of the plant was rocky and up a small rise. The sun was low and the shadows long. Muutsi talked loudly, nervously. She did not care for this area; I could tell from her voice that this place worried her. There were too many dark shadows for hiding.

I pulled at a sage root to step up on a large rock, but the root gave way and my foot slipped back. I reached again for another, larger root and first heard the sound, a solitary rattle. It was coming from beneath the large rock, right at my feet. I needed to move back quickly but in searching for my next stepping place, realized the ground was moving around me—I had disturbed a nest of young Kwasinabóo with their silent striped tails.

"Paha!" I could barely get the words out.

JUNE 28. SAN FELIPE. CROSSED BRAZOS ON A ferry. With the help of his two sons, a strong-armed Mexican man used ropes, pulleys, and mules to pull the wooden barge across the river. His sons lured the mules forward with corn and sugar cane. They talked and joked around with each other while they worked, like they was having fun.

Guess some brothers can do that.

Today, we arrived at this bustling little village. They was building cabins and a new hotel. Boats were coming and going on the Brazos. Wagons and horses, families and single men, slaves and freemen raced past us like thirsty cattle to water.

In the noisy one-room tavern, Wilbarger introduced Pa and Uncle to Austin's secretary Sam Williams, a quiet, smart-lookin' New Englander. He was impatient with the slow plod of us southern farmers. I aimed at sitting with the men, but Billy took the last chair at the table and smirked, so I stood at the wall.

As was their pattern, Pa and Moses-Smith stubbornly asked dozens of questions. Williams, glancing regularly at the door, reached his limit quick and spoke up in a voice that surprised us. "Misters Hornsby, Mr. Wilbarger is accurate in his belief, and I feel merited in advising you to see as much land as you can for yourself before settling. I have not seen the leagues beyond the Bastrop settlement myself, but his honor, Colonel Austin, assures me they are among the most fertile in this country. We may talk this subject well past the coming Sabbath, but it will spread no further light on the facts."

MUUTSI MOVED QUICKLY. SHE HAD A LONG stick in her hands and spoke excitedly, but she was so far away and the land was difficult, especially given her age. From the tree line, I heard a familiar whoop, a warrior's call. It was Isawura. He had been watching us and knew the signs of danger. He spoke calmly, quietly as he made long strides toward us. "Be still Wʉkʉbuu. Stop old woman before you fall."

It felt like forever but he finally made it to where I was standing. The young snakes were all around my feet. Isawʉra lifted me to the safety of the large rock with so little effort and so quickly, that it felt like a dream, but I will never forget the look on his face as the adult Kwasinabóo sunk her fangs into his ankle, as did several of her young. Isawʉra made a small noise. He looked me in the eyes, his face taut, his jaw set. For the first time, I could see the soul of this strong warrior. Another bite and he made a smaller sound. His eyes at once brave but longing. Isawʉra knew he was already dying.

He was heavy and could not ride in his condition. It was all that Muutsi and I could do to help him over the long distance back to camp. He tried to keep us from thinking of the poison that now ran through his body. He asked about the medicines we were preparing and jokingly asked about one that might bring a young woman to love a young warrior more than anything else.

I felt the heat in my cheeks.

This was the first time I had been so close to Isawʉra for so long. I could feel the strength of his arms over my shoulders. By the time we reached camp, his color had changed, his lips were pale, and he was sweating heavily. Muutsi did all she could but the poison of the Kwasinabóo was stronger than her medicines and stronger still than Isawʉra.

My Sun Mountain was dying.

JUNE 29. AS WE MAKE OUR WAY NORTH, EACH hilltop and rise presents a new view to our big family, and with every mile through forest and prairie, creek bottoms and riverbeds, I'm sure we older boys, Pa, and Moses-Smith is all worried the same: when will we see Indians? Will there be trouble? Are they watching us right now from the shadows?

Mr. Wilbarger, on the other hand, seems perfectly at ease. He never reaches for his gun at the sound of deer in the bushes or the sudden flutter of a flushed turkey or quail. When we camp at night, we Hornsbys notice every sound and hardly sleep. Though he don't drink spirits, Wilbarger sleeps like a drunken man and snores up a storm.

Out of earshot of Ma and Mattie, Pa talks to his own worries. "Josiah, we ain't soldiers. At least, not this lot of us, though my father and his father fought plenty. What are the chances we can stick to farmin' and stay out of all these troubles you're describing?"

Mr. Wilbarger tried to be soft with his words but the tenor of his voice spoke to the serious topic. "Not much chance of that, Mr. Hornsby. We gonna need you, your brother, and the boys here to help us take a hold on this land. Else it's a sure thing them Comanch and others are gonna push us out. Heck, the Mexican government could change their minds about us any time. They've done it before. If it'll make you feel any better, I'll help learn the boys to shoot."

Billy jumped in, "Heck, we all can shoot a mouse out the top of a pine tree, sir. Well, most of us anyway, 'cept Mal." Josiah wouldn't let that pass. "This ain't the same as hunting critters, little or large, Master William. It's a whole different thing to get one shot at a man that is bent on killing you and your kin."

At breakfast on this, our third day, Wilbarger talked about the Colorado. He said the injuns have their own words for it. They call it the Great Clear River. Billy was thinking hard. I knew by the way he sat and stared at nothing in particular. Finally, he was out with it. "Mr. Wilbarger, how far away is this big river, this Colorado?" Wilbarger said we'd see her tomorrow with any luck. Billy was like a dog on a scent. "Why aren't we shipping all this stuff up that river instead of haulin' it across this prairie? Wouldn't it be faster and safer?"

We all stared at Billy. This was a smart question, a man's question. My older brother was actually showing some sense but I wasn't going to let it stand. I kicked at the dirt and spoke up. "Billy, Pa has thought this out. Mr. Wilbarger has made this trip a hundred times. Why you gotta go mess with things?" Billy stood and pointed right at me. "Shut your trap. You just mad 'cause I thought of it first."

Mr. Wilbarger stood. "Now hold on, boys. It's a good question, Master William. The Colorado is plenty wide in most places, but there'd be two things against us. One, we'd be headed upstream and we haven't enough man power to row or use a pole for all this. The other is, that darn river is tough to navigate for any distance. She's a dozen hands deep in some places, and less than one in others. The Brazos is better for navigation but it winds north for some ways after San Felipe. It wouldn't help us go west." I figured I should get in on this conversation, show I was thinking too. "Mr. Wilbarger, how often you seen that great clear river over her banks?"

The answer was a bit sobering. "Well, Malcolm we been beside her two full years now. Spring is the main worry. She'll rise three or four times each spring I imagine. One of them is likely to be a roller for sure. We've lost a few citizens to her fury, that's the truth. All these rivers are to be respected even in the winter." Then, of course, Billy had to barge in. "What's the matter, Bookweevil, you scared of some old rising river? You more chicken than man. It's a wonder Ottilee Jameson ever gave you even a hoot."

I couldn't sit there and take the ribbing. I could feel my face burning. I stood and walked toward my big brother aiming to hurt him somehow. Good thing Moses-Smith saved my brother from a whipping by stepping between us. Pa put a point on it. "Men, boys, we travelin' today or spending the rest of our daylight jawing like a bunch of old maids?"

As we moved out, I thought about them Mexican boys at the ferry. I didn't see how brothers could get along like that and I reckoned I never would. Pa broke my sour thoughts with some good news, but he done it quiet so none of the others could hear. "Mal, I heard in San Felipe that the Jameson's are making plans for heading this way. It's likely they'll end up in Mr. Austin's newest colony like us." I tried to be calm about it, not show my excitement. "Their ma all right? Everyone coming?" Pa nearly smiled, "Their ma is fine, boy. I'm sure all the Jameson children are coming." I sat taller in my saddle.

Nothin' my old fool brother could do was gonna push me out of my sunshine.

ISAWʉRA HAD NO CLOSE FAMILY IN THE Penatʉka. Like my father and aunt, the band had adopted him as a boy. For this reason, I had to help Muutsi and my father with the preparations as the young warrior struggled for his last breaths. This was one medicine lesson I did not want, but Muutsi insisted.

I am glad Isawʉra had his eyes closed at the end. I felt bad for having shown him little warmth. I could never see his spirit in his eyes and did not wish to look into them again as he left this world. He had given his life for me—I had never given him anything except for some food and a smile. As his life faded before us, Father bent Isawʉra's knees up to his big chest and my paha used a horsehair rope to bind his body in this position.

We wrapped one of Isawʉra's blankets around his body and used more rope to hold the blanket tightly in place. Father and Wowoki placed the body on the back of Isawʉra's favorite mustang and had me ride behind him to make sure he didn't fall off. Wowoki and father rode close beside us to help. No one spoke a word.

We rode to a small cave that father had chosen and laid Isawʉra's body as far inside as we could. Father placed Isawʉra's favorite pipe and tobacco beside him, and we covered his body in stones to keep the animals away.

By the time, we returned to our camp, Muutsi had already begun burning all of Isawʉra's things: his teepee, blankets, clothes, harnesses, and weapons. His ghost could then go in peace and not be bound to this world.

Had I been Isawura's wife or had he a mother or sister among us, we would cut our arms or cut off our hair, or both. I did not do this. I wanted to be away from the fire, away from the memories, away from what might have been.

For days after, I begged Muutsi for work to do, medicine to learn. I walked around the camp looking for people who needed help. I gathered food and water. I cooked. I worked the skins. I cleaned and combed the hair. I spun ropes. I worked before the sun rose and after it had set. I would have worked without stopping but my paha would not allow it.

The women in the band tried to ease my mind. They told me I would find another husband; there were plenty of warriors available. I didn't want to hear it. Why should I marry now? My father was free from his promise. I was free to be a medicine woman like my aunt and take care of the people.

Muutsi and Father reminded me that tradition insisted I wait; that a medicine woman must have been married and passed her time to have children. I wouldn't listen. I insisted that I would be different. I worked with the medicines and any other task I could find until I was so tired I could not see the work.

Still, kwasinaboo and Isawura haunted my dreams.

JULY 5. BULL CREEK. THE LAND NOW IS different from them flat coastal plains. This land rolls gently into low and broad grass-covered hills, prairie land. Pa stops now and then to smell the air or get down from his horse and grab a handful of soil, rub it between his palms and hold it up to his nose. Over the last several miles, Pa nodded just a little after each testing of the air and earth. We is getting closer to the place he's been dreaming of, I'm sure of it.

Of course, we are all on edge. Every mile takes us deeper into Indian country, into the unknown. We watch the dogs for signs. We try to stare through every thicket, every patch of timber. Pa never goes anywhere without his guns. Ma tells us Hornsby boys daily that we have to look out for each other. Still, we's gonna have to learn to face danger on our own, and experience is the quickest lesson on the frontier. Besides, all their talk is putting more fear in me than just living it.

Today, Pa sent me on an errand 'stead of Billy. He said, "Take Reub with you, Mal. He's old enough to do his part around here. We all have to help." I was going to argue but I stopped when I saw Pa's stern look. I grabbed the canteens and my little brother's hand and headed for the creek. Then I said something I was soon to regret. "Come on Reub, let's see if we can't scare up some big snakes."

Moses-Smith grabbed the new rifle and a powder pouch, glanced at Wilbarger who nodded agreement, then stepped in front of us and spoke quiet enough for the women not to hear. "Mal, reckon you ought to take this with you. In case them snakes is walkin' on two legs. You see any dark men with long hair and war paint, shoot first and ask questions later."

I dropped the canteens and took the gun. I told my Uncle I'd keep an eye out. That's when Reuben Jr. saw his chance. He grabbed the canteens and took off toward the creek. Pa glared at me, all pained in the face, like he'd made a mistake in the choosing. I chased after my little brother and yelled, "Hold up there, Reub, an injun's liable to carry you off, boy!"

Reub giggled at the game and ran farther ahead. I couldn't help but laugh at my cotton-top little brother. He was quite a sight, mop of blond hair flying and canteens bouncing on his butt as he disappeared into the woods.

When I caught up with him, we'd reached a deer trail on the steep slope leading down to the creek; his head bounced forward, his feet slipping and sliding on the loose rocks. The canteens bounced and banged wildly behind him, but he was still giggling. I yelled at him to slow up and that's when it all went sour. Reub lost his balance and rolled right down the creek bank, canteens and all.

The good news was Reub rolled up against the trunk of a bald cypress and didn't seem hurt. Heck, I couldn't tell if he was still giggling or just sniffling. The canteens were scattered all over. The bad news was Reuben Hornsby Jr. had rolled over a big cottonmouth, bigger than I'd ever seen back home.

A FEW DAYS AFTER WE BURIED HIS FRIEND, Wowoki came to our teepee and asked Muutsi if I would speak with him. I gathered myself from my bed, tired from another night of little sleep to find Wowoki pacing outside our flap. "Sister, I will hunt today. The winds are good for taking a deer. You will join me."

I asked if he had Father's permission, but he barked that he was a warrior and did not need anyone's approval. So I asked him if we would just ride off and say nothing to our father. Wowoki clinched his jaw, shook his head, and moaned deep in his throat.

When we asked, Tupaapi looked away for minutes of silence. Finally, with a voice touched by sadness, he said, "Yes...go. If you must leave camp, best with your brother."

I sat across from him on the other side of his fire. Since we had buried Isawura, there had been many agonizing days with no words from my father. I was happy that he'd even nodded me into his teepee. He had a warning for me too. "Daughter, you are clever, but Wowoki is a warrior of many seasons now. Heed his vision. Learn from him; he has learned from me and the other elders. The day will be fruitful. It is good for the hunt when sister and brother join together."

COTTONMOUTH'S AN ODD SNAKE. MOST OF their kin prefer to be as far from a man as possible, but them cottonmouths, they stand and fight. I couldn't see his tail but the head looked to be nearly the size of my hand and ten paces from Reub's noggin. I spoke quiet but firm. "Reub! You need to be real still now and keep your head down, you hear? We're goin' to play a game if you ain't hurt too bad. You hurt too much for a game?"

Reub said he wasn't hurt at all. I told him to keep his voice low as I eased down to my knee and checked the percussion cap on the rifle. Then I said, "Don't look up. All right then, we're playing the frozen game. You remember the ice in Vicksburg?"

The snake was on the move. He slithered slowly toward my little brother. I still couldn't see his tail. He had to be over four-foot-long. I had to keep talking to my brother to keep him still. "You remember them night crawlers frozen in that ice, Reub? You freeze like them worms and win this game and Billy will whittle you a gun. You hear? Keep your head down."

I had to move. I couldn't shoot the snake with Reuben right in the line of fire. Of course, being a Hornsby, that boy would not hush up. He asked me if I was sure Billy would whittle him a gun if he freezes and wins the game. Then he asked me what exactly the game is. I had to shut him up with something like. "Hush, Reub, and be still, for god's sake."

I pitched a few pebbles down the slope, stepped to my right and eased back down on a knee. The snake stopped and turned in my direction. I pulled the hammer all the way back, held the rifle to my shoulder, aimed down the barrel and eased the trigger. The gun fired and jerked hard against me. Reub looked up, saw the snake and screamed. As soon as the smoke cleared, I realized I'd missed. The snake was movin' again, straight toward my noisy brother.

I ran, slid down the bank, and turned the rifle around in my hands so I was holding the warm barrel. By the time I reached the snake, it had raised his head only four feet from my little brother—striking distance. I found my footing and swung my rifle with all my strength, catching that snake under the head and sending him flying into the flowing creek below. Then I just sat in the dirt and stared at my little brother. He was dead silent except for sniffling the tears back.

In seconds, all the men in our party were at the top of that creek bed and priming their guns. I stood, scooped my little brother up into my arms and climbed towards them. Reub stopped his crying and pointed to our older brother with a question. "Billy, Mal said if I's still you'd whittle me a gun! Have you started yet?"

Well, every one of them men shook his head 'cept my uncle. He laughed aloud, smiled at us boys and sighed. Pa yelled back toward the camp, "Ma! Mattie! You and the babies can get out from under the wagon. It's just your sons stirring up trouble."

Billy yelled to ma something about me shooting up every bit of Texas except where I aimed. I hushed him and said I just took a ten-foot cottonmouth that'd surely had Reub if it weren't for me. Billy had to ask, "Where's this big snake now? Guess we're lucky you didn't shoot Reub or the canteens." Reub jumped down from my arms walked up to Billy and hit him on the leg. "You big mouth, where's my gun?"

That made me smile.

SIX

Good Winds Change

LIFE IS FULL OF SURPRISES, SOME ARE GOOD, some terrible. This hunt with my brother turned to the darkest kind.

Wowoki rode hard southeast, out of the hills and toward the Great Clear River as fast as his horse would carry him, showing off. I tried to keep up. He would get so far ahead, and then circle back for me, laughing. We rode south along the Kuna-itu creek that cut into the prairie, staying hidden in the line of trees. Occasionally, we ducked out into the sun for its warmth. Without warning, Wowoki reined in his horse and stroked his neck to keep him quiet. He signaled to dismount as I too heard the faint neighs of an approaching mule. We tied our horses and continued on foot, crouching low and stepping carefully.

Then the stranger came into view.

It was a Taiboo walking a mule along the opposite bank of the stream. I wasn't sure which was worse, his smell or his sour song. He would sing a little and spit brown juice. I'll never forget his strange song.

"I'm a goin' to the shuckin' of the corn.

I'm a goin' to the shuckin' of the corn.

A shuckin' of the corn and a blowin' of the horn.

I'm a goin' to the shuckin' of the corn."

Wowoki signaled to lay down and wait as the man passed. He didn't pass. He stopped right across the stream from our hiding spot, sat down on the upper bank and pulled a small tarnished container from his coat.

The man was round and red-faced. His breathing was loud and labored, his hair long and scraggly. The facial hair in front of his ears was so thick and red it looked as if he wore the tails of two squirrels. His clothes of tanned deerskin showed stains from many suns of sweat and no washing. Juice ran down his chin from both sides of his mouth and onto his shirt. He was so swollen and red-faced, I thought he might burst at any minute as would an over-ripe melon.

He set a long rifle down beside him. In his belt, he carried two flintlock pistols. As he pulled off his boots, I saw a huge knife made of steel. It reflected the sun before he stuck it in the ground. He smelled even worse with his boots off.

I looked at Wowoki, held my nose and smiled. He didn't smile back. We watched the man remove his socks, pick up his rifle, tiptoe down to the stream, and slowly slide his feet into the cool water. Then he yelled in a voice that sounded like metal against metal. "Whew! Beth Ann, yer a-killin' me and my feet."

His mule had a white belly and leggings, and as she grazed, she walked with just a trace of limp in her left front leg … probably a thorn or bruise. The man yelled at her again, "See you don't go walkin' away, BethAnn. We'd be home if it weren't for yer dang fool wanders."

Wowoki signaled to stay there, that he was going upstream. I shook my head and held on to his arm. I knew what he was after, that mule. Besides, I did not want to stay there alone. Wowoki grabbed my arm and squeezed. I could read his eyes. *I am a warrior. I do not fear this man's weapons. He will never see me coming and is too slow to catch me.*

I whispered. "Don't go, brother. The signs are bad. Let's go to the horses and leave this Taiboo who smells stronger than the onions that grow on the banks." Wowoki pulled away from my grasp. I watched him work his way low along the tree line, cross the stream and slip up the opposite bank.

The man yelled again, "Beth Ann, get yer mangy mule hide back! I'sa gonna beat yeh from here to de river or my name is not Jacques Boucher. Now you made me sad, mangy mule. " Then he started another song, this one slow.

"Fais dodo, colas mon p'tit frère.

Fais dodo, t'auras du lolo.

Maman est en haut.

Qui fait des gâteaux."

A warrior would never sing such a sad sounding song out here. What was this Taiboo? How could he be so large and not a warrior?

As I watched, Wowoki crawled slowly along the tree line on the opposite bank, his rifle slung across his back. He fell to his belly and slowly eased forward until he was within a pace of the mule. He stood, stroked the mule's nose and neck, grabbed a handful of her mane and leaped up on her back, but the mule whinnied, her leg gave way and she dropped to her front knees. My brother tumbled over the mule's head, his rifle landing in the grass.

The Taiboo was on his feet and carrying his rifle at his shoulder faster than I imagined possible for such a big man. "I gonna skin yeh alive, yeh son-of-da-blind-dog messin' with me mule. Allons danser!" He stopped and dropped to a knee.

"Killed more dan dozen of dem from the Creek tribes in eighteen and fourteen ..."

Wowoki scrambled to his hands and knees just as the Taiboo fired his rifle. The lead ball struck my brother and flipped him over. Boucher rose and walked slowly toward Wowoki while reloading his rifle. His voice shook but he kept walking and talking. "Dem Brits thought dey help dem injuns beat old Andy Jackson. Why we killed eight hundred of dem at a cost of only forty-nine of we's own."

He stopped when he saw Wowoki on the ground. "Dat will teach yeh to mess with da man's mule!" He pulled his long knife from the ground and walked toward my brother. The closer he got to Wowoki, the more his voice shook. "Now yeh gone done it. Yer scalp is gonna make des all worth da trouble, boy."

AUGUST 11. CAMPED NEAR BURNAM'S Crossing. Life is full of surprises, some bad, some good, some wonderful. Ma and Pa told us this morning that Ma was due to have another baby. On account of her grief, the promise of another child made Ma seem to forget all the trouble in bringing them into this world.

Then, we men rode off to be among Texas royalty.

The deer scattered, and squirrels and blue jays scolded us as we rode along the Colorado in the quiet of the morning. A thin layer of fog rolled across the water. Wilbarger had arranged a meeting between Pa, Moses-Smith, and Stephen F. Austin at Burnam's ferry crossing. Me, Billy, Tom, and Tom Elder tagged along. Even if I wasn't too keen on Texas, I was excited to meet the man who'd brought so many folks to settle her.

Billy ribbed me about it something awful. "Better lookout Pa, Mal's gonna run you and Uncle right over before we even get close. What you frettin' about, Bookweevil? Mr. Austin is a man same as me, pa, uncle, and Mr. Wilbarger. He puts his boots on just like us, don't he?"

I told my fool brother that I wasn't fretting. I just didn't suppose we should have such a busy man waiting on us, that's all. I also pointed out that he'd left me out of his list. He said, "Gotta be a man to be called a man, Weevil."

Still, I'm getting better at this game myself. I hit right back at him. "That don't make a lick of sense. Guess you gotta have a brain to talk any sense. I did notice you slickin' your hair back with Mr. Wilbarger's lard back there. Maybe you hoping Mr. Burnam has a daughter. Course, she'd have to be blind." Billy tried to kick me, but I seen it coming and eased my horse out of range.

Then, he tickled himself silly. "Least I know how to talk to a girl, little brother. What would you say? Have you read any books? Do you like blacksmithin'?" I just shook my head like always when my big brother acts foolish.

As we rode, Mr. Wilbarger told us Burnam's Ferry was a gravel-bottomed ford at one of the many shallow areas of the river, south of the little village of La Grange. They used a ferry only when there was a need to cross high water. When the river was rolling hard from rains upstream, no one went near it. Mr. Burnam is building quite a station there including a two-story brick inn and store. He is a veteran of many fights with local Indians, so his station on a La Bahía Road cutoff is a welcomed sight for road-weary settlers and traders, his reputation for bravery a comfort.

We made good time and arrived early. The big house was nearly finished at the first level. It had wooden floors and smelled of fresh mortar, cut wood, and plaster. The stamp of our boots echoed in the broad entryway as the Burnam's youngest children scurried in and out of the house playing a game of tag. A young black servant—couldn't tell if he was a slave or freeman—led us into a big dining room. Tom and Tom Elder sat on the stoop outside.

We was surprised to find two well-dressed Mexican men—one older, one younger—seated at the table set with bread, butter, jam, cheese, and coffee. We didn't know what to do right off. We stood and stared for a few uncomfortable minutes until Wilbarger entered and spoke up. "Señor Seguín, Juan. ¿Cómo estás?"

The two strangers stood and smiled. Each extended his hand to Josiah. The elder took Wilbarger's hand in both of his own. "Hola, Señor Wilbarger. It is a good day to see you. It has been too long, no?"

Wilbarger made proper introductions. "Señor Don Erasmo Seguín, friend and benefactor to our empresario, and his son, Juan Seguín. Please allow me the honor to introduce the Hornsby men who will be joining us in this great adventure you call Tejas." We all shook hands. The way Mr. Wilbarger introduced these two men, as if they were some sort of Mexican dukes or counts, made me self-conscious. After all, we was dressed in the same dirty boots and clothes we'd been wearing on the trail for days. They was dressed in proper coats and ties, dusty yes, but more civilized just the same. Wilbarger seemed to sense our uneasiness. "Señor Seguín, I beg of you to forgive our appearances. We have been riding steady from Velasco and were eager to meet with you and Mr. Austin without delay."

Mr. Seguín smiled and bowed again. "Ciertamente, Señor Wilbarger, our business of establishing profitable haciendas across Tejas does not require such formality of un hombre del abrigo, eh, a man's coat." He turned to his son for help in translating his next words. The younger Seguín bowed slightly, "My father says it is not the cut of the cloth but the cut of the man that will bring us success." We all chuckled and bowed to each other—a little less stiff now. Juan stepped back and waved us all to chairs at the table. "Please, join us in having Señora Burnam's coffee, bread, and jam. I assure you it is the best this side of the Brazos. Our host is with his honor, Señor Austin, at the river. They will return soon but urged us to partake in their absence."

Billy and me grabbed chairs at the table. Pa cleared his throat and nodded toward a bench against the wall. I moved to the bench. Billy huffed and glared at the younger Seguín, then poured himself a tin cup of coffee, grabbed a slice of bread, and slammed down on the bench next to me, kicking my leg in the process. I paid him no mind. Our Mexican hosts fascinated me.

The elder Seguín had thick grey hair and a broad moustache, his skin tough and leathery. He sat up straight, noble but gentle in his manners with an easy smile like he was an officer; maybe even a general in an army at one time. Juan, his son, was clean-shaven with a more serious face. He paid close attention, nodded often, but spoke only to translate for his father.

Wilbarger had told us that only a month before this visit, a Mexican official tasked the younger Seguin with organizing a Ranger company to patrol the San Antonio de Béjar area. He would lead other men, many older than he was, in warding off Indian attacks and keeping watch over outlaws tempted to test the law. I wondered if I could handle such a responsibility. I had my doubts.

My thoughts was broken by the sound of boots in the hall.

AS THE MAN GOT CLOSER TO WOWOKI, I jumped up and yelled to my brother." The Taiboo stopped and turned. "Y'all! Tryin' to flank me, no?"

He pulled his pistol from his belt, cocked the hammer and took a quick shot in my direction. The lead ball whizzed over my head and shattered a limb behind me. Then he continued up the bank toward my brother. I stood, ran down the bank, and splashed across the stream. The Taiboo had straddled my brother with his legs to keep him from moving. I watched him pull Wowoki's hair above his forehead and start to cut into his scalp. I found a good rock and threw it, hitting the big man on the back of his head.

He stood, rubbed his head and stared as I searched for another rock. "Why, yeh just a little girl injun, ain't ya? Well, yeh gonna make a better prize than his scalp, but I's gettin' both." He turned toward Wowoki, who had gotten up and was now running upstream. Hoping to convince the smelly man to follow, he stopped and taunted, jumping as best he could and yelled insults, but the Taiboo did not follow. He focused on me as I splashed my way back across the stream carrying his boots. "Drop dem boots, girl!"

I dropped the smelly boots and ran toward our horses. I could hear him splashing across the creek, his wheezy breath, and crashing steps through the brush. I changed course to hide behind a big oak, but it was too late. The Taiboo grabbed me by the hair. I yelled at him and sunk my teeth into his big forearm. He slapped me across my face so hard I fell to my knees, dizzy. He pushed me down and sat on my back. I could not breathe. He pulled on his boots, then picked me up by my hair, and with one swift movement of his arm threw me over his shoulder. I tried kicking him but couldn't do much damage. As he splashed back across the stream, I screamed and tried to bite him through his buckskin coat. The taste and smell made me sick.

Once on the bank, he pulled my head back by my hair and forced a branch between my teeth. "Bite me again little stinker and I's break dem teeth outta yeh head." I looked for Wowoki, hoped to hear his signal.

There was nothing.

The Taiboo turned toward the tree line with one last taunt, "I hope yeh dying slowly out der, injun ... and full of de pain. I take proper care of yeh girl now, yeh hear?"

WILBARGER JUMPED TO HIS FEET AS TWO
other strangers stepped into the room, one well dressed with an
air of confidence and formality, the other with dust and plaster
on his shirt and trousers. Wilbarger rushed forward, "Ah, our
gracious host, Mr. Jesse Burnam and our empresario, our
baron, our future king, Mr. Stephen Fuller Austin. Sir, your
timing is perfection."

Mr. Burnam tipped his hat, slapped some dust from his
pants and stepped back out of the room just in time to keep one
of his toddlers from racing inside. The well-dressed stranger
laughed off the compliment. "Be careful, Mr. Wilbarger, you
will have my head in a noose or at the very least, my backside
in a Mexico City prison for such talk. Señor Seguín, Juan, good
day to you both." Then he turned to us. "Ah, these must be the
Hornsby men that I have heard so much about. I believe we
have somethin' in common sirs. I understand that your father's
given name was Moses, as was mine, god rest his soul."

Pa and Moses-Smith eagerly shook Austin's hand and
then introduced me and Billy. Mr. Austin looked both of us
square in the eye and gave our hands a firm shake. He was
thirty-seven years of age—same as my pa—yet they couldn't
be more different. Pa looked straight through most men; he was
hard inside and out, and had little time for small talk or
pleasantries. Mr. Austin seemed younger and kinder, less
aggressive or maybe just more charming, especially when it
came to business. Austin was Pa's height but more sparsely
built. Pa kept his beard long and thick. "Time spent shaving is
time lost on the land." Austin looked to shave his whiskers
daily, revealing a strong chin. Both had dark hair, Austin's hair
being more auburn and unruly. From how smartly it was tied, I
judged he regularly finished his outfit with a bow tie.

After a whole mornin' of talk, all the food was eaten
and the tin coffee cups empty. As we stood to end the meeting,
Mr. Austin shook everyone's hand, including Billy's and mine.
He stepped between us, patted us both on the shoulders and
spoke in a fatherly fashion. "My friends, I present to you the
future of our fine country. These young men, their brothers and
sisters, their cousins, represent all that is ahead of us. We must

not be discouraged by the occasional Indian depredation. We must not let changing fortunes that come and go as do the winds force us to yield to trifling difficulties. Let every man do his duty, for our country and for our future. Brindemos por México!"

Everyone cheered and clapped. I felt my face flush. Until now, I'd resented my pa for moving the family to this rugged place, for leaving grandfather and others I cared for. In a single morning, Mr. Stephen F. Austin chipped away at the coldness I felt about our travels and replaced it with a spark of excitement about this place the Seguíns called Tejas.

As we saddled up, Mr. Wilbarger held back to speak with Mr. Austin in private. When he rejoined us, I sensed a bit of dread in his demeanor. So did Pa. "Mr. Wilbarger, you look a bit ghosted, sir." Wilbarger spoke in his slow teacher's voice. "Mr. Hornsby, our empresario has just informed me that settlers were attacked on the very trail we chose to follow from the coast, just a day or two behind us."

I thought on this for much of the days that followed. If the Jameson's were headed to Texas, might they take the same path? Ma would have us praying for 'em. I'd be praying for my dear Ottilee, but more than anything I wanted to be beside her, protecting her.

THERE IS SOMETHING WE CANNOT HOLD BUT is more important than all the horses, rifles, and blankets to our people, more important than the nʉmʉ kutsu; it is our freedom. If I bind your arms and legs while you sleep, you will complain very little, but when you wake, you will fight and scream until your arms, legs, and throat are useless. The People are always awake in this way. Without this freedom, we enter the long sleep with the kooipʉ. I was a captive, my freedom gone.

As the sun slipped below the horizon, the big Taiboo carried me with my hands and feet bound, to his tall square tent of wood that smelled of manure and rot. This is where he kept his animals and he had dropped me on the disgusting floor. He lit a lamp and stepped away, then came back with rings of steel attached by chains. He measured the dark iron against my legs and chose the smaller of the two.

Once he had secured the iron rings around my ankles with steel pins, he jerked me to my feet and dragged me out into the dark. The shackles were heavy and cut into the tops of my feet as I tried to walk. The short chain made it difficult to keep up with the Taiboo's long steps. We stopped at a tiny log-covered hole in the side of a small hill. From a strip of leather around his neck, he pulled a big key and unlocked a padlock on the door. The large black hinges squeaked and groaned as he yelled, "Martha, get up out of der, damn yeh!"

A black-skinned girl stepped out of the dark interior. Boucher held up the lantern and pulled me forward. "Yeh gonna keep an eye on des little fillé, Martha. She get away, I reckon I sell off yer boy der to pay for losses, yeh hear? Yeh hear me wo-mon?"

When I looked at the frightened girl before me, I felt a deep yearning to be in camp with my family and as far away from here as possible. Her clothes were ragged. She smelled as bad as Boucher. A baby cried from somewhere in the dark dugout. The girl didn't speak; she only nodded her head slowly, more ghost than alive.

Boucher towered over her. "Martha, yeh good for nothing 'cept making babies, ain't yeh?" He grabbed me by my hair and pulled my head down to the low entrance. "Des home now, girl." My buffalo pendant slipped out of my shirt. He reached for it and tugged at my neck. "I like des. You steal it from a dead white woman? Maybe someday I take it back." He pushed me through the entrance and turned to Martha. "She yours now, yeh hear?"

I tripped on the shackles and fell to the dirt floor. A tiny fire in one corner barely lit the space. In the other corner on a thin pile of hay was a bundle of tattered blankets. The girl stepped into the dugout and stood resolutely between the bundle and me, her hands in fists.

The squeaky door slammed. I heard the sound of the big iron hasp and lock closing on the outside. I stood and pounded on the door and screamed as loud as I could until my arms and voice were useless. It was no use. I was a captive.

That night I could not sleep. Somewhere out there, my brother was hurt, maybe dying. The prairie would be dark and quiet except for the wind in the grass and trees. He would close his eyes, draw the night air into his lungs and try to remember all that our father had taught us: to make decisions slowly with all the knowledge we can gather.

First, where is the enemy? Gone with his sister and horses. For this—when he recalls the day and the loss of his sister—he will likely yell at all the living things in the night. For this, he will search for any weapon and think only of revenge on the Taiboo, but his body needs rest.

I tried to send him my thoughts. Turn back to Father's lessons, brother. What are your surroundings? The tree line hides you. The creek will lead you north to our great river. The night is clear. Once across the river, the moon and stars will lead you back to camp, should you choose that path. What is your physical condition? Your wounds will ache. You have lost much blood, but there is water nearby, wild grape and fruit from the naseeka. Should you track the Taiboo and try to save your sister, or hold your pride and get help at camp? What of your rifle? Should you search for it in the dark?

I know you will growl and pound your wounds with your fist in anger. Father has taught us to take charge of our emotions or they will blind us and force poor decisions. Wowoki, you must now mind this lesson. This is a time to think, not worry. You need water and food, not fear. You must get back to the Penatuka, get healthy and get help. There will be no honor in it and it will be difficult to face our father, but you must make a warrior's decision. It will be a long and lonely night for both of us, but I will be strong.

You must be strong too.

OCTOBER 14. BASTROP. MOMENTOUS DAY. PA never whistles, sings, or hums, least not that any Hornsby ever heard, but this morning he whistled one of Billy's old marching tunes from the moment he stepped outta bed. The little ones followed him about the cabin in their nightclothes like ducklings.

Before mounting his horse to join me and Moses-Smith, Pa smiled through his thick black beard and moustache, kissed Diana on the forehead, then gently touched Ma's pregnant belly and kissed her on the cheek. He reached and mussed Daniel's hair and spoke loud enough for all to hear. "That's for luck, Danny. This will be our day, Mrs. Hornsby, I feel it."

Ma nodded. "Yes, Mr. Hornsby, it is an excellent day for settling on where we will raise these gypsy children." I love my ma when she says things like that. Pa smiled, tipped his hat, and yelled at the older boys and slaves out in the field that he expected a productive day, that there'd be no foolery on account of his absence, and if they must fish, be sure it's a reasonable hour. Then he spoke directly to my big brother. "William, I know you aim to be in town to see that girl of yours. Mind you don't stay late and leave your ma to all this on her own." All 'cept Billy waved their hats and nodded. Billy kicked at the dirt.

We met Wilbarger, Mr. John Webber, and Mr. Austin on the north end of Wilbarger's bend in the Colorado. Mr. Austin was also in a cheery mood though he seemed plagued with a cough. He greeted us as fellow Texians and charmed all as was his way. "Progress awaits, my friends. Mr. Hornsby, I see you have brought Master Malcolm to keep us in line. Malcolm, I do declare you've grown a hand taller since I saw you last."

Mr. Webber's mule carried packs containing heavy surveying tools. I rode behind, taking inventory of the equipment in my head: sixty-six feet of iron chain, dozens of iron stakes, a Jacob staff, and the compass. I was born for this sort of work.

Mr. Webber is from way up in Vermont. He served as a private in the War of 1812, and was in Austin's colony by '26, mostly to avoid resentment for marrying a former slave. I had heard this in the town gossip, but had never met him. Like Pa, Mr. Webber hoped that, in the process of surveying and laying out the sections, he would find suitable headrights for himself. He shared the same worries as every colonist and was not afraid to talk about 'em. He asked Mr. Austin about the reports of squatters south of the river.

Mr. Austin was diplomatic to a fault. "Mr. Webber, it is a quandary. While we need every man, woman, and child to help us hold our place here, we cannot afford to cross the Mexican government at too many junctions. Much of that land is marked for influential citizens of Mexico, same as us, only with a deeper, older sense of ownership. Every empresario in our young state has sworn to protect their rights. Makes it hard to turn a blind eye in these cases. What's your feelings on this matter, Mr. Hornsby?"

Pa was quiet for a bit. Then he spoke low like he does on serious topics. "I understand the desire. Ain't much different from our own: run a profitable farm and provide for one's family, but what them squatters is doing is tainted with thievery. I apologize for my strong words, but there's just no way around the truth. And just like every form of thievery, most often it hurts more than just them that loses directly." It was about the only somber note on an otherwise bright day. Pa had every one of us thinkin' in silence for a bit. He could do that.

We made decent time working our way west along the winding river to where we'd stopped the work before, 'bout nine miles from Wilbarger's bend. Here, the Colorado made another deep southern turn. It was about the length of Wilbarger's but a third wider, nearly two miles across. We tied the mule, and removed the tool packs too prepare for the day's work.

As I had several times now, I carefully assembled the compass: a circular flat piece of wood with a cavity in the middle to hold the compass card and a needle. All this I set in putty and protected with a glass pane. Two wooden arms held the sighting bars. Then I screwed the entire compass unit and the sighting arms on top of the Jacob staff and carefully stuck the staff in the ground.

While the others set up the rest of the equipment and kept guard, Mr. Austin and Pa mounted up to ride ahead. Pa stopped and turned. "Malcolm, if you finished there, mount up and come with us, I have something to show you." Austin snapped his horse in the rump with his reins and yelled out.

"Your future awaits, Master Malcolm."

IN THIS TAIBOO PLACE, MY DAYS WERE THE darkest that I'd ever known. One night in my sleep, I saw Wowoki banished from the camp. He had no fire. The rain soaked him as he tried to sleep beneath the dark sky. My Father and Aunt were there too, yelling at him "You are no warrior. You are no warrior." Every word twisting his body as if a knife was sinking into him. With each cut, he screamed. "She's alive! I know she is alive, and I will find her!" but Tupaapi and Muutsi would not listen.

They changed into four-legged meat eaters and were joined by a pack of others, part wolf, part lion. They circled him and showed their teeth. They growled, but Wowoki stood and faced them with his spear. If one attacked he pushed the beast back, but the others would get closer.

Then he was out on the prairie alone on his horse riding slowly, his head limp bouncing as if riding in his sleep. I was there. I stopped his horse and pulled on his leg to wake him. He did not wake. I yelled his name and beat his leg. He did not wake. I pulled myself up on his horse facing him and lifted his head to look into his eyes. They were dark and empty without spirit. He was alive and dead at the same time. I heard myself singing the death song, but I could not bind his legs or wrap him in his blanket.

Then the dream changed. Wowoki was rushing from one Taiboo camp to another on foot. He would run up a hill or into the woods near a square wooden tent, and make the bird sounds we'd learned from our father. Then he would listen for the answer, but there was none. He was making the sounds for me! My brother was alive, and he was searching for me. The dream woke me and though it was still dark, I stood at the large wooden door and made the birdcalls as loud as I could. Perhaps the dream was a sign that Wowoki or my father or my aunt were outside calling for me. Perhaps this dream was meant to warn me so that soon I would be free and with the People. I kept calling.

No one answered.

WE RODE SOUTH, FOLLOWING THE RIVER'S bend along the tree line of post oaks, black jacks, and pecan, then along a bluff above the sand-lined water. Pa and Mr. Austin discussed the area, its value in the coming years and the fact that, as a home, it would be farther west than any other on the north side of the river.

I watched as Mr. Austin bounced in his saddle while he talked. This far out in the prairie most kept their voices low. Mr. Austin paid that rule no mind. I always listened closely to his words so I can write them in my book at night. "I tell you, Mr. Hornsby, it's a paradise. Dozens of natural springs, one just a few miles up this river that is colder than a winter in the state of Connecticut. Caves full of bees and their honey. There's a mountain of a hill along the river that affords a man a view to behold. I believe the land to the west with its confluence of natural beauty and resources would be a prime spot for an establishment of some size and importance."

My Pa was losing his patience. "Colonel Austin, no offense, sir, but I am finding that my attention is better spent on the here and now." Mr. Austin cleared his throat. "Well, yes, of course." He pointed to a large live oak bent long ago to parallel with the ground. "Pay close attention to that bent oak, Master Malcolm. This is a landmark for those warriors using this river bend as a winter camp for decades before us. Mr. Hornsby, you are aware that we are not the first to ride across this particular Eden. There may be disagreements with those who come before us."

Pa ignored the comment and pointed to a clump of small driftwood in the top of a tall oak along the river's edge. "Mr. Austin, I believe there is proof of how fertile this section will be. If I'm not mistaken that is driftwood from flooding which means this land has layers of rich sediment." Mr. Austin turned and shaded his eyes. "Sir, I believe that to be a large bird or squirrel's nest, but I admire your optimism." Pa dismounted, grabbed a handful of the rich black soil, held it to his nose, breathed deep, and smiled. "Well sir, either way, this suits me fine."

"Very well Mr. Hornsby, I will have Mr. Williams draw up the necessary agreements. You have made a fine choice, sir. Master Malcolm, I believe your horse to be standing on the site of your future estate. How do you find it?" I wasn't sure how to answer but felt my Pa staring at the back of my head. "I guess it feels a little like home, sir."

Mr. Austin asked if I was prepared to defend it. He said there are others who claim this spot. They will certain come a calling. How's your firearm skills coming along?" Pa cut him off short. "Mal ain't much for fighting sir, if that's where you're navigating."

I never been so embarrassed in my life. Must've turned five shades of red. Pa was telling the most important man in Texas that I, well, that I ain't never killed a man and that he wasn't sure I could. I eased my horse away from the two of them slow like. My heart was pounding through my chest. All I could think of was Covington County and walking through our meadows.

I wanted to go home, my real home, in Mississip.

I LISTENED TO FOLLOW THE THUNDER AS IT came closer and closer that first morning. The lightening lit the sky before the sun rose. The wind whipped the trees against the roof or our tiny cabin. When the rain came it was first big round pieces of ice rattling on the roof and bouncing through the slits in the walls. The baby was screaming. The girl Martha held him and rocked back and forth singing a song and occasionally barking at the ice and rain.

When the rain came in full it poured through holes in the roof and walls and began to fill the cabin floor. The People would never build a camp that would flood like this. The rain didn't stop. Soon the water was up to my knees.

The baby continued to cry. Martha barked at the weather more and more. The wind howled through the cracks. I put my hands over my ears and tried to scream this terrible dream away, but when I opened my eyes, nothing had changed.

Then I noticed that the baby had stopped crying and his mother was staring at me, not in a fearful way, more as if she understood me. The rain was cold on my legs. It made me shudder, but the look of understanding from Martha gave me just a little warmth.

NOVEMBER 23. DOG TIRED. WE DON'T STOP from sunrise to sunset nearly every day. Make's time pass quickly, but the Jamesons is taking forever, so time is just torture. They're missing all the progress. Bastrop is growing every day. There's always something new. Still, there are two things the town is best for: supplies and gossip. Ma is not interested in gossip, so she ain't so happy in town. Lucky me, then, to have drawn the short straw to go on a supply run with her.

The general store is now a wood structure instead of a tent, and the hub of activity. Heck, we couldn't get our wagon even close. I had to walk Ma across the muddy streets, though she wasn't one to complain about such matters. Once inside, Ma pulled out her list and put me to work. "We need five pounds of flour son and be sure to avoid any critters in there. Mal, see if Mr. Conley has baking soda. I've missed having a Sunday cake for your pa twice now. I shan't miss it again, Lord help me. Now, Malcolm Morrison Hornsby, you are not to go near that hard candy. Your uncle gives you children enough of that sinful stuff to kill the horses, but please do check on the tobacco for your father." I told her a man can only carry so much in his head and his arms. She just said, "Son, a man does not complain to his mother, now does he?"

I seen two men playing at checkers in the back of the store. I didn't recognize them, but new folks comin' in by the wagonload. Only, these men looked to have dark news. The oldest of the two had bandages around his head, fresh ones. I could see bloodstains. His pal, about my age and stature had cuts and bruises all about his face and arms. These boys had gone to the dirt with someone or something, that's for sure. I tipped my hat. "Morning, sirs. How is it you come to look so worse for the wear, if you don't mind my asking?" The youngest snapped at me. "You Austin colony boys always so nosy?"

I begged their pardons. Then I explained that we share news around here that might affect more than one. You know, wildcat taking calves in the area, or worse. One of them saw right through me and came to it. "You talking about Indians, boy, ain't ya?"

I nodded my head. Then the bragging commenced. They started in like they'd won a war all by themselves. "Well, you're looking at two men who bested them yesterday. Must have been a hundred of them no good heathens comin' after us, but we fought them good."

People in these parts always say the Indians they crossed come in the hundreds, but I suspect if a hundred Indians was on or near a trail, there'd be a lot more folk who would see them. I pushed for more detail and asked where they come across 'em, and that's when their news took a turn that near dropped me. The older of the two said, "We's on the trail up from Burnham's." The older man stood slowly. The other side of his scratched-up face was black from bruising. I could barely make out what he said on account of he couldn't move his lips much, but I got the gist of it. He'd lost everything he had. Everything but what he had on. His wife and son, gone. I lowered my head, removed my hat out of respect and said I was sorry for his loss, but all I could think about was Ottilee and the Jamesons.

I grabbed that flour as quick as I could and walked quiet-like to the front of the store. Ma asked about the supplies that I'd failed to gather. "You ask about the baking soda and tobacco? We don't need to be here 'til tomorrow, do we? Besides, I have some news for you. I just heard that the Jamesons are on Mr. Austin's list and should be at the mouth of the Brazos in the coming months. They'll be crossing at Mr. Burnham's and here among us before you know it."

The only words I could get out were "You sure?" Ma didn't see my face or hear my worry.

"Well, of course, I'm sure. Why would anyone just make up a story like that, son? Now you just hold onto that for a moment." She turned to the proprietor. "Mr. Conley, we need to talk about that woolcloth you ordered for me last month—I have sewing to do before this baby comes in the heart of winter and I mean to see it done."

I couldn't breathe. I felt dizzy, like the store was spinning around me. I made up my mind right then to go south and wait for the Jamesons and help them get here safely. We was in the wagon heading home before I could work up the nerve to tell my ma. I said something like, "Ma, I'm dropping you off, packing me a possibles bag, and headed down to Velasco to meet up with the Jameson's when they arrive. They'll need, well, they'll need another set of hands to help 'em moving to these parts. Wouldn't you have appreciated some help when we made the trip?"

Ma put a dim on my plans right off. "Malcolm, you're likely weeks ahead of them and, besides, you will have to discuss that with your father, young man. Only he can judge as to how much work he has for you right here." I huffed a bit and shook my head. Ma spoke slowly and right in my ear. "Malcolm, you may be old enough to make this decision from your own porch, but you will have to cross your father should he be seeing the situation from another. Is that clear?"

I set my mind to it. The minute I finished helping Ma get the supplies in the house I would find Pa and tell him straight off of my plan and my being committed to see it through.

I'VE BEEN A HEALER FOR AS LONG AS I remember, I know a lot of spells and medicines, but sometimes the seeing and feeling is more than the knowing. Sometimes, we have to make a choice between what we desire with every sinew of our bodies and what we must do to take the sickness from someone who needs our help.

In the dugout cabin, the night fire was nearly out, and Martha's baby was sick. I heard it in his cough and felt it in the heat from his little body as we slept next to each other in the hay and dirt. Martha didn't know what to do. She used strange words, not Taiboo words. She chanted and danced around her sick baby boy and pulled at her hair in frustration.

We both rose to the sound of the lock on the door sliding open. I wanted to run into the fresh air but had to shuffle up and out of the dugout, the chains on my ankles ringing softly. It was cold out. I heard other squeaky doors and watched dark figures climb slowly out of two larger cabins nearby, all women and girls, all ghost like. Martha stepped out holding the baby and began to cry. The shadowy figure yelled in a language that sounded familiar to me. "Niñas, rápida, rápida."

The music of this language and the memories it conjured made me feel warm and cold at the same time. As my eyes became used to the morning twilight, I saw that the shadowy figure was just a boy, a Mexican boy who looked to be my brother's age. He was dark skinned like me. His hair hung nearly over his eyes below a tan hat made of straw. There were spits of whiskers on his face.

The rest of the slave women stood around as Martha pulled on the young man's arm and tried to show him her baby. The young overseer stared at my shackles and me. "¿Quién eres?" Hearing this old language was frustrating: it sounded so familiar, and yet I could not understand the words.

Martha's baby coughed and cried. She lifted her shirt and tried to feed him, but the baby would not take the milk. Tears streamed down the faces of both mother and child. The other women spoke in hushed tones and pointed. Martha waved her fist above her head and chanted, "Yālä käyāla! Yālä käyāla!"

The boy shook his head. "I am sorry, Martha, no entiendo." He tipped his hat to me and spoke slowly in the Taiboo language, "I am Alonso, overseer for this farm. The master said he had a new slave, but I did not expect someone as you."

I wanted to tell him about a medicine for the baby. I shuffled to a nearby tree and pulled small bits of bark from the trunk. "Puha!" Everyone stopped to stare at me. Even the baby quieted. No one seemed to understand. I dropped to my knees and made motions as if I was digging. "Tʉkʉ ahwerʉ!"They just stared. I felt the heat in my face and my anger grow. I pulled at my hair and moaned. Then in my frustration, a word popped out of my mouth as if I had spoken it every day of my life, "Medicina!"

"Medicina?" said the young overseer. I nodded, pointed to the woods and then to myself. "Medicina!" Alonso helped me to my feet. He looked down at my shackles and sighed, "Cómo va a trabajar en eso?" I didn't understand the boy's words then, but I have learned them since. He gently held my arm, pointed to the woods and said, "Vamos a ir por la medicina."

In a damp thicket of cypress and red cedars around the springs, I found the milk vine roots for the medicine. As I dug with a Taiboo spade, Alonso stared at my swollen ankles and shook his head. From where we were, I could see the tree line of the Great Clear River in the distance behind him.

I felt the balance and weight of the shovel in my hands. I was thinking that if I hit this young Mexican on the head hard enough, I could make it across the meadow before he woke, even in these shackles. I glanced back at Alonso. He studied my face. I held up the root, pointed two fingers to my eyes and toward Alonso's, and then pointed around the thicket again. "Medicina."

DECEMBER 3. LONELIER THAN A PREACHER IN a saloon. I told Pa about the strangers in the store and their story about the trail from Velasco. He thanked me for not alarming my ma but said he couldn't spare me going down to meet the Jamesons, not with the baby nearly here. I tried to argue but Pa gave me that stare, the one that'd sure enough start a fire in your eyes if you tried to look back at it.

Then I was dumb enough to go and try talking to my brother 'bout it. I said that Pa would certainly let him go. Billy was nothing but a smart mouth. "You want me to go down and save your girl, Bookweevil?" I should have known better than to ask, but I kept at it. "No! That ain't what I meant, and you know it. Maybe you could talk to Pa for me?"

Billy sounded more like an adult than a brother. "Mal, Ma is having that baby any day now. Come spring, you'd be crossin' them rivers when the currents are killers. Besides, you gonna just ride out of here on your own with everything hanging over our heads? Pa told me about them Indian attacks down south. You gonna take on them hostiles all by your lonesome? What you gonna do, throw books at 'em? All for some girl? Some girl that may not fancy you one hair?"

Now he was heading down the wrong path. I asked him what exactly he meant by that. He said we been gone awhile, Ottilee ain't sore on the eyes, and maybe she's even traveling right now with her new beau. I could see Billy was thinkin' on something other than me and Ottilee. Best I asked him plain. "What's in your head, William Hornsby? You ain't no angel, but you ain't usually this cruel."

He confirmed my suspicions. "Women are all the same, little brother. They'll string you along as if you are the biggest fish in the pond and the only one they want to hook. Then snap, they cut that line and fish another pond before you can whistle a tune. You know that Jane girl I fancied in town. She done married a man twice her age just because he got a farm and horses and slaves."

I felt real bad for my brother. His eyes would light up when he talked about that girl, but I told him that Ottilee ain't like that. He just shook his head and said, "They all like that, Weevil, don't you see? Ottilee is just the same. The prettier they are, the more ponds they have to fish."

I wanted to crack Billy's head on the tree next to us, but I held back. I knew I was right. I knew Ma, Pa, and Billy were missing the point, knew I had to see this talk through. I took a deep breath and another shot at it. "It's not just Ottilee, Billy. It's the whole Jameson family and everyone ridin' with them. They was our neighbors and it wasn't that long ago, was it? I know I ain't no big hero like you, brother, but I can shoot. We've traveled that trail one more time than they have. I know the blind spots, the draws to avoid. And I can figure my way out of a jam if I need to."

Billy turned and walked away while scolding me. "Mal, you're as thick as a plank. You ain't going. There's too much at stake right here. Listen to your big brother, I'm not telling you somethin' you don't already know." Then I said something terribly mean. I yelled that he wasn't my brother, and that he was nothing to me except misery, every day. I shouldn't have said them words.

I watched him walk away, knowing he might just be speaking the truth.

ALONSO WORKED HIS WAY AROUND THE thicket looking for more vine. He stopped and knelt at a plant with promising leaves, his back to me. I stood slowly, raised the shovel above my head and eased forward, quietly shuffling through the leaves and limbs toward him.

Once behind the boy I raised the shovel higher. Then we heard it: Martha's baby was crying loudly, and Martha was yelling. Alonso looked toward the farm then at me. Behind him, I saw a flash of red, yellow, and black slither toward his bared calf. "Kwasinaboo!" I brought the spade down and sliced the snake's head off, just inches from Alonso's leg. The boy sprung to his feet, grabbed the shovel from my hands, and stepped toward me. I stood still.

He reached and carefully lifted my mother's wooden-beads. They had fallen out of my shirt in the commotion. Alonso gently held the beads and turned the cross at the end in his fingers, "¿Señorita, cree como yo?" He stared into my eyes and I into his. There was so much kindness and questioning. He was no warrior, but with him I felt safe.

In two days, Martha's baby had improved. He was eating regularly, sleeping soundly, and without fever. He squeezed my finger and tried to pull it into his mouth. By four days, he had noticeably put on weight and I had a new status. In the fields, the other women took turns sharing food with me. Alonso smiled and bowed just slightly in the mornings when I climbed from the cabin. He'd retrieved the dead coral snake and spread the colorful skin on our door.

When he spoke to me, out of earshot of the smelly man, he would say, "No perteneces aquí. You do not belong here." Still, I found myself staring north toward the Great Clear River and the freedom it promised. I rubbed my mother's crossed charm until my fingers ached.

Then one night from the dugout, I thought I heard my brother making the birdcalls. I sang back, "Taka, taka!"

No one answered.

DECEMBER 6. TODAY WAS FULL OF WAITING and new faces. I tried to read to pass the time, but my little brother had other ideas. I watched Danny pull his coat collar up around his neck to protect against the cold mist. He stepped up onto the overturned bucket, looked down the road and stepped off—stepped up and off, up and off, until I reached out and held his arm. "Danny, I'm trying to read." Then I guess he had to get his restlessness out by talking. He looked up at me from beneath all that hair and hat. "Billy says books are for worms and weevils."

I told him he shouldn't listen to Billy, especially about books. Our brother wouldn't know a good book if it jumped up and smacked him on the butt. Danny laughed, and then he came to the point. "When she coming, Mal? Pa said if it rains again, ain't gonna have no birthday; if that midwife-lady don't come, ain't gonna have no birthday today."

I tried to get my words in—the boy was talking up a storm and acting more nervous than a groom waiting for a mail-order bride. I told him this wasn't much rain, and that Pa was just pulling his leg about the midwife. Danny wouldn't let go of it. "Pa also said my birthday have to wait fer Ma to have that baby."

I mussed his hair and tried to reassure him. "Today is your birthday, little brother. Ain't nobody gonna take that away from you. Heck, you might get the best birthday present ever." Of course, he had to go guessing. "What's that, a pony?"

Daniel can sure make me laugh. I answered him, "No, a little brother or sis" and he said, "'Ready got one of them. Don't care much for another." That's exactly when we heard a horse-drawn wagon. Danny leaped up on the bucket. "She's here! She's here, Mal. The midwife-lady is here for my birthday." A wagon pulled by two skinny mules turned the bend in the road. A woman sat on one side of the seat, a shawl draped over her black hair. When she saw us Hornsby boys, she rubbed her wooden rosary beads, crossed her chest, and looked up into the sky.

Driving the wagon was a boy about my age, with dark hair hanging over his eyes from under a wide-brim straw hat. He carried his rifle across his lap, pulled the mules' reins, and talked quietly to them. "Niñas, lento, lento."

MY AUNT USED TO SAY THAT WE ARE LEAVES in the wind; flying, floating, stuck in a draw or the fork of a tree, swirled in one spot until the next wind comes along and frees us. Alonso may have been that wind for me.

I heard him ring the bell outside our open door, and then I heard Boucher giving him a fit, so I peeked out through one of the cracks. Alonso tried to calm the big man. "Señor, lo siento, my old horse is lame. I have walked most of way." Boucher raised his fist as if to strike, shook his head, and jerked the bell from the young man instead. Then he rang it hard in Alonso's face.

I hated that bell. Every morning I yearned to wake in a warm teepee or at hunting camp with the People. Every morning Alonso's bell would snap me out of the warmth and comfort of that vision. My life as part of the People was slipping away. I had dreamed Muutsi made medicine and danced me into a thin line of sage smoke that floated out of the shackles and through the open slot below the big door. I woke knowing the dream had slipped into another sun.

I would try not to give up. A battle does not always test only our physical strength. Wowoki and Father would come. When a warrior is fighting to keep what belongs to him, he becomes a mad mountain lion, but even the lion must wait for the right time to strike.

Boucher had ordered the other slaves to make me look as much like them as possible. They cut half of my hair, braided the rest, and wrapped the braid tightly on top of my head, covering it all with a handkerchief. They took my buckskin clothes and replaced them with a long dress of thin calico, leaving my feet bare. For some, such torment might have brought tears, but instead I tried to grow stronger. Day by day, I worked to turn my anger into bravery, my loneliness into strength. I struggled.

The cold season in the fields was hard. We women cleared land, burned underbrush, rolled logs, split rails, carried water, and lifted rocks. We worked from before sunrise to our nightly meal and sometimes after. The animals on the farm often had easier days. Certainly, they were cleaner. What made it worse was that Boucher had welcomed a couple of his old Creek-fighting friends to his farm in the guise of hospitality: an old Taiboo, tall as I ever seen but with only one good eye, and another who sounded and looked like Boucher, only he was smaller; maybe Boucher's brother.

I was sure it was to keep my rescuers at bay. The scruffy pair drank and yelled a lot. They fired their rifles and pistols at imagined Comanche behind every tree. The two appeared little threat until the taller one pointed out that I was making the birdcalls in the night from my dugout. Boucher silenced me from then on, by tying a big stick between my teeth. For extra measure, he strapped my wrists together behind my back with rawhide every night.

I had to sleep with my hands behind me—the pain burning in my shoulders.

DECEMBER 7. WAITING AND WORRYING 'FORE the best came about. During the worse of Ma's troubles, we boys either sat, wrestled or played to pass the time in the barn. I fiddled with a few bent nails and a couple of old locks. Keys and locks are a wonder to me. Billy sat and tried a new tune on his tin whistle, a Christmas tune, one he'd heard someone singing to the piano from inside a La Grange saloon. The singer sung in German, but Billy liked the tune and said he caught the words "O Tannenbaum" in the chorus. I was amazed at how he could turn a tune after just hearing it once. Uncle Moses-Smith had run a secret errand. Pa slept on a pile of hay—he hadn't slept much in the last few days being up with Ma so much.

The Mexican boy stood alone and watched us all. We Hornsby boys weren't sure what to say to him. Guess he wasn't sure what to say to us.

When I finally got one of the old locks to open, I celebrated. As usual, my brothers just ignored me, but the stranger noticed. He slowly walked to my makeshift workbench on a board in a pile of hay. He started in Spanish, but I reckon he seen on my face that I didn't understand much of it, so he asked in English if I'd just opened the lock without a key. I popped open the second lock and answered, "Heck yeah! I could do this with my eyes closed. Try me?"

He sat beside me and shrugged. I told him to close the locks while I turned my head, and then hand me the lock and make sure I wasn't lookin' as I opened it. Billy stopped playing his whistle and watched as I opened both locks, one after the other, without turning my head to look. Billy shook his head and went back to his music.

The Mexican boy asked me to perform my magic feat over and over. Finally, he grabbed my elbow and asked if I could do that with other locks. I told him, "I reckon. Maybe. Have to try to see." It was then I put out my hand and introduced myself proper. He said his name is Alonso de la Garza. I recognized that name. "Say, don't you work for old man Boucher?"

Alonso answered, yes, but not today. He said his mother's work was God's work and I wondered aloud if old man Boucher would see it that way. Alonso just looked down and shook his head. I felt bad, so I offered go with him to Boucher and talk about the baby an all. His answer surprised me. I even made out most of the Spanish in it. "No. I have something importante, more important. If you will allow me to speak of en privado?" I glanced at my younger brothers throwing hay at each other and my older playing the same notes over and over, and I reckoned being outside would suit me just fine.

Me and Alonso leaned against the south side of the barn, enjoying the warmth of the sun. Without looking, I continued to open and close one of the locks. We watched Tom and Tomas Elder, hoeing in the field. I should have been out there with them, Billy too. But the only times Pa didn't make us work was Sundays and days when Ma was bringing a baby.

Alonso is smart on lots of things. I was pointing and talking about the corn and cotton we'd plant in the spring. He made suggestions on the best seed corn we could choose for this soil. We was joking and laughing. It was like I'd known Alonso for years. Then I seen Tom charging up to the barn with a look as mean as one of Pa's. I tried to introduce him to Alonso, show I was teaching him my lock tricks and he was teaching me, but Tom was seeing it a different way. "You's teachin' him to laugh at me?"

I reached for my friend's arm. "Now go easy, Tom. We ain't laughing at you." He looked around me but didn't pull out of my hold. I kept at it with the cool water. "You're all heated up, Tom, but we ain't slighting you, I swear." He finally looked me in the eyes but I didn't recognize my old friend. It was like he'd become a man overnight while I wasn't looking.

He pulled me hard away from Alonso and spoke quiet. "I'm sorry, Mal. Guess workin' on our own out here is crossin' me. I got to ask you, Malcolm, what hold Master Hornsby have on us now? Slaves ain't legal in Texas. That's what de houseman say in town." I told him it was best not to listen to them folks in town. That there's more to it. Tom glanced at

Alonso. "Yeah? Maybe so, and maybe you should watch who yer mixin' with. He don't look no better than them soldiers down south." I nodded my head. "Yeah, I remember, Tom, but they was prisoners forced to be soldiers. Alonso here same as us, making his way on the land and he seems to have a good head for it." Tom wouldn't let it ride. "Well, you watch him just the same, looks like trouble."

Mattie got me out of the pinch. She yelled from the house to say I was needed inside. Ma was struggling and she may need strong hands to hold and a good talker to ease her fretting. I ain't never seen her so worried. "Malcolm, there's likely times you will need to close your eyes or turn your head. Mind yourself now and don't alarm your mother one bit, you hear?"

THIS WAS NO LIFE FOR A PENATᵾKA WOMAN. I thought of my mother and imagined how brave she had been as a captive. The Penatᵾka took captives, as did most of the Comanche bands. Those brought into the band from the outside worked hard and often at the worst jobs. Some Penatᵾka, those with dark hearts, would mistreat captives, but many times, the People treated them more as family than livestock. This dark-skinned group and the smelly white men was far from being a family and the work made little sense. I understood the essential seasons of the Penatᵾka: times to hunt and times to trade for what the hunt did not bring to the fire, but this work, this life on the farm, was different; it had a different rhythm and purpose. I could not see how this work clothed or fed anyone.

There were a few bright spots in my darkness, one being Martha and her healthy baby boy who Martha had named "Boo" after Wᵾkᵾbuu. It was an honor. The other bright spot was Alonso, his use of my mother's language and his occasional effort to show me kindness.

I eased out of the dugout. Alonso stepped quickly to remove the gag from my mouth. "Hola, Señorita." There was a different music in his voice. He spoke firmly to the master as he untied my hands. "Señor Boucher, I would very much want to talk to you of bringing another to help catch thief of pollo, eh, chickens." I glanced up into his eyes. He looked directly at me and winked.

Boucher spit and mumbled. "Listen to me, yeh little span-yard, I don't need no one dat can do yer work fer yeh and take more o' my money." Alonso stood with his back to Boucher facing me and whispered, "Lo siento." It was quiet, soft, but there was promise in his eyes and in the music of his words.

I tried not to smile and risk giving the promise away.

IN THE HOUSE, MA WAS HURTING, MOANING long and low, and I could see the sweat on her face. Alonso's mother sang a soft song in Spanish as she worked. She stroked Ma's hair and spoke in a soothing tone. She'd had Mattie make a special liniment that filled the house with a warm and welcoming smell, and most importantly, she had Ma talking names—thinking about anything but the pain. "If it be a boy, and I feel it surely is, we are partial to Thomas, but Lord knows I haven't the slightest idea of a middle name. And if it's a girl, I believe Sarah Ann will do just fine."

Señora de la Garza talked up a Spanish storm, but she had ma in a good place. Ma even asked the midwife questions about herself. "What is your full name, madam? If I may ask." Señora de la Garza smiled and shook her head. Ma tried her Spanish. "Your nombre, Señora?"

"Oh, sí, sí. Es Señora Adelita Santana Francisco de la Garza."

Señora de la Garza was captivating my ma. It was as if there wasn't a baby involved at all. Ma's mind was somewhere else entirely, and that was pure magic. "That is quite a mouthful. Say it again, it sounds like a hymn."

Señora de la Garza smiled again and shook her head. Ma insisted. Senora de la Garza stood and said her name with pride. "Adelita Santana Francisco de la Garza." Ma acted like she'd found a four-leaf clover. "Francisco. I love the sound of that. You suppose Francisco would make a suitable middle name for a boy? Mattie, what do you think?" Mattie nodded. Alonso's mother smiled and went on about her work. I don't think she understood a word Ma had said.

As darkness arrived, Uncle Moses-Smith came home leading a small pony. He'd missed the birth. Thomas Francisco Hornsby came without further incident, the newest citizen of Bastrop in the Mexican state of Coahuila y Tejas.

Daniel had both a baby brother *and* a new pony for his birthday.

We lit the barn lanterns. Billy played his whistle, and everyone danced and sang except Pa. He sat and smoked his pipe, full of the day's worries. Though he tried to hide it with the occasional smile, especially when his youngsters pulled at his arm to come dance, Pa was in a quandary. I worried about Ma too. Decided I'd check on her. When I stepped back into the cabin, I found her asleep, so I grabbed a chair in the corner and hoped to sleep a bit myself.

Señora de la Garza blew out a couple of candles and put on her shawl. Baby Thomas slept peacefully as she made the sign of the cross above his crib. She walked over to Mattie and reached for her hand. "La paz sea con vosotros." Mattie nodded and smiled. "Miss de la Garza, thank the lord you was here. You put the right spell on the misses, you sure did."

Señora de la Garza made a sign of the cross over Ma, bowed slightly to me, and then walked out the door. Alonso was waiting outside. They would stay in our barn 'til morning; too dangerous to ride home in the dark.

Later in the night, Ma woke with a scream and sat up in bed. Mattie was asleep on the floor at the foot of her bed with Diana in her arms. Pa, who had fallen asleep in his chair, raised his head and rubbed his eyes. "Mother, are you well?" Ma's voice was distant. "Husband, where are the children? Are they safe? I had a terrible dream. There were savages everywhere and the children were screaming."

Pa brushed her hair back from her face. "Easy, Mrs. Hornsby, easy. Mal's right here. Mattie has Diana, and the rest of your children are safer than hens in a stone coop. The newest addition is beside us and lookin' hungry. The rest is out in your barn with their uncle, brothers, and Tomas Elder. I imagine they're sleeping and snoring quite soundly."

Ma insisted Pa look in on them. Pa reached for her hand and held it gently. "You done well, Ma. He's as handsome as his brothers are and big as a lamb. I will hand him to you for feeding then be right back." Though I could tell she was fighting it, Ma fell right back to sleep while feeding little Thomas.

Pa eased back through the door, checked on Ma and sat back down with a sigh. I whispered real low. "Pa, Ma and little Thomas look well, don't ya think?" Pa looked up slow, tired. "You done well, Malcolm." Then he leaned toward me and kept his voice low. "Your uncle tells me that there was a few cattle stolen from Wilbarger's place where we got your brother's pony. I told your ma, but I didn't tell her that pens were broken down, and hogs shot with arrows—and that there were dozens of tracks from un-shoed horses along the river. Mr. Austin is organizing an armed group of the men without homesteads to look after us, but there ain't enough of them and there's little to no pay in it."

I asked, "You figure, me and Billy need to help?"

Pa didn't answer; he just looked down and sighed.

I HAD BEEN AWAY FROM THE PEOPLE FOR SIX moons. Every day was worse than the one before. Every day, I imagined a story I could not see: Father would rise early in the dark and ride with my brother to find me, but as the sun hid at day's end, Wowoki would walk slowly back up his hillside to eat and sleep alone. He would not enter camp until I returned.

Then the morning came that I heard my brother's birdcalls. This time it was not a dream.

When they arrived, my father sent Wowoki and another warrior to distract the Taiboo from the thickest bush while he checked the dugout cabins for me. We captives heard the warriors yelling and the gunshots from the direction of the spring. The plan seemed to be working except all the slaves were locked in their cabins.

All except me.

The Taiboo walked me out into the muddy field. Boucher—standing behind me—had a rope around my neck. The other two men held pistols to my head and stood close to me. I yelled to my brother that they would kill him. Boucher slapped me on top of my head and yanked on the rope. Wowoki threatened the Taiboo from the thicket, "We will eat your heart!" He took aim at them but did not pull the trigger. He tried again, breathing deep and aiming down the long barrel. This time he fired.

The lead ball grazed Boucher's brother in the arm, barely missing my head. The wounded man pressed his body against me. Boucher stood even closer to me and pressed the barrel of his pistol against my ear. It hurt but I did not move.

Father was somewhere in the camp. He used a birdcall to signal Wowoki to pull back. My brother continued to reload the rifle. Father signaled again. Wowoki ignored him and took aim for a long time, then lowered the rifle. In moments, my brother, father, and the other warrior were gone. They would not take a chance with getting me hurt or killed, but I was sure they'd return.

As the white men dragged me back to the cabin, Boucher slapped me on the head. "I should kill yeh and save me a lot of de trouble, no?" His wounded brother complained. "Dis ain't worth a few lousy meals and your old watered-down brandy. Dem Comanch is gonna skin us alive." Boucher stopped and stared. "Merde! You need to grow some bone in yeh back, mon frère. Dem Comanch come no closer while we holdin' this one at de end of our guns."

I do not know what my brother and father did after that. I am sure that Wowoki challenged my father and the warriors to join him in an attack on another Taiboo camp in revenge, but father would be cautious. To raise the alarm at another camp, especially one nearby, might only make it harder to get me away from this Taiboo. Wowoki would listen but continue to boil. For only a moment, I had tasted a breath of free air and seen my family.

Despite the danger, I would have to find strength in that freedom, and I did…for a little while.

SEVEN

Some Light Breaks the Darkness

MARCH 8. AIN'T WRITTEN IN SEVERAL WEEKS.
Winter here was difficult, enough to hold the Jamesons up a
spell and make farming a torture. Folks 'round here say we've
had more snow and freeze than they seen since setting up. It
was hard on the livestock, but it's past now. Mostly just rain
these days.

I sure hope the Jamesons land in Texas soon.

I was eight when I met Ottilee. She was only five. We
was at the Covington county dance; quite an affair in the
biggest barn I'd seen. There was garlands of pine branches and
Magnolia flowers all about. The place smelled like a whole
bottle of Ma's toilet water. Must have been enough lanterns to
light ten cabins. Black men and boys was playing the fiddle,
drum, and fife, while adults was dancing, talking the weather,
eating lots of food, and drinking plenty of spirits.

Me and Billy was playing a good game of mumble-the-peg off where we wouldn't bother a soul. I nearly had him beat for the first time in my whole life when this little cotton-top girl no taller than my shoulder come tripping by with her arms full of a big cake. I think she figured she'd take and eat the whole thing.

Well, wouldn't you know it; she tripped over her own darn feet and lost that cake to the barn floor. That ain't the worst of it. Poor girl managed to find a sharp rock with her little knee. Thing bled bad. I could see she was afraid of crying and raising too much of a ruckus on account of that cake. She was brave for that so I had to help her. I offered my handkerchief and fetched her a cup of lemonade. Billy just shook his head and snorted like an old angry bull.

When she looked up at me and asked my name, that's when I first saw them blue eyes. Never seen eyes like that. Haven't since. I didn't answer. Then she asked, "Why you starin'? Cake on my face?" I don't remember saying one word that made a lick of sense. She asked me again, "You gonna tell me?" I shook my head like I didn't remember the question, but mostly I was afraid of the gibberish that might come out of my mouth. She never gave up. "Your name. That's what I asked you, ain't it?"

"Malcolm Hornsby, from Covington County." I said.

She just laughed. "Ain't most them from Covington County?"

"I reckon, just thought you should know."

"Well, I'm Ottilee Jameson. We just arrived so maybe I ain't to say where I'm from just yet. That your brother walking off?" Sure enough, Billy had lost interest.

I couldn't move.

It was like them blue eyes had me staked down to that very spot. She turned her head like a puppy to a whistle and asked, "You gonna be my shiny knight, Malcolm Hornsby?" I managed to get one word out: "What?" She just kept flooring me with questions. "My ma always talking 'bout my daddy being her shiny knight. That you?" I pretended to think on it for a bit before I answered, "No, I don't reckon so." That's what I said anyway, but I was fibbin' for sure.

From that day on, all I wanted to be was Ottilee's shiny knight.

I HAVE BROUGHT MANY CHILDREN INTO THIS world. I have saved many more, but I've never had my own children and for this, I have regrets. Still, I know from watching it too many times the bond between a mother and her child can bring a terrible pain should it tear.

After being so close to my freedom, I felt my spirit moving away from me. I had not bathed in weeks and my head ached. There were sores all over my body. Often the food we were given went right through me. My life in the smelly man's camp was unbearable except for the times with Boo.

Martha's son grew fast. He was so big he was beginning to walk and always beside her or me or within our sight as we worked the fields. Alonso snuck him food while the women doted on the boy. He was our charm. Boo had brought a certain brightness and new life to our dark world, but I sensed a change in Boucher, the way he looked at the boy as if he was more nuisance than help.

Alonso and I were helping Martha and Boo into the wagon one day when Boucher stopped us. He had a bag of chicken feed in his hands and a smile on his face, and he was staring at Boo as he spoke to the young mother, "Martha leave de boy here today. It's time he learn to feed dem chickens. He no live and eat on des farm for nothing."

Martha held Boo tighter, looked at Alonso, and shook her head. Boucher stepped closer and spoke firm. "Span-yard, hand me down de boy now. He feed de chickens. I bring him to de fields." Martha looked at Alonso and shook her head.

Alonso gently reached for Boo and spoke soft. "Just the pollos, Señorita."

I looked deep into Alonso's eyes for a sign. Martha was looking too. Slowly, carefully, she placed Boo into Alonso's arms. The boy fussed and reached for his mother, but she forced a smile and caressed his cheek.

In the fields, Martha hardly worked. She constantly watched for Boucher. She would turn from the planting to watch the trail to the cabins and bite her lip. Alonso smiled and shrugged but it did not help. Soon Martha was making little sounds and slapping her leg. Then we all heard the hooves of mules and the squeak of a wagon. A stranger was visiting Boucher's farm. He was a small man, middle-aged, with a long black beard. He drove the mules past us without even a glance. A young black woman, perhaps a house servant, rode in the wagon bed behind him, looking jostled and miserable.

Martha watched the wagon intently. As it passed she started walking toward the cabins shaking her head. There was one word she was sure she understood: "no." With each step, Martha repeated it louder and louder as she quickened her pace. "No, no, no!"

APRIL 2. HORNSBY'S BEND. NEAR FINISHED shingling the roof on the new cabin today. Ma and Pa were in town. It's been raining so much, we've had to work soaked to the bone nearly every day. We was taking a breather today when Billy decided we should climb a big oak to see if we could spot the river level from there. I was pullin' Josephus to the next branch when I looked up to see Billy was already four limbs higher. He teased, us but I assured Joe that Ma have our hides we come home with a broke arm or worse.

The big live oak stretched its limbs nearly twice as wide as they were tall. It must have been fifty feet at the top—the perfect spot to look out over most of the bend. Tell ye the truth,

I was getting a little nervous at that height. The tree limbs gave under our weight and the tree was swaying in the wind.

As we neared the top of the big tree, I saw glimpses of the land our pa had claimed. It was a paradise. We'd already seen every sort of wild beast: snakes, lizards, toads, buffalo, deer, coyote, red wolf, cougar, bobcat, armadillo, squirrel, beaver, opossum, ring-tailed cat, badger, fox, raccoon, and skunk. Pressed into the banks of the river there are large pockets of clay for making bricks and pottery. The tops of the bluffs are home to stout oaks for building.

Looking near straight down, I had a good view of the cabin. Our new home is made of two one-room cabins several paces apart on a common floor with their doors facing each other. Some of the neighbors helped build her. I loved the work. I stayed busy keeping the axes, adze, saws, drills, and knives as sharp as I could make 'em.

Once most of the walls was up, the last hewed log was the longest—the length of both cabins plus the space between. Lifting it required all the men together and a pulley system called a block-and-tackle that I had mastered.

At the end of each day my hands were sore and blistered, my back and arms ached, but the excitement of working with steel and machines made it hard for me to sleep at night. All I could do when I laid down was think about the work needed for the next day. I was last to sleep at night and first up in the mornings, laying out the tools and equipment, oiling steel, and sharpening more cutting tools. Pa said I was earning meals for two men every day.

The building took five days of constant work from sunrise to sunset and under torchlight at night. The men slept in tents, the women in the unfinished cabin. By the sixth day, most of the neighbors left to take care of their own.

It's good for us younger men to know how to build a house, how to use machines and the labor of friends to put a roof over a family's head. I wonder if Ottilee will marry me, a blacksmith, and live in a cabin I built. I'm sure she will, me being her shiny knight and all.

From the grand tree, we looked down on Tom and his pa, Tomas Elder. They was still workin' with Moses-Smith. Lately, Tom and me have spent less and less time together. I yelled out to him and he looked up but went back to his hammering. It didn't feel right him still working and me lollygagging in a tree with my brothers. I eased back down the tree but Joe whined that he didn't want to get down. I tried to sound like my pa, "There's work to do, Joe." Then glanced up at my big brother in the top of the tree. "Darn it. Billy can look after you, I guess. Hey, Billy, I'm goin' back to the cabin to help. You look after Joe now, you hear?" Of course, Billy couldn't leave it alone. "Go on, you scared cat, Mal Hornsby. You're just lookin' for an excuse to get down cause of this wind."

I whispered to Joe as I eased down past him that he best slide down behind me. Billy wasn't gonna help him none. Then an acorn hit me on the hat, then one hit my arm, then another hit my neck, all in a row. Joe hid behind the trunk of the tree but I was defenseless against the rapid fire and I knew right where it was coming from. The dogs were barking. Billy threw acorns at Tom, Tom's father, and Moses-Smith on the roof. They threw back what they caught plus a few bent nails. Even Joe was throwing acorns. We laughed ourselves silly. Good thing Ma and Pa were away; they was intent on sleeping in that cabin we were supposed be roofing. They might not have found our jocularity so entertaining.

BEFORE WE COULD STOP HER, MARTHA WAS running down the trail toward the cabins. Alonso chased after her. The rest of us followed. By the time we reached them, Boo was struggling to get out of the slave's arms in the back of the wagon and Martha was running and yelling. Boucher slapped one of the stranger's mules on the flank to get him moving, stuffed a bag of coins into his coat, and ran to stop Martha before she could block the trail. "Martha, we gon' be all right. No cause to worry now."

Martha struggled and screamed in the big man's arms until she lost all her breath and gave out. The wagon raced past us. I seen Alonso was feeling the heat inside. He tightened both fists and his neck was red from the blood. He faced Boucher's direction and reached for the knife he carried in a scabbard on his belt. I grabbed Alonso's arm and pulled his hand away from the knife. Alonso jerked away. I grabbed him again and whispered, "Need you here." Alonso relaxed his arm, turned, and watched Boo and the wagon disappear over the hill.

Martha fell to her knees and sobbed.

APRIL 6. HAVE TO WRITE BUT HARD TO SEE through the tears.

Ma and Pa stayed two nights in Bastrop on account of the river being unpredictable. By the time they came in sight of the new cabin the next day, we'd finished the roof. Everything seemed so alive around us in the bend. Especially the mosquitoes. There were suddenly clouds of 'em. Evil mosquitoes.

When I seen my mother and father, knew something was wrong. They stopped a bit from the house and talked, then Pa stepped down and Ma drove the mules to the barn. Pa called for me and once I'd walked up, he said he wanted my help locating the best spot for the well. I reminded him we'd done that only the week before. He didn't use his hard voice but was firm just the same. "I want to talk it over with you again."

We walked several steps back down the hill away from the house. I couldn't figure his aim. "Pa, you ain't thinking we dig this far from the house, is you? We'd have heck carrying that distance every day."

Pa shook his head a little. I could tell he was deep in the thinking and there was plenty wrong when he said, "Mal, I need to talk to you about something else." Pa had never called me Mal much. It didn't set right with him to give us nicknames. Then he come out with it. "While we's in town, your ma and I heard some news. Now, it could just be a mistake. People like to talk and lord knows they like to spin a yarn, but this one, well there were witnesses that seemed to know what they saw. They had the fear in their eyes still."

I had no idea what the news was but him pulling me aside was weighing heavy. He tried to come straight out with it. "Son, it's been raining all around us for days, filling every creek and river across the territory. I'm just gonna give it to you clear now, you're old enough to hear it that way. The Jamesons and several of their party, well, they was crossin' the Colorado below Burnham's. They didn't know about all this rain up river you see. The river had a flash flood that surprised even their guide. Most of the party didn't make it, son. The few that did is the one's that told us in town."

Pa reached and took hold of my neck, not like when I'd done something wrong but gentle like. I don't remember what he said from there. I do remember jerking away from his soft hold and yelling "no." Must have been a dozen times or more. I remember wanting to hit him for something I didn't even understand. I remember asking, "Where is she now? They have a body? If they don't have a body, maybe she's all right and just lost!"

Then I remember walking in the mud until I couldn't walk no more. Billy said he found me on a deer trail near dark. He had me drink some of Pa's spirits and led me back to the house slow and easy. I don't know how I even took in any air for several days after. I couldn't eat. Don't remember sleeping in the new loft. Don't remember where I was or what I was seeing most days, except one thing, only one thing: Ottilee's blue eyes.

THERE WERE TIMES, ESPECIALLY IN THE OLD
Penatʉka days in Texas when our elders would walk away
from our camp and never return. They might have lost a
husband or wife, or were alone with no one to look after them,
and chose to burden another no longer. Today, we call this
nabekʉkatʉ; it is the Comanche word for what the Taiboo call
suicide.

Life on the smelly man's farm was its darkest now.
Without Boo, the light had gone for all of us women, but
especially for his mother. She would not eat, would not move
from our cabin, even after Boucher kicked at her legs and
yelled at her. She didn't make a sound, just laid there in the
dirt, a ghost but alive. I was afraid we would lose her like the
elders.

Alonso did what he could. We all took turns spooning
soup and tea down her throat, forcing her to swallow. After a
few days, she seemed a little stronger, enough to sit and talk,
mostly in her own language but occasionally she'd stand,
smiling and saying "Martha fly" which didn't make any sense
to me at the time. Then she'd collapse and mumble what
sounded like a death song deep into the night until she fell to
sleep. Still, she would not leave the cabin except to relieve
herself.

Boucher grew impatient. He yelled at her every day,
several times a day. He tied her to a post and whipped her. She
never made a sound in those whippings.

Alonso did everything in his power to distract the giant
man or keep him away from our cabin. Then one day, while all
of us except Martha was working the field, she walked away.

When we returned to our cabins that night, she was
gone. Boucher and his friends locked us all inside and went
hunting her. With the sunrise they returned pulling the poor
girl behind them by a rope around her waist. Alonso told us
that Martha had just started walking down the road to find Boo.
She didn't run when she heard the men behind her, she just
dropped to her knees, looked up at the heavens and yelled
"Martha fly." Alonso said he heard the men talking about it.

Seems the sounds that Martha made that night was so mournful it put a scare into those Taiboo.

The next morning, I woke to find Martha dead. She had removed all her clothing and hung herself by her ragged old dress from the rafters in our cabin.

I sang the death song over her and grew angrier with each note. I promised myself then that I would find my strength, do more for my freedom and the freedom of all of these women, even if the Taiboo killed me.

APRIL 10. WE'VE SPENT THE LAST TWO DAYS looking for the Jameson's bodies downriver from Burnham's. Pa said I didn't have to go along. Ma begged me not to go, but I … I needed to know for myself.

After fighting all the snakes and mosquitoes, we found Mr. and Mrs. Jameson three miles or so down river from where they'd tried to cross. Their bodies was so roughed up and swollen, it was hard to make out exactly who they were 'cept for the rope Mr. Jameson must have tied between them for the crossing. That rope likely drowned them both. Guess it was best they died together.

We never found my Ottilee. Billy tried to give me hope. Said she could have made it and was wanderin' back upstream but I heard some of the other men saying her body could be in the gulf by now.

Pa took me aside and said that in these situations it was "best to remember someone you love as they were, not as you see or imagine after an accident." Pa never uses the word "love" lightly. It jolted me.

Still, the ride home seemed awfully long as all I could think of was her strugglin' in that current and me not there to be her shining knight.

IN ALL THIS DARKNESS, THERE WAS ONE DAY shortly after when we once again heard a little laughter in the Taiboo camp. We were all in the field planting seed when it began a firm rain. Just enough to make the newly plowed earth a pot of dark brown slop.

Alonso slipped in it first. He was running to bring us more seed bags, had his arms full and his feet flew out from under him like he was on ice. Those seed bags went flying too. As we ran to help pick up the seeds, we began to slip and slide ourselves.

Pretty soon, every one of us was covered in mud, seed, rain, and smiles. You'd try to stand up and just end up slipping right back down. We made a mess of them rows, but for a little while we weren't scared of what Boucher would do. For a few minutes, we was just a bunch of girls and their Mexican friend laughing and playing in the mud, like little children.

Boucher whipped us each with a stick, made us fix the rows and replant the seeds on our hands and knees, but I don't think one of us girls wasn't smiling beneath our frowns.

APRIL 27. BIRTHDAY. FOURTEEN NOW. BEEN sick with the seasoning two weeks. Can't get out of bed. Head aches something terrible. Sometimes I'm hotter than a rock in the sun. Then I'm freezing. Every muscle and joint seems to hurt. I can't eat; don't even want to think of food. Ma has Mattie workin' day and night with cool cloths on my head and arms when the fever has me cooking. Then they are piling on the blankets to fight the chills.

I wish I could be busy with anything, even the lowest of the farm chores, just to keep my mind from thinking about the Jameson's accident. Ma is going to buy a book in town to keep me from dwelling on things. Right now, I'd prefer just to close my eyes and never read or think again.

Guess life ain't never that easy.

Been trying to write. Ma asks me nearly ten times a day if I'm writing in my book. She says it always does a body good to let the darkness out somehow and it might as well be in the ink. So, here I go.

The Last Victor

by Malcolm Morrison Hornsby

I've seen you and your last rattle
Take the breath away
Winning war without battle
No fair in your play

When the resting places fill
And we've lost all life
Who, pray, will be left to kill
No child, man, or wife

In the days of king and knight
One could stand for all
You and me, then, the last fight
I stand you fall

Take my breath so they may breathe
Fighting in fairness
The victor must take his leave
When all the fair are vanquished

BOUCHER WHIPPED US ALL AGAIN WITH HIS willow stick for that day in the mud, but something was starting to change. We girls were starting to stand stronger in these whippings and make less noise about it. Sure the tears still ran down our faces, but we turned away so the smelly man couldn't see. Even though it hurt something awful, we stopped yelling out nearly as much.

That man would stand in the shade while we cooked in the sun and yell at us "four and thirty, girls, four and thirty!" You see, we were meant to plant those seeds at four inches apart in the rows and in rows we'd plowed at 30 inches apart; but when we were sure he wasn't looking, we'd plant those seeds anywhere we pleased, just as a little revenge. We'd spit on the seeds when he wasn't looking. One of the girls even relieved herself in one of the rows all over them seeds.

When the sun had set on days like that, as you eased your sore old body down to the dirt and straw for sleeping, you might feel a little smile coming on because on that day you had just a tiny bit of power.

MAY 28. FEELING BETTER. WALKED A BIT around the farm today. The seasoning seems to have passed, but Ma warned me it could come back any time. I can't blame the illness for all the dark thoughts I've had lately. Had a lot of time to think on things these last few weeks while stuck in bed. I can't help wonder what happens when we die. Hardly have a new litter of piglets without one or two not making it. Seen calves born dead. Coyotes take chickens, leave the feathers. Cats take mice. Death is all around us, but all we know of it comes from the local preacher and our bible.

I figure, next to love, losing someone you care about is the most difficult stew of feelings a man can feel. Maybe that's why we need God and the Gospel, just so we can explain the weight of love and loss somehow. Don't think Ma would appreciate my questions, though, so I'll keep them to myself.

While I was on my back, Tom visited, but only once, mostly just to bring fresh water. He didn't say much. Alonso called, several times. It was good to see him, good to have the distraction. He had a proposal for me that I agreed to without even thinking. He needs help, he said, from a friend who is good with locks. It was clear that there would be some danger to it, that's for darn sure, but I didn't care then in my fevers and I still don't. Reckon I'd had old man death whisper in my ear a couple of times in just a few weeks. Wasn't much he could do to scare me anymore. Alonso said it'd wait 'til I was myself again.

That time is coming.

MY PAHA ONCE TOLD ME THE STORY OF THE old cruel crow and the healing woman. The healing woman was in her last seasons but would not leave the people for they had been very sick. She needed a crow's feather for some special medicine that would help her through her winter, keep her strong for the people.

Early one morning, she found a very old crow with a lame foot and asked him for one of his tail feathers. He refused. His heart had grown dark and cruel from years of struggle with his lameness. He did not eat as well as the other crows. He had no mate, for no other would have him. All this had made him bitter. He would help no one.

The old healing woman told the bird that he was the most handsome and bravest crow she had ever met. He refused to help her and limped a few steps away. She told him that she knew dozens of female crows that would be his wives, and if he would share just one of his tail feathers, she would introduce him. He refused and continued to look away.

Then she spoke of fields of corn in the Taiboo camps where he could eat until he was full most every day. This caught his interest. He looked at the old woman with one dark eye, stepped closer and asked her where these fields were. She shook her head as if she could not tell him this great secret. The old crow came closer and stared at her as if to read what she was thinking. He couldn't. He begged and promised to share several tail feathers to know this great secret. Now she had him.

The healing woman spoke so softly that the crow moved even closer to try and hear. She said the words again but even softer. The crow moved closer still and turned his head away so he could hear better. The healing woman took a firm hold on one of the old bird's tail feathers, then yelled, "Fly there toward the rising sun! Fly now!"

Her yell scared the old crow so much that he took off toward the sun and left one of his tail feathers in the healing woman's grasps. She used the well-earned feather to give her strength and help the people for many more moons.

I knew I must use such a trick on Boucher, fool him into sharing his key or setting us all free, but I never had to go to such lengths. Alonso and a Taiboo warrior would bring me the medicine I needed.

JUNE 12. ASKED PA TODAY. HAD TO TELL A white lie or two, but it's all for the right reasons, I figure. Waited until the clearing of the five acres below the cabin was nearly finished. All us men were at it. I was on a saw with my pa. I raised my voice over the noise. I told Pa I would be over at old man Boucher's through most of the night. He didn't like it much. Said he don't care for that man. I told him that Alonso would be tryin' to catch a coyote or fox, maybe even a wolf, in the act of raiding Boucher's chickens and that two is better than one for staying up.

He stopped our sawing and give me the lookover, then asked me one question after another. Had I'd told Ma? I promised I would. Was I leaving before sunset? Was I riding Jackson? Then he insisted I take the good rifle and strongly recommended I stay as far from that Frenchie as I could, except to be paid—and that amount better be worth the time away from our farm. I assured Pa I had thought of all them things.

Back in the cabin, I had an even tougher time of it. Mattie rocked baby Thomas as Ma packed my saddlebag slowly, carefully, as if she might postpone the trip all together. She started right in on me. "Malcolm, must you go?" I told her I had given my word. She said she didn't like me riding alone. I reminder her that it ain't much of a distance and that I'd be riding mostly in daylight. Then I tried to distract her from her worrying. I asked her to put extra cake in the bag for Alonso and fibbed that Alonso's family needed a bit of lard. Said he's too proud to come right out and ask, but I seen they need it.

She makes it a lot harder than Pa does to keep the truth from her. She buttered me up, something terrible. "The good lord's charity is in you, Malcolm Morrison Hornsby." and, "You've grown into such a handsome young man. Some young woman is going to be lucky to have you as a husband. I know you still miss your dear Ottilee, God bless her soul, but it will hurt worse if you don't start letting go. Lord knows I have climbed this same mountain too many times." Mattie was nodding her head and confirming every word, "That's right. Lord knows. Amen."

Then Ma surprised me with something else she was thinking. "Son, you're back on your feet now—and, well, you should be thinking about settling with your own family someday, that's all I'm saying. Don't put it off too long." Then she smiled and hummed a hymn as she wrapped another helping of cake into a small cloth and eased the package plus a small tin of lard into my bag. She set the bag over my shoulder and let her hand rest on my neck. "Please tell Señor de la Garza that next time he'll need to come here for dinner to get more of Miss Mattie's cake."

Before she let me off the porch, Ma made me promise to be home for breakfast and to take our Bible. Though I pointed out I would be in the dark most of the time, she insisted "Malcolm, lord knows it's as good a readin' as any, and I'll be comforted knowing you have it."

WHEN THE SUN WARMS US, WE WALK THIS land in the light of life. Still, the dark spirits are always close, always looking for a chance to steal our sun, bring us closer to death. I have cured many who carry this ghost sickness, those who are dead but walking. It felt nearly impossible to cure myself. My spirits would rise with the new strength we women had found, but then fall when I was alone in my cabin and thinking of Boo, Martha, and my own family. I had given up much of my hope. It was as if the river was only at half its level.

Something in Alonso's eyes and in his voice in the last few days had begun to change this. He seemed stronger, more warrior than boy. He had more hidden smiles for me. He looked me directly in the eyes more often and there was hope there—the hope I had lost.

What I could not understand was why. It felt as if I had lost my ability to read the signs, Alonso had grown stronger, while my powers had faded. Father once told me that to lead you must learn to follow. Perhaps this was the sign.

Perhaps I should follow the Mexican out of my darkness.

JUNE 13. SO TIRED I CAN BARELY KEEP MY eyes open but I must get this all written down before I forget a moment of it. Last night was a humdinger. A story I'll tell to my children and their children.

The sliver of a moon barely made shadows of us two on the hill above Boucher's raggedy farm. I watched the cabin and dugouts for the last lamp to go out. Alonso sat beside me using a molcajete, a small stone bowl, to crush chips of limestone into a white watery mix.

Alonso had a plan for nearly everything. I ain't never seen someone so clever. It all started quiet and dull, so much so, I decided to take a nap, but the night turned into a real barn fire after that.

I woke with a start. Alonso was gone, the moon had set and I was alone in a deep darkness that gave no comfort. Then I heard the footsteps slow and soft as if sneakin' closer. I reached carefully for my rifle, added a bit of powder and eased the hammer back. My hands was shaking as I whispered, "Amigo?" There was no answer. I steadied my hands, pulled the rifle tight against my shoulder and full-cocked the hammer. Lucky for the both of us, Alonso finally answered.

I told him I'd nearly shot his fool head off. He just started in with his instructions like he'd done this every night of his life. "Lo siento. All sleeping now. We go." Well, I couldn't let him have all the lead so I asked him if we shouldn't remove our boots. I figured we's meant to leave bare tracks like injuns. Injuns is easy to blame for most things. He whispered his approval.

It was so dark that I had to hang on to Alonso's shirttail as we walked. Before I knew it, we was standing at the door of one of the dugouts. As Alonso spread lard on the hasp and big door hinges, I unfolded my handkerchief and held my tools up close to my face to see which end was which. I signaled for Alonso to hold the lock up so I could work on it without it clanging against the hasp. I held one nail inside the lock as always, and turned the other. The lock didn't open. I tried again from a different angle, no luck. "Tarnation. It ain't working."

Alonso whispered, "Keep trying, amigo" and that's when we heard it. Someone was movin' inside the dugout. I was just praying this wasn't a trap when Alonso whispered, "It's her, she hears everything, even when she sleeps." Then, just like that, the lock popped open. Alonso could hardly contain himself. "Si. Bravo!"

I slowly opened the hasp and eased the door back. The lard did its job. The big door didn't squeak a bit. The smell comin' out of that cabin would have choked a horse. Sure enough, what looked like a little girl stepped into the doorway. Alonso gently reached for her arm. She jerked away. He reached again just as gently and spoke so softly I barely heard him. "Amiguita, estás libre. Vamos."

She stepped up out of the dugout slowly to keep her shackle chains quiet. Once she was clear of the door, Alonso untied her hands and removed her gag. In the starlight, all I could see was her outline. I reckon she was tryin' to make me out as well. I spoke in a low whisper. "I need to get them locks from your legs," but when I dropped to my knees, she stepped back. I took a deep breath. This wasn't going to be easy and the one luxury we didn't have was time. Lucky for me, Alonso whispered in her ear, then eased the girl toward me. She dug her toes into the dirt and pulled back. Alonso gently eased her forward. "Vamos, mi amiga."

I used a hand vise from our barn to straighten and remove them pins that held the heavy iron cuffs around her ankles. I couldn't believe this little girl was carrying all that weight on her legs. She let out a sigh as I pulled them away. Then she spoke quiet like. "The women vamos." I heard the Spanish words, but her accent wasn't like Alonso's.

Alonso sighed and whispered "no." She said it again. Her accent was definitely not Spanish, nor was it black sounding. I started to understand then what we was on to in this adventure. There had been rumors in town that old man Boucher had himself a Comanch captive, but I didn't believe it. She stepped toward him and raised herself up on her toes so she could look Alonso right in the eyes. With his fingers, he indicated that she would leave with me and that he would stay.

She shook her head and pointed to all of the dugouts. "Todos!" Alonso shook his head, "No, Señorita, imposible." Then he said words that seemed to strike a nerve with her. "Vamos, Penatɨka."

That proved it. She was Comanch head to toe and from the toughest of them, too. Even in the dark, I could see her eyes widened and she almost smiled. She turned to study me more closely. I pointed to myself and whispered, "Malcolm." She stepped toward me, stood on her toes, looked directly into my face and said, "Mal-cuu." She pointed to her chest, "Wɨkɨbuu."

Alonso added, "It means hummingbird." Wɨkɨbuu stepped closer to me and whispered, "Vamos, Mal-cuu." It was just then, out of the corner of my eye, I seen a light flash in Boucher's cabin. Someone was lighting a lamp. I grabbed Alonso and pointed that way. He looked and then pushed us both toward the rise where I'd left Jackson. We moved that direction in quick steps, while Alonso turned to the last part of his plan: he would paint injun-looking symbols on the door and leave a feather. That should put the fear into old man Boucher to leave Wɨkɨbuu and her rescuers, that being us, alone.

I pulled on my boots and climbed onto Jackson's saddle. When I turned to lift the girl up on the horse, she was gone. Then I heard it: a voice in the dark. It wasn't Alonso's or the hummingbird girl. It was French sounding. "Who dat der? Mon frère, dat you?"

I LISTENED TO THE FOOTSTEPS AS THEY approached my cabin. I was afraid it was Boucher and his friends looking for trouble with one of us girls, but the whispers were different, younger, softer.

I heard a faint metal sound and the door shifted just a little. Then I heard a strange Taiboo word, "Tarnation." I didn't recognize the voice, especially in that whisper. I did recognize the next voice; it was Alonso's. His words made my heart jump and my whole body shake. He said, "Keep trying, amigo."

I eased up to stand as slow as I could so as not to wake anyone else. I had to hold my feet wide apart to keep the chains on my ankles from making any noise. Just as I got to the door, it opened silently to let in the cool night air and the boy's smells. There was no moon but in the starlight, I could just make out Alonso in his hat. Another boy about the same size was standing back a ways like he was unsure of what might be coming out of this hole in the earth.

Alonso untied my hands and took off my gag, then he touched my arm and eased me forward toward the Taiboo who spoke in a nervous whisper. "I need to get them locks from your legs." I remember when he dropped to his knees it reminded me of Boucher and I stepped back.

Alonso stepped from the cabin and whispered in my ear, "Vamos, mi amiga" but I wasn't ready to trust this stranger. Alonso touched my arm and nodded close so I could see him. I eased forward toward the other boy. The fresh night air and having my hands and mouth free gave me courage.

The Taiboo boy used a tool to remove the heavy iron cuffs around my ankles. Then I begged Alonso to wake the others so they could join us. Alonso whispered "no." With his fingers, he told me to leave with the other boy and that he would stay. I stamped my foot and pointed to all of the dugouts, begging that Alonso free all of us. Alonso shook his head, "No, Señorita, imposible." Then he said words that made me understand, "Vamos, Penatɨka."

I studied the other boy as close as I could in the dark. He pointed to himself and said, "Mal-cuu." I could tell he was introducing himself, so I pointed to my chest and proudly whispered, "Wɨkɨbuu." Alonso pushed us both toward the rise beyond the fields. Someone was awake in Boucher's cabin. The Taiboo boy and I ran quickly but I felt a sign, so I doubled back to ensure we weren't being followed.

Lucky I did. Boucher or his brother was easing toward that hill with a gun in hand. I found a good-sized tree limb on

169

the ground and snuck up on him but I stepped on a stick that gave me away. It must have been Boucher or his brother 'cause he whispered loud and with fear, "Who dat der? Mon frère, dat you?" I didn't give him an answer except a good knock across the back of his fool head with that tree limb, then I ran as quickly as I could up that hill.

JUNE 14. I EASED BACK DOWN OFF JACKSON'S back and tried my best to see through the darkness. Then I heard movement and seen what looked like a man about ten paces from the hill. I wasn't sure if he could see me or not but I ducked down just the same, holding tight to Jackson's reigns and praying he stay quiet. I was sure it was Boucher himself.

Just then, there was muffled sounds then a loud whack and moaning. I stared hard but couldn't see. Then out of the dark came Wukubuu and Alonso, fast. As soon as they got close, I seen a big knife in Alonso's hand. The little injun girl just stepped up and jumped on to Jackson's back. Alonso whispered, "Vamos, amigo," but seeing that big knife felt like trouble. I asked if he'd tangled with Boucher. He said no, it was the brother. That eased my mind a bit. Then Alonso said something that made me smile. He told me that this little girl had picked up a big limb and knocked old Boucher's brother into the next homestead. Said he had to take the knife from her as she pulled up the man's hair.

I reckon she saved our bacon, but I was a little nervous about riding with her behind me on my horse. I climbed up into the saddle in front of the girl. She was breathing heavy. For a moment as she moved to get balanced on the horse's back, she put her hand on my shoulder. It made my stomach twitch; I'd never been this close to a girl anywhere near my age before. She had a certain lightness, a balance to her.

We rode hard heading southwest at first, but by a hundred paces, it was obvious that Wukubuu was upset. She yanked on my left arm as if to turn the horse north and said something that sounded like, "Pahabitu! Pahabitu!" I didn't know what to make of it. She pounded on my back and pulled my arm again. I glanced back at the girl. I remember saying it then, "Tarnation."

Wukubuu seemed puzzled with my word. I heard her trying to mimic me under her breath. "Ter-na-un, ter-na-un." It was funny so I said it again, "tarnation, except you got to say it with feelin' like it's the last bit of mud on your boot. TAR...NA...TION!

It was hard going in the dark. We was both quiet as we made our way through the thick growth to near the river. As soon as I stopped, the girl leaped from the horse and ran down the bank. I tied Jackson's reins to a branch and followed her. When I reached the river's edge, I saw Wukubuu out in the water, washing with plants from the river bottom. She had jumped in, calico dress and all. I reckon it was a good thing 'cause she did smell something awful.

I was stuck. Didn't know exactly what to do. I tipped my hat and quietly eased back up the bank. I reckon she needed time to herself. Then it dawned on me, I couldn't take her to her people—they'd kill me for sure—so I made a big decision.

As the sun started lighting the horizon, I walked along the river line toward home struggling to carry my saddle, rifle, bridle, and saddlebag where I stashed Ma's bible. I was thinkin' and talking to himself like a man that was touched. What will I say to Pa about the horse? I'll have to say that me and Alonso were camping and Comanche stole my horse. No. Maybe I'll just say "injuns." It don't make sense to single out one particular tribe. How'd Alonso say that name, "Woo-Cu-Bu?"

By the time I reached home, it was coming on light. I was bone tired but knew I couldn't sleep—not that Pa would have let me. Ma said she was worrying sick about me, but something in that night air must of lifted that seasoning right off my shoulders. Pa came in and went straight to the question,

"Where's your Jackson, Malcolm? You walked back from old man Boucher's?"

When I was a boy, I'd have froze right on that spot. I ain't never lied to my ma and pa before, but this mornin', I knew I was a man and sometimes a man has to bend the truth a bit. I bent it quite a ways. Told Pa, we had a heck of a time last night. There was two of them foxes, not just one. We's lucky we put out several snares, but one of 'em bit Alonso and broke loose from the snare on his bad foot. We chased that animal in the dark. I tell ya, it was like two cat's with their tails tied chasing a mouse. Must have been quite a show, but while we's chasing him both Jackson and Alonso's mule slipped their ties and wandered off. Can't blame 'em. We'd a scared a whole herd I imagine, but we got that other fox, Pa. Had to hit him in the head with a big limb to finish him, but we got him."

Ma and Pa was starin' at me like I'd swallowed a whole frog. Pa just took it in stride, said he reckoned Jackson would mosey home today or tomorrow.

Tarnation. Don't imagine I'll be seeing my Jackson again.

WHEN I WAS A YOUNG GIRL, I FOUND A BABY bird who had fallen out of his nest. I gathered him up and kept him in one of my aunt's small baskets for his protection. I tried to feed the bird but he ate very little. Wowoki made fun of me. He said I was just waiting for the bird to get big enough so that I would have a friend. After only a few days, I was sure the bird would die because he had eaten so little, but something incredible happened. I woke to the sound of his wings against the basket. I took the basket outside and slowly opened the top. The young bird did not hesitate; he flew out of the basket and out of sight. It is one of my favorite memories.

He was free.

That night, I had forgotten the Taiboo boy. It felt so good to be clean that I lost track of time and finally crawled out of the cold water. I pulled my hair from the tight braids, lay on the bank, and stared at the stars as exhaustion claimed me. When I woke, it was still dark. I sprang up and whispered "Mal-cuu," but there was no answer.

I moved quietly through the brush up the bank and found his horse still tied to a branch, but with a small rope instead of his leather bridle and a blanket instead of his saddle. I wrapped the blanket over my shoulders and walked through the brush in ever-widening circles, calling, "Mal-cuu? Mal-cuu?" You see, I couldn't afford to be out alone in the daylight. Boucher would be looking for me. I called one more time for the Taiboo boy, then mounted his mustang.

Before I crested the hill hiding our camp, I smelled cooking fires, heard children playing, and dogs barking. Before I rounded the rocky ledge, the whinnies of mustangs filled my ears with anticipation and made the Taiboo's horse nervous. He slowed and pulled back against the rope halter. I eased him forward.

Once clear of the ledge, the camp came into view. The teepees, fires, and corrals of my people spread out before me. Normally, they would have moved camp by now. They had stayed and I was home.

I remember watching Muutsi shuffle to bring me new clothes as soon as I had ridden into camp. It was like a dream. Then she took the slave clothes and threw them into her fire. As I watched them burn, I thought of being separated from everyone, everything I had known before. The distance had helped me understand my place among the People. Father had always told me I would lead in some way. Now, I was ready to try.

I stood beside the Taiboo horse, patiently waiting for my father to speak. My whole body felt tired and sore, but being back in camp gave my head and heart a comforting heat, as if I were melting in the warmth of the People. Dog inched closer, unsettled by my absence and unsure of my new smell.

Finally, Tupaapi stepped out and approached me. He looked me up and down, pointed to my feet, and said one word, "Wutui." He walked back into his teepee and emerged with his best woolen blanket for which he had traded several skins. He wrapped the red and blue striped blanket around my shoulders. It was soft and warm on my neck and arms, and smelled of my father.

I tried to hand him the end of the rope halter – the mustang would be my gift to him. He would not take the rope. He stepped slowly toward the nervous horse, eased the Taiboo's blanket from his back, walked to the nearest fire, and dropped the blanket into the flames. Sparks flew into the air.

He walked back to me and took the rope in his hand. "Now, this is a good trade." Then he yelled out a celebratory whoop and all in the camp stepped forward to welcome me.

All except my brother.

JUNE 21. TRYING TO HIDE MY EXCITEMENT, especially around my parents and big brother. Uncle Moses-Smith can tell I have a pot on the boil, but he don't push none. That was some adventure with Alonso and that Penatuka girl. Keeping my book o' pages hidden better now so my nosy brother don't find it and let all my secrets out.

Can't help but wonder if Wukaboo has made it back to her people. I sure hope she treats Jackson well. I know them people the same that makes a lot of trouble for us Bastrop settlers, but she didn't seem so bad. Why do people always have to fight over things that ain't that rare? There's plenty of land and water. More than any man or woman, old or young, could ever need in one lifetime.

We've had three new families move into our stretch of the river. All seem like good stock, some stronger than the others. Reckon they'll make it. Seen one of the families has daughters Billy's and my age. Ma sent the two of us over to deliver a basket of welcome. I seen the sisters looking at us from their tent, heard their giggles. Billy tried to pretend he didn't notice. I imagine we'll be helping them build their cabin here in the next few weeks.

Maybe we'll meet the girls.

THE WELCOME FEAST WAS EXCITING. I FELT like a warrior home from a victorious battle. I watched for Wowoki. Father assured me that he was well and was busy with his horses, but days had passed. The sun was setting again and still no sign of my brother. Then I heard it. Wowoki, his face and horse painted for battle, rode along the edge of the camp whooping and standing on the horse's back, showing off, celebrating in his own way, a warrior's way. Now he was free to take revenge on the smelly Taiboo, free to regain his lost honor.

I looked to my father and asked for a horse. "My brother will fall and hurt his head if I do not teach him how to ride." Tupaapi chuckled. "Go, my daughter, but not far."

I heeled my horse and raced to the top of the hill where my brother waited. Upon seeing me, he started riding back and forth again, hard. I tried to keep up but couldn't make the sharp turns. My brother teased me. "Huutsúu Kwanaru, our father's sister has much work for you." His spirit frightened me—a dark fire burned in his eyes. His breath was sharp and threatening. "Brother, I see you wear the war paint. Is this to welcome me home to a battle?"

Wowoki heeled his horse and galloped past me yelling. "Why are you here on my hill? Is there not a baby to bring into the world or skins to ready? I wear the paint as I choose."

I waited for the right moment to guide my horse directly into his path, but the frightened animal held back, and without thinking, I yelled the Taiboo word, "Tarnation!" Wowoki pulled up and glared at me as if I had grown another head. I looked down. Wowoki moved his horse closer. "Now that you are home, I will have my revenge."

I sat as tall as I could on my horse. I was free now from being a slave, from being a captive with no words to speak. I looked directly at my brother and shook my head. Wowoki guided his horse to circle me. He stuck his chest out and huffed through his mouth. My brother was a warrior. He had risked his life for me on many occasions. I was being disrespectful and I knew it. I also knew that what my brother was planning was not the path. I had friends in that camp. I looked directly at him and spoke. "Brother, in their camp there are those among the dark ones that showed me kindness. There is a Mexican. And a Taiboo who released me from the smelly man's chains. He gave me his horse without trade."

Wowoki screamed. "And with his Taiboo words, what else did he take in return? What of my honor and the honor of the People? Have you thought of this?"

My voice gave my fatigue away. It sounded to me like begging. "Brother, I have honor too! Some of those in the Taiboo camp protected me. They helped me come back to the People. What honor is there in repaying this with death?" Wowoki held up his hand without turning, but I would not stop. "If you had listened regarding the mule, we would have no need to talk of any of this."

He softened but only a little. "Sister, do not speak this way to a warrior."

"I am speaking to my brother; a warrior who I hope grows stronger and wiser every day. Only one Taiboo is responsible for all of this." Wowoki turned his horse to face me. His look was menacing. "More will do the same." I shook my head, rode back down to camp and yelled to my brother as I rode, "When does this stop, Wowoki?

For much of the next day, Tupaapi sat quietly, carved new pipes and squinted to watch me work a buffalo hide. I couldn't wait to do something for the People, something I had chosen. He watched as I stretched the hide on the ground and fastened it down with wooden pegs around the edges. To rid the skin of remaining meat, I scraped the hide with a flat-bone scraper – a family tool handed down by Father's mother. When finished, I proudly carved another notch into the handle to signify, as did my mother and grandmother, that another hide would soon be ready. The notches nearly covered the handle. I was home with the People.

I was free.

EIGHT

Life's a Hard Study

NOVEMBER 16. IT FEELS LIKE WINTER HAS
joined us to stay. It's colder than I ever remember in Missisip.
Still, it's fun watching the little ones enjoy the snow. We have
a couple of great hills for sledding. But when watching the
little Hornsbys slip and slide ain't an option, being idle is
torture. All I have is to think on is things I'd rather forget.

Been sick on and off as well. Alonso's mother is trying
to poison me with all the potions and remedies that she's
convinced my ma I should have. Some of them make me sleep
for days, others give me dreams that I can't explain. I don't
know the words she uses, but there's plenty of them in her fast-
talk to Ma—words like peyote, cinchona, cayenne, snakeroot,
jengibre, sage, and mostaza. They packing one or another in a
plaster on my chest, neck, or head, or choking it down my
throat.

If a man is sick

Health near disaster

Nothing will get him from bed more quick

Than another darn plaster

They always at the praying and candles as well. Ma ain't leaning Catholic, but she ain't about to stop no prayers or put out no candles till they burn all the way down. She says she wouldn't want to waste them. I'll get out this bed tomorrow, take a long walk, and maybe keep Ma and Señora de la Garza off their knees and away from them candles for a day or two.

What will I do with the rest of my time? It's like being in prison I guess: three square meals, but darn glad when it's past. I must get stronger, get out of this bed. Get on with my life. Alonso says the trick is to keep moving, even if only a few steps, he says, it's a few steps further than you were before. Alonso has a way of looking at things in a simple fashion that suits me.

He keeps reminding me that families don't start on their own. He says it's like huntin only without a weapon or any mind to killing—more like preparing yourself to be captured.

Maybe I can visit them neighbor sisters if it warms up and I'm stronger.

IN ALL MY YEARS OF HEALING, I HAVE SEEN this sickness in many. It follows a great dark wind in a life, whether battle, death, or a terrible wound. It is also true for those who became captives of the Penatʉka. At first, they would not eat, they cried, moaned in their sleep, babbled in words that had no language. Once the dark spirit passes over a person, it is difficult to heal. I knew this sickness too from my return to the People.

I should have been my happiest back among my own, but I struggled.

One evening, I stood at a respectful distance as my father worked his horses. My thoughts were cloudy as if I was standing in my sleep. Dog sat beside me. He had stopped his constant sniffing and settled back into his old routine of following me about the camp. Tupaapi pulled the Taiboo's horse from the herd and walked him toward me. He stood silent in his way for some time, and then spoke directly. "The young Taiboo who gave you this one must be sad for his loss, but there is a balance: his sadness, my happiness."

I knew my father was trying to brighten my spirit, trying to break through the dark wind that had taken his daughter so many moons before. I forced a bit of a smile and pushed myself to answer, "Does this horse whisper such things to you, Father?"

He smiled with his eyes and nodded ever so slightly, but I sensed a burden he didn't share. I tried to stand taller and speak firmly, "I have wronged you, Father. You have lost a great opportunity to gain horses, blankets, and more. I will marry now, as you wish."

He looked up at the half moon and stars around it. I could hear his deep, steady breaths. I watched the firelight dance on his cheeks, graying hair, and the small shadowed lines at the edges of his eyes. Finally, he began a song. He stretched out and swept the sky several times with a cupped hand as if capturing a trail of stars.

When the song was finished, he spoke. "Yes, the bounty would have been great. As great, perhaps as all the stars I sing into my hand, but a man cannot catch the stars in his hand, can he? I grow older and weaker. My eyes will soon no longer be the eyes of a warrior. Our numbers are smaller, there is less game, and more people from all directions that fight for what is left. These things age my spirit more. Perhaps it is best to have my daughter with me until my time is done. Wukubuu, I have lost you once. To lose you again or to have you caught up in the winds of another man's choosing would not ease my heart. Our moon is the brightest in our sky, but he travels alone and I am sad for him. Marry when you wish."

I looked into my father's warm smile and felt safe again, stronger. The dark spirit would lift from me. I knew this now. What I didn't know was that my Father had a task for me. He stepped closer and lowered his voice. "Little bird, I do need your help with something else involving marriage. The young women are all so afraid of your brother. Your medicine is strong. Have you the right spell?" I nodded my head and smiled.

I knew exactly what to do.

JULY 28, 1833. HAVEN'T WRITTEN FOR QUITE some time. Missed my birthday this time; turned fifteen. Was sick, of course, but soon as I was up to it, worked harder than ever on the farm. Last few months, we was fightin' four big storms. Had to work on the roof early this morning with Pa to repair what the last storm brought us. From up on the roof, I stared at a full field of nearly ripe cotton spread out below the house. In the rising sun, it was a long narrow field of bright white, looking like snow in the middle of the summer. I watched the light change as the sun climbed and remarked about it to Pa.

"Son, if you don't hand me that cedar shake, we'll still be up here admiring the field when the harvest starts tomorrow. Besides, it's gettin' hot already."

I tossed the wood to my pa and yelled down about the field at Tom who was splitting the shakes. Tom just kept at his work as if he didn't hear me. He's been like that. I asked Pa if Tom and me could go fishing later on. Pa cleared his throat. "Mal, Tom there has other chores." I knew by his careful words to leave it, but I couldn't stop myself. "Pa, all I ever do around here is farm work. You said there'd be more smithin'. There ain't. Now I ask about fishing for Tom and me." Pa held up his hand. He pulled the last nail from between his lips and hammered it into the shake.

He said we'd talk about this real quiet now so as not to upset Ma. Said she's a baby coming and he and her don't always see eye-to-eye on this subject anyway. Pa looked tired. Ma was pregnant again. It was the twelfth time and getting harder now on both of 'em. Pa has a way of saying things without saying them outright, but this time he made it real clear. "Mal, starting tomorrow during harvest, Tom, Thomas Elder, all the blacks, they gonna work after sunset under the torches, even Miss Mattie. We ain't got enough hands. Tom's full grown now. Thing's is going to be different between the two of you."

I looked down at Tom. We'd known each other, worked and played beside each other all our lives, but Tom was crossing a line. It made me angry, angry with myself and with Tom for being different. I watched our two dogs wrestle and chase in circles around Tom's feet. Then I spoke these words without thinking. "Them dogs has got it better."

Pa looked at me sideways so I changed the subject. "Grandpa said I was meant for other things. What about black smithin' in town? You said I'd be welcomed to ask Mr. Johnson about it." Pa didn't say it in a hard way, not as he has before, but he was firm. "Malcolm, I can't spare you. We just getting started in all this. Maybe at the end of the season. Understand?"

I was full of my own thinking. I understood all right. My best friend is not my best friend anymore. Sometimes it's like he ain't even a man anymore. Looks like I ain't never going to be a blacksmith like I want. I'm going to be stuck in this black dirt the rest of my days.

That was when Pa held up his hand and whispered so I knew something wasn't right. His attentions were on three riders approaching the house from the east, from the shadows of the woods. It pays to be alert out here. In a matter of minutes, you might be fightin' for yours and the lives of your loved ones. Pa touched me on the sleeve. "Mal, ease down and get my rifle, and don't bother your ma with it. You hear?"

I STARED AT THE LITTLE HAND HOLDING MY arm. The small pinto whinnied and shook his head to scatter the flies. Pʉ-na petʉ's son was now a boy of nearly three full seasons but the horses scared him, especially this one making noise while he was sitting on its bare back.

The boy tried to squirm off the horse's back and into my arms. I stepped back and let him fall slowly to the dirt, knowing it would scare him more than hurt him, especially since he still had a hold of my arm. Then I lifted him and set him on the horse's back again, his face streaked with tears and dust. He yelled. "I not go!" I brushed the dirt from his legs. "Someday soon Huuhwiya will ride with his father to hunt, to fight."

He yelled "No!" and squirmed again, but this time he leaned toward me and saw that I would not catch him. He sighed and eased up square on the horse's back. Now I could teach him more. "While you tame this pony, would you like a story?" He nodded.

"When our people came down from the Takabi Mountains, a great warrior led them and all were afoot. The people used the dog to carry what they would not carry themselves. There were no horses in the mountains, no buffalo, and…" I had to stop the story. The horses around us had begun to complain. Something, someone was spooking them. Then I heard a familiar whoop at the edge of the herd. It was Wowoki. He was showing off, jumping from one horse's back to another, stopping only to ensure I was still watching. He worked his way closer, whooping with every leap.

It didn't take long for Huuhwiya to notice the approaching warrior. The little boy tried to stand on his horse's shoulders but quickly sat as the animal shrugged and whinnied. I grabbed my young friend and shifted him slowly on to my back. In an instant, there was another whoop and my brother landed on the back of Huuhwiya's horse, laughing and calling to me. "Huutsúu Kwanaru, busy with babies again? This one has made the horse smell. You should do better job or our aunt will punish you." I told him that he scared the horses, but little else. Then I suggested it was he who had soiled the horse's back.

He laughed. "Brave talk from a woman to a warrior."

I pushed the toddler toward my brother. "I have a soiled child as my spear."

He leaned away. "No, you win, sister. I cannot defeat this weapon. Wʉkʉbuu, give the boy to Muutsi or his mother and come with me."

I declined. I had started a story and it would be bad medicine to not finish. Wowoki persisted. "A short hunt, perhaps along the river? While the sun is low we can keep in the shadows."

"It is not our way, the hunt. That is for those who hope to be warriors." I teased.

"I *am* a warrior and will decide myself what is the way. We have not hunted together for some time. It is good for the hunt when sister and brother join. Tell me, what signs do you see?"

I looked back toward the east and shaded my eyes. I heard the faint cry of the hawk. It came from the south, from near the river. "The hawk hunts there as will I, but first you must complete a task for me."

"You make demands of your older brother?"

Wowoki was falling right into my trap. "Perhaps you fear what it might be."

"I have no fear."

"None?"

"You are testing my patience sister."

I had him.

No one would have dreamed this next sight. The men and women at their fires stopped and stared. The warriors working on their weapons and pipes stopped and stared. Those in their teepees sensed the change in the rhythm of the camp and stepped out to investigate.

Wowoki crawled around the camp on his hands and knees with Huuhwiya sitting on a small blanket across the warrior's strong back. The younger children followed them, each hoping he or she would get the next ride. The People laughed and pointed. The young women of marrying age watched more closely. Their smiles had a different meaning.

I felt stronger. My medicine was growing beyond spells and potions, but I knew that my brother was still bent on his revenge, on regaining his honor. No medicine would cool that fire.

AS IT TURNED OUT, RIDERS FROM THE TREE line were not a threat. Josiah Wilbarger was among 'em. The two others, Bill Strother and Thomas Christian, were also local residents. They'd rose before the sun that morning to beat the heat and meet a newcomer at our place.

J. D. Haynie, a young arrival from Missouri, had contacted Mr. Austin who sent a message to Wilbarger asking if established Bastrop men would help a new settler. Haynie was bringing Mr. James Standifer, married but undecided on his own land. The two of them didn't arrive until late in the morning. That gave the established men time to trade stories and catch up with news while they helped work our fields.

Ma felt good enough to venture out in her bonnet. She brought us cornbread and blackberry tea. She spoke with our neighbors as if she'd known them all her life, sending best wishes to their wives, checking on their youngsters. Mr. Christian had a baby on the way, so Ma had to mother him, or more like grandmother him. There was talk of the expectant mother's appetites for odd foods and the signs it brought. Mr. Christian said his wife was longing for plums or cherries, but,

Lord knows, he didn't have room for no twins in their house with six already.

Pa cleared his throat loud enough to indicate he wasn't happy to have his pregnant wife in the hot summer field. Wilbarger took Ma's arm to walk her back to the house. They wasn't ten paces from us when Ma's bonnet blew off her head. Mr. Wilbarger caught it and was handing it back when he froze. Ma had that look on her face, the seeing look. She talked slow and quiet. "Josiah, you will be mindful out there, won't you? I don't care for the feel of this wind. I believe it bears bad tidings. It is a trifle, I know, but many a little makes a mickle."

Wilbarger turned, tipped his hat, and tried to reassure Ma. "Mrs. Hornsby, you have enough to worry about these days. There will be five of us, maybe more if any of these fine Hornsby men care to join us, and we ain't goin' that far. We'll be close enough to hear your mid-day prayers, I reckon." Ma said she'd be praying for them just the same.

Haynie and Standifer arrived just before lunch. The five men joined us Hornsbys for our mid-day meal. It was exciting to sit next to these older, rugged men and hear their stories. Haynie and Standifer asked many questions. They was from farm country in Missouri and Tennessee and seemed nervous about being out on what they viewed as the edge of the wilderness. Billy whispered, "Maybe we can get Pa to let us go along. Them boys is so green they liable to die fallin' off their horses before any injuns ever get 'em."

I bumped my shoulder into Billy's and made my own joke. "They're complaining about the heat like little girls. Maybe we ought to get them some bonnets for their trip." Billy snickered and nodded. Tarnation. I made my brother laugh.

Wilbarger, Strother, Christian, Haynie, and Standifer were away by noon. Billy wanted to join them, but Pa refused to lose the help in the fields. Ma waved from the porch and as the men rode away, she looked up into the trees as if the leaves flickering in the wind would show her a better sign. I guess they didn't.

She just shook her head and stepped back into the cabin.

WOWOKI'S NEW WIFE, PUKUTSI, HAD MOVED into my brother's teepee. She brought more laughter to our family and companionship for my aunt and me. And she lived up to her name: stubborn. As the flower season neared its end, her belly showed the signs of their first baby and we were all happy. Even Wowoki smiled briefly at the news, but my brother's dark spirit had changed very little.

This warm season was ripe for revenge.

He still argued with our father and every other elder. The younger warriors feared him, though they would never admit it. I watched them avoid crossing paths when he did not see. I heard their whispers when he passed. Wowoki wanted to push all Taiboo from our territory and capture any that remained. The other warriors were just as eager to gain honor in fighting the white-skinned but were more patient. They wanted to trade, expand their families, hunt and train their horses. Wowoki had no patience—he would fight every day if he could, mostly against the Taiboo, but also with anyone who confronted him, except Pukutsi. Though he spoke less often of it, revenge on the smelly Taiboo that had captured me was always in his eyes when we were together. It darkened my spirit too. With Pukutsi, he was calmer, a different man, but for the rest of us, Wowoki's spirit was dangerous, even when he'd set out to be different.

I remember we heard news from those traders from the Waco tribe that a few stray buffalo had wondered further south than usual, ahead of the herds. The warriors formed a small hunting party and asked Wowoki to lead them. He jumped at the chance and surprised me with a request to go along, not as one who would take the skins but as a seer and to bring good medicine to the hunt. Perhaps Pukutsi had recommended this.

We rode for some time in the direction the traders had described, toward the great clear river, but with no luck. We had traveled far from the camp and many of the warriors were ready to give up and return. Wowoki would hear nothing of it. He spoke to the others as if they were children, teasing them about needing their mothers. The warriors hit back, making fun at his expense, by pointing out that he had brought his sister along. Wowoki raged.

I watched the blood rush to his face. He drove his heels into the sides of his mustang, whooped, and raced ahead of us. We rushed to follow. By the time, we caught up he had stopped on a hill and dismounted, pulling his horse behind tall rocks. Something had caught his eye.

We followed his lead and quietly walked our horses up the hill. In the far distance, we spotted a small group of buffalo grazing on a grassy hilltop. Wowoki had spotted something else. He cautioned us to stay low. We saw the smoke of their guns before we heard the shots. A Taiboo hunting party, perhaps ten men or more, had stepped out from the trees and brush and killed all the buffalo in minutes.

Though they were much too far to hear or even notice him, Wowoki stood on the hilltop yelling threats to the white men. "Taiboo. We will have your hearts in our bellies before the sun fills the sky again. We are coming for you. Prepare for your death."

My brother turned back to face us. "Sister, we will make quick work of those who steal from the People. There will be scalps, saddles, weapons, hides, and meat to take back to camp. What are the signs telling you?"

I looked away to cover my true feelings. The Taiboo were at least twice our number, heavily armed, and they had the high ground. We would have to go around them to set a trap but it would be dark soon. The other warriors were quiet. Why not bring more warriors and take even more scalps, more spoils to the People, in the next sun. I tried to sound firm. "Perhaps a good meal and long sleep tonight will bring more spoils to you and your warrior brothers in the next sun."

Wowoki did not speak. He snorted at me and the warriors, mounted his horse, and turned his back on the Taiboo. We would return to camp, but there would be no sleep for the warriors and they knew it. They would fill the night with songs, food, and pipes. They would challenge each other, and tell stories of past victories and honor. They would build their rage together as one builds a fire. The Taiboo taking the buffalo was only the spark.

Like the nakuyaaru, these young warriors would burn their way across the prairie if they could.

JULY 29. AS THEY RACED INTO THE LARGE meadow west of our cabin, Haynie and Standifer came into the sunlight looking like cats with their tails afire. I yelled to Pa that Mr. Wilbarger's party had found trouble. Pa locked the dogs in the barn and rushed to meet the men before they got too close to the house, too close to Ma and the slaves. Their frantic ride through the brush left the men with scratches all across their arms and faces. Haynie had lost his hat and his head was badly sunburned.

They caught their breaths, drank their fill of water, and chewed a bit on some bread and bacon to settle their nerves. Finally, Standifer worked up the nerve to tell us that all three of our neighbors, Wilbarger, Strother, and Christian was dead and likely scalped. Mr. Haney held his face in his hands and walked quickly away, but I could still hear his sobbin'.

Pa took command. He sent Billy east along the river to summon the neighbors in case the hostiles should attack again. Moses-Smith rode north and northwest but only as far as the next neighbors, the Walters and Rogers. It was getting late and being out in the dark in small numbers was dangerous.

This is the story that Haynie and Standifer told to us, at its roots. By mid-afternoon, Wilbarger, Strother, Christian, Haynie, and Standifer had slowly made their way northwest, stopping here and there to point out the features. In some places, the area to the northwest of us is as rich as our bend. For a few hours, I imagine it was practically a picnic.

Then it all went cockeyed.

I TRIED TO SETTLE INTO THE RHYTHM OF THE Penatuka, but our everyday life was changing. There were new sicknesses that my aunt and I could not fight. Our game, our food, was getting harder to find. The Taiboo camps were growing every day. Wowoki was nearly mad for revenge, but revenge is a knife with two edges.

While my brother was out on raids with the younger warriors nearly every day, my father's health was failing him and he was losing that most precious of valuables, his pride. It was more and more difficult for him to see clearly at any distance and almost impossible for him to hunt alone. When he returned empty-handed, he would praise the game for their cleverness.

At night, my father, Wowoki and the other warriors would stay up under the stars preparing for battle. Each of them painted his face, chest, arms, and horse. Across his chest, Wowoki painted a buffalo with a scar on its face.

After their war song, each warrior spoke of one another's bravery, of who would inflict the greatest revenge on the Taiboo. It was not custom to speak of oneself in such a manner, but bragging on a comrade or teasing was. As the drummers beat their rhythms and sang, Tupaapi pushed Wowoki and the other men into a frenzy of boasting and challenge. The men yelled and whooped.

In the mornings, when the warriors went out together to attack an enemy, father would insist on joining them, but I knew they were careful to keep him behind and as far from harm as he would allow. I was not there, but I heard the stories

190

often. I did not realize it at the time, but one such story was of a raid that started a chain of events affecting many that I loved and cared for, and added another layer of pain to our lives.

My brother and five warriors had spotted a Taiboo scouting party. They suggested to Father that he stay behind to keep watch on the trail. Wowoki said Father looked in the distance and bragged that he would go and find more Taiboo and take more scalps than all the other warriors take together.

Wowoki and the warriors surprised five white men in a thicket by a stream, taking horses, guns, scalps, and saddles, while suffering no casualties or wounds themselves. Two of the Taiboo escaped, but the warriors already had their hands full of rewards and did not give chase. When they rode back to where my Father should have been, he was missing, his tracks leading south toward the river.

He was alone and headed right toward the Taiboo camps.

THE MEN SAID WILBARGER WAS THE FIRST TO notice the fresh tracks of unshod horses and caution the others. He pulled his rifle and quietly directed the men to ride the trail nose-to-tail the same direction as the tracks. He tried to calm the men with his local prairie wisdom. Standifer said he'd never forget Josiah's words. "Better we face 'em than have 'em at our backs."

The tracks led up the west side of a creek most call Walnut for the Black Walnut trees that line it. The brush was thick and the tree limbs low. As the trail became less clear, the tracks were harder to follow. Wilbarger stopped and silently signaled they were turning back.

They worked their way along a spring-fed branch of the creek and stopped for a rest in the shade of oak and pecan. Quietly, whispering when they spoke at all, they ate their johnnycake and drank from canteens. Each took a turn at a watch, though here next, to the creek, the thickness of the brush limited their vision considerably.

By the time they saw movement in the bushes, the air around them was full of yells, gunfire, and flying arrows. Bill Strother, on watch at the time of the attack, was the first one killed; an arrow pierced his heart. Thomas Christian, desperately searching for his horse, took a hot ball of lead to the thigh and fell.

Mr. Wilbarger, wounded both in the calf of one leg and in the hip, tried to pull Christian to cover behind a tree but their attackers had surrounded them. The air was full of so much gun smoke it was difficult to see.

After the initial shock of the ambush and seeing the others wounded, Haynie and Standifer ran and climbed on their saddled horses. Wilbarger yelled to them, urging a stand but his pleas were lost in the chaos. The Indians moved from the bushes, screaming and all painted up. They finished Christian with knives.

Haynie and Standifer looked back when they heard Josiah yell again. They saw him shuffling toward them but after a few steps, he dropped his rifle, grabbed his neck, and pitched forward. A bullet had passed through the poor man's throat. At that, the two farmers heeled their horses and raced away through the brush toward the river. Standifer said he must have repeated one word a thousand times, as they raced to get as far away as possible: Comanche.

As soon as the news spread, the neighbors began to form a defense at our home. If the Indians did not attack again, a small party would go out in search of the bodies and bring them back tomorrow. Ma didn't seem surprised, just terrible sad. She sat on her bed and rested her head in her hands. "I've known since this morning's bad wind. Lord help us. We must get word across the river to Alonso and his mother. Go see to your pa, son. There's much to do." I stepped out of the cabin and walked toward the barn. Half of me wanted to help find them that did this and exact the rightful revenge.

Half of me wanted nothing of it.

WOWOKI TOLD TWO OF THE WARRIORS TO
return to the camp with their bounty from the creekside attack.
The others would stay with him. Following my father's tracks,
they worked their way between the hills and across the river
slowly to avoid notice. By the time they made it to Boucher's
farm, it was nearing dark and apparent that no one was there.
There were no lights, no smoke from the chimneys, no sounds.
Even the livestock were gone.

Wowoki whooped and pounded his chest. They would
take as much of value that they could and burn the rest. From
the barn and dugouts, there was very little to steal. As they
neared the main house with their torches, Wowoki had a strong
sense that something was wrong. It was not a trap, he was sure
of that, but something, some smell or sound, made him
hesitate.

At twenty paces from the main cabin, he found his
answer. There was a steady, labored breath in the shadows near
the square teepee. Wowoki recognized the sound—this was a
man and he was dying. Wowoki signaled for the others to wait.
He crouched low and eased forward. As he got closer, he could
see the outline of a man resting against the trunk of a tree. The
figure raised his hand as if signaling then dropped his hand in
apparent exhaustion before he said, "Son."

The word shot through Wowoki's heart. He recognized
our father's voice even in the weak whisper. "You must
prepare my body." Wowoki said he insisted that he and the
warriors would take my father back to camp, that Muutsi and I
would heal him, that our medicine was strong. My brother
asked why he attacked the Taiboo alone. Father said that he
needed to see if he could do it. If he could put on the paint and
defeat an enemy.

Wowoki tried to get him to stand. He said they should fight the Taiboo together. He said that there are many of the Taiboo, but they are like minnows and we are the fish. Father would not stand. He answered my brother. "The river is not empty when one fish dies." Then he grabbed Wowoki's arm, nodded slightly, and went limp. Wowoki said Father was missing a section of his scalp and was bleeding from gunshots to his chest and stomach. Wowoki yelled as loud as he could so that the sound would echo across the prairie forever. Then he sang the death song and swore he would kill every last Taiboo, even if he had to do it alone.

JULY 30. COULDN'T SLEEP LAST NIGHT. DON'T know if it's on account of me feeling poorly or just all the excitement. Seemed like torches and noisy activity surrounded our house from sunset 'til sunrise this morning. The night was full of firsts.

I'd never seen my pa kneel with Ma to pray. Sure, he says the blessing at the dinner table, but as far as I know, Reuben Hornsby will go to his knees for no one. This was different. Ma is due a baby in months, it's harvest time, and the safety of close friends had been threatened, maybe some even killed.

Ma made every member of the family along with Mattie and all the slaves kneel on the porch and pray with her. I held Ma's hand. It was warm. She looked at me with alarm and spoke under her breath. "Malcolm, you're as cold as a winter's day and pale. Mattie will make you a poultice." I whispered back that I was all right and we had enough to worry us.

She turned her attention to the others. Her voice trembled and her Scottish "R's" rolled. "May the spirit bring peace to this house, this day and all days. Look after us, Father. We are your sheep and need our shepherd, now more than

194

ever." Pa prayed softly, patiently for a man who was itching to get on with preparing a defense and leading a burial party for one of his closest friends.

More neighbor men, wives, and children than I ever knew we had, kept arriving, including the Wells sisters. Some of the men took turns keeping watch along the tree lines. Others cleaned their rifles and pistols. Tom and me brushed down and fed horses. Tom didn't say a word the whole time. It was like workin' with a ghost. I felt dizzy and tired but tried to help as much and as long as I could.

When I sat for a rest, Tom sighed and shook his head. It made me angry enough to stand for a fight but I didn't have the strength. I yelled at Tom to get the work done and stop being so lazy when we's all in such a state. Then I stomped out the door, feeling worse than I ever felt about my words.

The slaves roasted a wild hog over the fire. Tents went up around our cabin and barn. Despite cautions from all of us, Ma busied herself to exhaustion. I reckon it was as much to help the men get ready as to keep her mind off the dangers that seemed to be closing in on her family. She fell asleep on top of the bed covers with her shoes on. The other men and women continued for a couple of hours and then settled in.

I stepped out into the warm night, heard voices from around the side of the barn and walked slowly that direction. When I recognized my pa's voice, I stopped and stayed out of site. It was Pa and Billy. They was talking about me. Pa said I was old enough to see the consequence of crossin' paths with injuns. Billy said I was more fragile than a fly's wings, all milk and water and wouldn't likely stomach the sights. Pa didn't answer. I could tell he was thinking it through. Then he said he was leavin me here 'cause ma would be calmer. I wasn't sure I disagreed with either one of them.

Finally, all but the posted guards settled into bed. I couldn't sleep and laid in my bedroll imagining the worse for our lost neighbors.

Not long into the night, Ma woke. I plainly heard Ma and Pa whispering in the dark. Something was wrong. Pa lit the lantern. Ma stopped whispering. Her voice was hard. "Mr. Hornsby, it was more than a dream. I have seen him as clear as I see you now. Josiah is alive. You must go to him tonight. He is gravely wounded and alone, but he is plainly alive."

Pa tried to speak as soft as he could. "Mother, how can we ride tonight? There is no moon to speak of. In the dark and with such a large party, we'd hardly ride quiet enough to keep the savages from takin' advantage." Then Pa must have blown the lantern out as if dotting the end of his sentence. Most everyone fell back to sleep, but not Ma. She lay awake and quiet as long as she could and then climbed out of bed, lit the lantern, and packed provisions for the men.

Before the sun was fully up, everyone woke to the sound of Ma singing one of her hymns. She sang loud enough that even those sleeping in the barn heard her. "From my fierce enemy in safety do me guide, because I flee to thee, Lord, that thou may'st me hide." That was Ma's way of saying there was work to be done and it wouldn't wait.

An hour later, Pa, Uncle, Billy, Joseph Rogers, John Walters, Bill Webber, and a reluctant James Standifer were ready to ride northwest and bring back the bodies of our friends. Surrounded by the wives and children, Ma yelled to the riders from the cabin porch to wait a moment. She sent Mattie with two sheets, an old pair of Pa's trousers, and one of his old shirts. Pa turned his horse and rode up to the house to ask Ma why she was sending these old things.

Ma lowered her voice so only Pa and us nearest would hear. "Mr. Hornsby, you will use the sheets to bring Mr. Christian and Mr. Strother, God rest their souls, as properly as you can, and as I told you, Mr. Wilbarger has lost his clothes to those savages. You will bring him here as quickly as you can, and in those old things so as to protect the women folk's modesty."

Pa knew better than to argue. He nodded silently and tipped his hat, then eased his horse to the barn to speak with us who stayed behind. "Keep an eye out and your guns close, Tom, boys. Mal, watch after your Ma, ye hear."

As Pa rode away, I noticed J. D. Haynie standing in the shadow of the barn door looking down at the dirt below his feet. He couldn't bring himself to join the others nor face my father either.

I couldn't blame him.

WOWOKI AND THE OTHER WARRIORS BOUND my father's legs and washed the blood from his face and head. The others told me my brother never spoke but that his breath was hard and hot like a trapped nʉmʉ kutsu bull. Even on the ride to bury Tupaapi no one spoke. The warriors rode slowly far ahead and behind Wowoki and our father, both out of respect and to protect them should there be a Taiboo attack. They rode through the night. The moonlight must have cast sad shadows as their horses slowly chose their steps.

Wowoki told me much later that it was the most difficult ride he had ever taken—torn between helping our father's ghost go in peace and realizing he would never hear his voice, his wisdom again. However, he could not show his worries to the other warriors.

UPON THEIR RETURN, PA TOLD US THEY'D followed the dead men's trail, eyes watching every tree, creek bed, and wallow, ears pricked by any hint of attack. He quietly instructed the other men to keep Standifer centered among them as they rode. It was vital he guide them to the attack site as quickly as possible and he would need all the courage they could give him. Once they found the spring, they dismounted and worked their way down the creek bed. It didn't take long to find what they all dreaded seeing.

Billy and Standifer kept watch and held the horses. The others quietly shooed away the turkey vultures and wrapped the bodies. It was less than a day since the attack but the exposure and the nature of their wounds made it difficult to tell the dead men's identities without close inspection. Pa was the first to notice that his friend Josiah Wilbarger was not among them. Then he saw what looked to be a trail of something or someone dragged toward the creek.

With Uncle and Rogers behind him, he quickly worked his way along the trail to the bank. On the opposite bank, the grass grew more sparsely, replaced by thicker brush and cactus. The fresh trail all but disappeared.

Once they'd secured the two bodies over the packhorses, the other men joined the search on the far side of the creek. Billy said he seen those that had pocket watches check them often. As the sun rose to midday, he kept close to Mr. Standifer who seemed more and more eager to give up the hunt and ride back. Billy put his hand on his shoulder and suggested they talk about the sort of land he was looking for, but Mr. Standifer would not be distracted. Billy said he glanced all around him, eased down on one knee and confessed that he wasn't cut of the right cloth for this business. Wasn't meant for killing or seeing it done, not this way. Billy said he didn't have an answer.

Meanwhile, Pa and the others was still at it. Joe Rogers eased his way through a clump of sage, something at the base of a large oak had caught his eye. As he moved closer through the brush, it was clear this was a man wearing little clothing. Rogers dropped to one knee and cocked his rifle. He gave a whistle warning to the others and aimed his gun at the dark-skinned man only twenty paces away. The man raised his hand, his voice barely over a whisper and said, "Please don't shoot. I'm a sight to be sure, but, tis Josiah Wilbarger, I swear."

When they reached our place, it was late afternoon. Ma and a couple of the wives were waiting outside. We eased Wilbarger off Billy's horse and let him rest on the porch. Pa's old clothes were short on him, but I imagine they kept him warm.

Ma had seen right.

After greeting Mr. Wilbarger up close, the other wives quickly excused themselves and stepped back into the cabin. Mattie kept her gaze to the floor, set bandages, poultices, and a pot of hot water on the porch, and backed away. Ma stepped down off the porch, gently held the wounded man's hand, and spoke to sooth. "Mr. Wilbarger, I sent these men with the conviction that …" Ma stopped and wiped a tear from her cheek. "… with the help of our Almighty, they would deliver you to this refuge. I thank him now that you are safe. If you will allow it, we must tend to your wounds and pray." Josiah blinked both eyes and nodded ever so slightly. Ma looked at Pa for something positive. "The others, Father?"

Pa looked down and shook his head.

IN THE DAYS GONE, AFTER A LOVED ONE DIED we would burn everything that was his. We would have to kill a warrior's horses, burn his pipe and blankets, and bury his weapons. All memory of the dead must go with the dead into the dust or he would come back as a ghost.

Word had come before Wowoki and the other warriors rode slowly into camp with my father's horse. Perhaps one of our hunting parties had crossed their path. I didn't know. I didn't care. All I knew was that my father was dead; everyone in the camp knew. Wowoki and the warriors had buried him in a rocky hillside.

It was difficult not to see my father, not hear his voice, not to look at his old gentle eyes when he was looking directly at me. It was difficult to keep from speaking his name. It was difficult to keep from feeling that, if not for my capture, my father's dark dream would never have come true.

I used my knife to cut my hair, almost to my skin. Muutsi did the same. She started a fire to burn Father's belongings and we threw our hair into the flames. Wowoki avoided us. It was better that way. Muutsi had spoken no words except when threatening to kill Wowoki, and she did this several times a day. She blamed him for the loss of her brother, though she did not mention my Father's name. Muutsi sang her death song low and sad, and slowly cut small lines in her skin up and down her right arm as she sang. She sat so close to the fire I was afraid she would catch in flames at any moment. She sang for hours, until she was nearly asleep sitting up.

The next day, a Waco trader who also traded with the Taiboo came to our camp. He told us Taiboo were gathering men to fight the People, and that they may be at war with the great fathers of Mexico to the south as well. He spoke of Mexico refusing a treaty. He said that the Mexican warriors in the area were being more vigilant and forceful. He said the Taiboo were forming war parties everywhere, not just to fight the People but to fight these Mexican warriors too.

Wowoki was there listening, asking questions. When the trader was finished talking, my brother yelled so that everyone in the camp could hear. "The Taiboo will be looking for war in too many places and their war parties will take them from their camps. While they are away, we will attack their families. We will take captives, horses, and scalps. We will clear them off this land. And then we will welcome the buffalo back to the places such as the big bend in the great clear river."

I thought of Malcuu and his family. They had not killed my father, and if not for them, I would still be a captive. What would my Father say to that? I would never know. Muutsi and I turned our backs on Wowoki and walked away.

JULY 31. MARGARET WILBARGER TRAVELED by wagon with a neighbor couple to our cabin. When they arrived, the man bragged that he'd "find them injuns and give 'em a war if they want it." He said we'd "give the pox to every last one of them men, women, and children, and wipe them bloodthirsty killers out once and for all!" Even with all the anger and worry we was feeling over our friends, that talk turned my stomach, especially when he's talking about women and children.

Don't seem right.

Mrs. Wilbarger didn't stay long. Mr. Wilbarger was deep asleep when she arrived. It's likely he didn't see the horror on her face, didn't hear her sobbing in Ma's arms. He didn't see her politely decline lunch and sit in the wagon alone until the neighbors joined her. Ma shook her head as she watched them roll away.

Pa was fast at work today. He sent Billy and some of the other men to cut posts. He had me, Tomas Elder, and Tom gather up the surveying tools and start marking lines around the cabin for building a small stockade. Pa had it in his mind it would enable those behind the walls to shoot out in any direction from well-protected positions.

Since our time here, Pa had tried to keep his mind on making ours a profitable farm, but a war is a hard thing to hold back. In the midst of our work today, he put his hand on Tomas Elder's shoulder and spoke quietly to him. "Tomas, time you learned that shotgun, you reckon?"

After sunset, Ma was out with Mattie helping feed us men. Everyone was quiet. Seemed the whole night was quiet 'cept for the big fire. Ma started humming one of her hymns. I looked Billy square in the eye and he knew what I was saying, even without the words. Ma had seen right in her dream.

We'd saved one of our own because of it.

IT WAS HARD TO GO ON WITHOUT SPEAKING to my brother, but Muutsi would not hear of it. I wanted to ask him so many questions, questions I should not ask. What did our father say before he died? Could I have saved him with my medicine or our aunt's medicine? Why did he fight alone? Where was my brother? But the questions just burned in my head instead. Wowoki was rarely in camp, and when he was, stayed far away from our aunt and me.

I felt as though I was in a terrible storm, blown about in the wind like leaves. I couldn't eat, I didn't want to work or hunt. Muutsi spoke very little, even to me. She'd make me tea but share it with no words, no touch, not even looking at me.

The elders decided we should move camp. This was happening more often now. The Taiboo were spreading quickly. There was fear that our hunting trails or the smoke from our fires would lead them to us. Wowoki had opposed the move. He called the elders children afraid of their own shadows. He pleaded with them to stay and fight, attack even, every sun, if that's what it took to rid our land of the Taiboo. I stood and listened outside the elders' teepee one night as he yelled at them.

They did not want to listen. Our band was growing smaller. Too many had gone. It made me think mostly of my father.

AUGUST 17. MR. WILBARGER WALKED A BIT today. He sat on the porch and whispered to us Hornsby men about his ordeal. I've tried to capture his story here as best as I can recollect.

He said he laid helplessly while his attackers stripped his boots and clothes from his body. He said it sounded touched but he was asking himself why anyone would want his long unders since he was sure they's torn and bloody. His wounded neck ached as someone pulled his head back by the hair. He saw shadows and sensed hands near his face. When the knife cut into his scalp, he smelled the blood for a moment as he slipped into darkness. He said he dreamed of his wife and children, his cabin and fields. Said his mind was fading in and out.

As he slowly woke, Mr. Wilbarger heard the wind and birds in the trees. His head throbbed. He reached to wave a fly away and grazed his head with his hand. It hurt. He felt his head and found much of his scalp was cut away to the bone. Sitting there on the porch with him, we could attest to that but we didn't let on, though it was hard not to stare at his bandages.

At this point, Pa offered to walk our guest back inside, but Mr. Wilbarger seemed dead set on telling his story in whole.

He said a layer of caked blood covered most of him. His throat was so dry he couldn't swallow and he knew he'd have to get to the creek for water. He tried to stand but went dizzy right off so he laid back down, dug his foot into the dirt, reached up to grab two hands full of grass, pushed and pulled to move. In this fashion, he was able to make his way to the top of the creek bank. From there, he inched his way around and slid slowly, feet first down the bank.

When his feet hit the water, the cold on his sunburned skin gave him a shiver. He looked down and noticed that the Indians left him one sock, perhaps because the dried blood made it impossible to remove. Water spiders and dragonflies scattered as he eased his legs into the stream and lowered the rest of his body until the water was just below his injured neck. By supporting himself on his elbow, he was able to take a drink and rinse his face. All his wounds burned in the water and pestering flies buzzed his head, so he removed his one sock to use as a sort of bandage around his head.

By sunset, he felt a little stronger. The night air was cooler. His sunburned skin chilled in the breeze. All he thought about was how to get to our bend, a good six miles away. He eased across the creek. Then, by going up backward and, using his good leg to push, he made it to the top of the creek bank and a few dozen paces further before his strength ran out. He lay beneath a big oak, stared at the stars along the horizon, and fell to sleep using a tree root beneath his tender head.

He said he'd "found his peace and prepared for his maker."

NINE

At What Cost?

JANUARY 21, 1834. SITTING BY THE FIRE ON
Ma's side of the cabin. Ma and Pa are up late and neither one
happy. Me, Billy, and Uncle Moses are heading out with a
militia in the morning. Time we did our part to find those
terrifying our neighbors.

In the lamplight, Ma is cooking. She does that when
she's upset. I swear she'd cook all night if she could. Right
now, she is stirring buttermilk and molasses into the cornmeal
mash as if tryin' to spin it into a little yellow twister right there
in the bowl. Pa is standing as close as he can while still
avoiding her arms and elbows as she works. They are
whispering but I can hear most of it. Ma said she knows we's
men now, but worried about my seasoning and Pa having to
make up for Billy missing his work on the farm.

Pa is standing still and silent, deep in his own thoughts.
Ma just stopped her stirring and let him have it. "Mr. Hornsby,

we have been together for nearly two decades. Brought children into this world. Buried two of them. We have traveled across this, the Lord's garden, together. I have never known you not to have a firm and rapid opinion on things, yet you now stand beside me quieter than a church mouse."

Pa glanced at me and I ducked my head. Then he answered. "Ma, I am more torn than you see on this. I can't spare them boys, you know that. There's too much to do around here, but Misters Strother and Christian is gone and our dear friend Mr. Wilbarger nearly with 'em. You said it yourself: they are men now. Times I think everything might be easier if they was still boys."

WOWOKI WAS GONE. HE GAVE SIGNS THAT HE would like to speak to Muutsi and me. We refused, so he dressed in his best earrings of Spanish silver, wore leather bands around his upper arms and painted his face ghost white. He also painted his biggest horse with red spots, yelling to any who would hear, "This is Taiboo blood! Each spot for all the blood I will spill."

Then he left the camp, alone.

Muutsi was losing more of her family. She sensed it. She made cuts on her other arm and her legs. She made strong potions from recipes she had not shared with me. They made her dreamy, almost ghost-like, but she did not sleep. She painted her face with chalk from the white rock and for two suns walked around the camp singing the death song—yelling at anyone who crossed her path, often mistaking them for her nephew. There were no warriors in her circle now. She must go on with only me, her brother's daughter, to look after her.

I remember waking one morning to see her sitting in our teepee staring at me. The white paint was gone from her face. Her eyes were bright, younger somehow, as if she had found a special medicine. She looked almost happy as she spoke. "Niece of mine, I would like to tell you the story of how a man and I were adopted by the Penatuka. I have made you a hot stew and have fresh water from the stream."

JANUARY 24. FOR THREE DAYS NOW, MA AND Pa have stalled our departure as long as they can. Finally, this morning we secured our saddlebags and blankets on the mule and were ready to say our good byes when a commotion commenced. Given the way he came barreling up from the prairie with no hat, the rider was lucky that Tomas Elder hadn't shot him from the new stockade walls, especially with half the men in the area gone with the volunteer militia.

Though the morning was cold, the man's horse was nearly dead. The animal's back and belly were wet with a lather that soaked through the cinches and skirt of his saddle.

Tomas Elder lowered his shotgun when he heard the stranger yelling from the tree line and all the way to the edge of the field. "Austin's arrested! Austin's arrested!" Then his wind gave out and he slumped forward on the horse's neck. The dogs chased his horse from the edge of the field to the cabin before Tom could get to him.

Pa did all he could to keep Ma from worrying over the unexpected guest and any news he might be sharing. With each baby, Ma felt worse. This last one is due in two months, so Pa was taking no chances. He lifted little sis, Diana, and sat her in Ma's bed with a request. "Little Bit, you hold Ma's hand now. Not too tight but don't let go, you hear. If she tries to get out of this bed, you holler like a lonesome old hound dog. Let me hear you." Diana just turned away and giggled.

The stranger sat outside on the porch in a tattered heap. He looked to be Billy's age. He had ridden so hard through the brush his clothes seemed as if he'd been wrestling a bobcat in a barrel. We stood around him, pushing and shoving for a better view while Tomas Elder tended to the young man's scratches with a wet cloth and bear grease. Mattie forced a few gulps of water down him and then, with Pa's approval, poured the rest over his head. This seemed to revive him a bit.

Pa dropped down on a knee and extended his hand. "Name's Reuben Hornsby, these are my boys." The young man tried to stand. Pa put his hand on his shoulder and eased him back down. "Rest yourself, stranger. We're due a baby inside any time now. We don't need another to care for. When you have your wits, we're ready to listen. Boys, give the man some air. Don't you have chores to do, the lot of you? Who's lookin' after them hogs today?" Pa didn't mention the militia. He was intent on getting news from the stranger first. "Did you say that Mr. Austin was arrested by the Mexicans, mister? We've heard those tales before, you know. What's your name?" The stranger held up his hand to shake, though he didn't have the strength to look up. "Name's Benjamin Franklin Highsmith originally from Missoura territory, sir. Been riding for three days. It's no shillyshally, sir. It's God's truth, Colonel Austin's in a Mexican prison. I know this to be the Hornsby fort. Folks in town told me I's best to tell you the news as fast as I could ride."

Pa looked steady in our eyes—me, Uncle, and Billy— then he looked down and shook his head. "You men best be gettin' on to meet up with that militia in town. This is no time to waste sunlight. Besides, ain't no telling who we'll be fighting next, injun or Mexican soldier."

I TOLD MY AUNT THAT TO HEAR HER STORY would be an honor and I was thankful for the food. With a sly smile, she warned me that for this story I would need the strength the food would provide.

She stood and began her story, waving her arms about as if she was a young woman again.

"*Wʉkʉbuu, when I was a child, there was a young warrior in my family who spoke with the animals. The deer and the fox knew him. The rabbit and the wolf knew him. The buffalo would stop and lower their heads to his honor, and when he hunted them, they spoke to him. They spoke of the honor to be game for such a fine warrior and the young warrior's family ate well and grew.*

"*But that winter, a darkness came to the People. Many men and women and all the parents—my parents, the parents of this young warrior—turned black and died. My mother died in my arms and I was barely big enough to hold her head up. My father dragged himself out of our camp through the snow so that I would not see his death, but I found him near the stream. He was on his side and held his knees like a baby. He had prepared his own body for his death.*

"*The young warrior, much younger than me, found me with my father. He said he would protect me, said he would hunt for me and keep me fed, keep me warm, but when he hunted again the animals would no longer speak to him. They were afraid of the sickness that afflicted the People. The deer, the fox, the rabbit, and the wolf just ran. The buffalo ran. Only one animal would speak to this young warrior; it was wasápe. The big bear stood on his hind legs and growled so loud that the whole world would hear him. He warned the young warrior that alone he had no honor, he could protect no one, provide for no one, not even me. He told the young warrior that he must leave this place, find a new band of the People.*

"*The young warrior ran as hard as he could, until he was running so fast that he could keep up with large hooved animals in a herd: mustangs. One of the mustangs spoke to him.*

"You have courage and strength, warrior. It would be an honor to carry you."

"The young warrior grabbed the mustang by the hair, jumped on his back, and came for me. He yelled for me to join him and we rode until we came to the camp of the Penatɨka. The rest of the mustangs followed. They too became a part of the Penatɨka band.

"After a few days, the young warrior went for a hunt. He was not sure of the signs. He had little hope this hunt would be different, better than the last, but he was wrong. The animals spoke to him again, and we ate and we were warm because we were with the Penatɨka. Our new People brought us hope and the animals saw the signs."

Muutsi sat back down with a very satisfied sigh and finished. "Now eat, my child. This may be the last meal that your paha cooks for you."

I did not eat. Not right away.

I sat directly in front of my paha. I took her hand and looked at her skin. I touched the cuts on her arms. I touched her short hair. "Paha, I am not a young warrior like my father was, but I will protect you. The animals do not speak to me, but I will feed you and I will keep you warm. You have many seasons left and many medicine lessons to teach me." Muutsi took my hand and lifted it to her wrinkled face. "My petɨ, I will stay a little longer but only because you have asked this of me."

APRIL 27. SIXTEEN TODAY. ALL MAN NOW.
Spending a week at home. Been on and off the trail with the militia for weeks, stopping and starting, men going home to take care of their farms. Sometimes we sleep at home in our

own beds but often out on the land. It is wearing heavily on my health and on Ma and Pa's patience. Ma had the baby while we was three day's ride away from the house. Miss Sarah Ann was born on March 21, but we didn't get the news until we came home. That's a sorry state. First time Ma's brought a baby when me, Billy, and Moses Smith weren't there to help.

Pa didn't make us work today, said I was to start my seventeenth year with a day of rest. Made me feel older somehow, but mostly restless. Funny, I thought as I got older, it'd be easier to sit and think on things, relax, maybe with a pipe or jug like Pa and Uncle. Maybe it's all the lying around I've had to do with the fevers—I ain't one to sit for too long in any fashion lately. Maybe this is the feeling that pushes a man to move on, try a new adventure.

Maybe when I'm rested enough, I'll go calling at the Wells' house tomorrow, just to be sociable.

WOWOKI HAD BEEN GONE FOR THREE MOONS now—a long time with no signs. I tried not to worry about him, tried instead to focus on the People and what I could do for them. One night, I dreamed of a river. The cliffs above this river were dense with trees. Eagles soared along the edges. The wolves howled in the night to celebrate their day's meal, and the numu kutsu covered the prairie like waves of water in the wind. Perhaps, this river would protect the Penatuka from the Taiboo. It would feed and clothe the people, and we'd be closer to the trading tribes we trusted.

I spoke to Muutsi of the dream first. She was eating a little better and had even done some ghost healing lately, but there was still little light in her eyes and she moved about the camp very slowly, often mumbling to herself. She would stand for hours on the nearest hill watching for her nephew. I told her the dream was warm and the river flowed happily along its path. I saw the People there.

We ate well and the children were safe.

Muutsi looked to where the sun rose and spoke quietly. "We have been in this camp long. When your brother returns perhaps." I tried to assure her that he would find us if we moved. He always does. I stood and stamped my foot to make my point. I would tell the leaders of my dream. The days are still hot and the grass still green, but within range of this camp, the numu kutsu are few. Instead, our hunting scouts had seen more bands of Taiboo men on horseback.

Muutsi's darkness returned. "Bah, they will not listen. They can't even get up to feed their horses." I was determined. "Good. Then they will have to listen when I speak, for according to you, they cannot run."

AUGUST 11. BOSQUE RIVER. WE'VE STOPPED again so I have time to write. River flooded most of the meadow ahead and the officers are looking for a way around. I'm not sure which is worse, the rain last night or the sun this afternoon, but I am tired of ridin' and not feeling too well. There's nowhere to sit or stand that ain't inches of mud, so we sit in our saddles. Our poor horses have the worst of it.

This summer has turned to a wet autumn. Most of the streams and rivers are over their banks. Most trails are sloppy wet. Snakes are regular, the mosquitoes vicious. The heat and wet air presses down on all the men. The hunt is slow and dull. It makes us cross with each other.

Our volunteer troop is only twelve men now. Half have given up after days of living in the mud and rain. One of us has drowned crossing a flooded stream. Some have become too sick to be of any fighting value. I'm close to that myself, if I'm honest. No one speaks of it, but many of these men, like me, have never been in a gunfight and ain't itching for it either.

This militia is bible-sworn-bound to find those that had killed Mr. Strother and Christian, scalped Josiah Wilbarger, and burned out old man Boucher. We are a hunting party, not for our supper, but for other men. The officers said they'd shoot any injun that put up a fight or the hint of one, even women and children. That talk made me nervous. So far, we've raided deserted Waco and Tawakoni villages, helped ourselves to stored food and buffalo hides, reclaimed a few head of cattle, but seen no Indians. It sure feels like they seen us first; there is nothing quiet in the way this army is operating.

One of the worse bits in all of this is one militia member particularly. As long as his brandy is near, the tobacco-chewing bear of a man, Jacques Boucher manages to stay committed to our group. He is constantly spewing his views on revenge and justice, but rarely does more than ride safely in the middle of our pack and whimper in his sleep, and he still smells like he ain't seen water in years. He darkens our nights around the fires too, telling the same old stories repeatedly. His favorite is, of course, his most recent tale of how he and his brother whipped fifty Comanch braves who'd made repeated attacks at his house. He drags a scalp out of his kit to prove it, but everyone knows it's cock-and-bull, that there was only one Indian and he was old, maybe blind. We'd also heard from Alonso that Boucher's brother had done most of the fighting while Jacques hid under a table in the cabin. Then they high-tailed it into town, slaves and all, for a full month before easing back out to his place to rebuild.

Billy joked that old man Boucher just as soon face a thousand screaming Comanch with us to do his fightin' as to meet one old, half-blind chief on his own. Ain't no way he's gonna quit this group and ride home alone 'less his thirst for spirits outweighs his fears. I'm starting to see Billy's jokes in a different light: man talk, plain and simple, with a touch of our uncle's humor.

Between the long rides and sleepless nights, I've been cleaning and oiling my rifle and my brother's and uncle's weapons too. Now, in the damp afternoon, the weapons are all wet again. I can feel the rust setting in, and the mosquitos are ready to carry us all off. Just today, I slapped at a mosquito biting the back of my neck. Uncle Moses-Smith eased his horse up beside my mare and said it looked like I got my first war wound on account of how full of blood that mozzie was. I wiped the back of my neck and stared at the blood on my fingers. It brought the butterflies back to my stomach.

Moses-Smith leaned a little closer and spoke low so the others wouldn't hear. "You figure there's injun blood in that? Might be a little coyote, a little black, a little of old man Boucher over there—which would be mostly spirits of course—and a pinch of Velasco gator, just for you my boy." I hadn't thought about that big gator for a long time. I answered that there could be Waco, Tawakoni, or Comanch blood in there. Moses-Smith sat back in his saddle, pointed to the fellows around us and said, "I wonder if mosquitoes fight over land like we do, Mal."

I lowered my voice and said I was asking the same question in my journal. I figured animals fight for their territory, but ain't we supposed to be above the animals? Ain't we meant to look after each other? Ain't that what Ma and the bible say? I figured instead of wading in this mud all day, we should be helping Pa out with the crops and that it's likely Ma is worried sick. Moses-Smith said a man ought to make up his own thoughts in somethin' such as this, and that my Ma and Pa know I'm a man now.

Billy rode up from scouting and reported to the Colonel that he'd found a way across about two hundred paces downstream. Guess we'll start again. Billy said something else too. He said they spotted at least one red devil mounted and riding slow due north. Cheers went up before Colonel Moore and his officers could stop the men from making noise and ruining any chance for a surprise attack.

Tarnation, we ain't soldiers of any substance.

OUR LEADERS WERE NOW ONLY OLDER warriors. Muutsi was right. They were very slow to move. Their wives were constantly bringing this and that to ensure their warmth and comfort. Their sons and daughters tended their horses for them. I knew they were meeting around the fire this night to talk of the People and our poor hunts.

I didn't plan on three of Wowoki's warrior friends being there too. They arrived after I had started my story and one of them cut me off. "Foolish woman, we do not need protection from the Taiboo. We do not move camp because they ride where we hunt. It is the other way. We will clear the earth of their smell."

He was tall, slim, and his face was long and narrow like a fox. His name was Tasiwóo because his legs dragged a bit when he walked. He never smiled. He was more sour even than Wowoki. It was no wonder they were friends. He said, "Why is there a girl here among warriors? Shouldn't she be caring for her brother's herd or healing the sick?"

Tasiwóo moved toward me, trying to frighten me with his stare. I did not look up. I spoke quietly, so quiet that the old men would not hear me. "You are not kaheeka. You do not have dreams. You do not see." Tasiwóo growled and moved closer, sticking out his chest and blowing his breath hard through his nose. "And you would have us leave your brother, our strongest warrior to follow a little girl's fearful dream?" I spoke louder, but still I kept my eyes to the fire. "One star is not the night sky. One warrior is not the People. We must do what is best for all. Wowoki would agree."

"Wowoki is not here to agree!" Tasiwóo had now moved to one pace from me. I could smell his breath when he spoke. He was so tall, I felt like a child beside him, but I was no longer a child. I stepped back from the fire and looked Tasiwóo in the eyes. At first I did not speak. I stared at his face as if looking for the ghost I was about to heal. Muutsi had taught me this: the ghost must know me, believe me, and even fear me. Then I spoke slowly, with purpose. "It is up to the elders. The People must eat. Our children must be safe. The river in my dream is only two or three suns away. We will camp there and the hunts will be good. And my brother will find us when he is ready."

Tasiwóo gritted his teeth and breathed deeply through his nose. He looked around at the elders and his fellow warriors. None returned his look. They knew I was right. This time, I was kaheeka just as my father had seen in his dream.

Still that night I could not sleep. All I could think of was my brother. Where was he? I decided then that I would find him before we moved camp.

AUGUST 12. KEECHI TERRITORY. I NEVER thought I could feel sadder than after losing Ottilee, but my head is all full of darkness and anger again.

After finally crossing the river yesterday, we drove our tired horses up and down the hills—in, out, and around the brush at a pace that made the animals suffer. We'd flushed Billy's young warrior on a big mustang with red spots painted on its flank. No one was sure of which tribe; no one seemed to care. The Indian disappeared into a dense thicket of oak, elbow-bush, and briars that grew around a wash between two hills. I don't know how he even got his horse in there, the brush was so tight.

Colonel Moore silently signaled to stop, dismount, and form a firing line in a circle around the thicket. William Mills, who'd lost his rifle in one of the rivers we crossed, led the horses back up the hill to tie them down. Boucher tried to go with him but Mills pushed him back toward us. We needed every man we had.

The Colonel signaled for the rest of us to leave hats and anythin' else that might snag. We was to ease into the thicket, guns primed and ready. Me and Moses-Smith moved forward. Billy stood behind and whispered, "Mal, let me go for you." I looked around at the other men, shook my head, and eased forward. Billy's voice softened a bit. "Bookweevil, you watch yourself in there. Ma will have my hide if I don't come home with you in one piece."

My uncle signaled for me to enter the thicket along a deer trail to our left and that he would enter straight ahead. I did my best to hold my rifle without it shaking. Every muscle in my body seemed to twitch. The bushes and briars were thick and prickly. I snagged my shirt and stopped to untangle. As I reached to pull my shirt loose, I saw a flash of movement ahead.

My heart pounded like it was trying to get out of my chest. I raised my rifle and cocked the hammer. I wanted to scan for danger but couldn't move the weapon more than a foot or two each side. I lowered the rifle and stared hard into the wall of dappled sunlit green. It was at that moment I heard the click of another rifle hammer, then a third. It was hard to tell exactly where the sounds were coming from.

A heavy boot snapped a twig, triggering the start of what sounded like the Fourth of July. Rifles fired from all around me in the thicket. The air was full of smoke and whizzing balls of lead that cut through the leaves and limbs beside me. I heard my uncle yell out, "Damn me, I'm shot!" so I pushed through the brush in that direction. I had to crouch and break through a snag of briars and brush. When I stood up, I was four paces from the warrior reloading his rifle. He looked to be Billy's age, had earrings of silver wire and wore leather bands around his upper arms. His face was fierce and painted white.

I raised my rifle, aimed at the warrior's chest, the gun barrel waving in circles, and then I fired. My lead just nicked his head, but I was so close that burned powder and wadding hit him in the face. He yelled at me and tried to rub the powder out of his eye, his head was bleeding something awful. He was plum crazy with the blindness. He raised his rifle to fire but was aiming all over. I was so shook all I could do was yell back. "Tarnation!"

The warrior stopped dead still. He strained to focus, like he was trying to recognize me or something. Then I heard my uncle. He must have been looking at the Indian from another angle. He yelled, "Mal, get out of there! Right here's the injun. He'll kill us both."

Meanwhile, the men we'd left in the circle around this clump of brush heard the shots and dodged stray projectiles. They saw the gun smoke but couldn't see us, worse yet, the Indian. Evidently, hearing Moses-Smith yell, Boucher slipped behind another man and grabbed his arm. "Shoot, yeh eejit, that's liable to be the Comanch."

Moses-Smith gave up on reloading his rifle and backed out of the brush the way he came in. Just as he broke free of the briars and into the open, Boucher pulled hard on the volunteer's arm again. His gun fired. The ball shattered Moses-Smith's right elbow on the same arm where he bore the earlier shoulder wound.

In a heartbeat, Billy was pulling Moses-Smith from the brush while desperately straining to see through the smoke and yell for me. "Malcolm Morrison Hornsby, where the hell are you! Are you shot? Mal? Damn it, answer me!"

I was afraid to answer, afraid to move. The Indian was still trying to focus on me but I noticed he hadn't raised his rifle. I took that for a chance and started backing out of the brush. I came crashing out of the brush and froze when I seen my uncle. Moses-Smith was pale and bleeding. His right arm a bloody mess, face twisted, and eyes pressed closed. I turned to my brother. Billy glanced up the hill in Boucher's direction and snarled. "Ask that sorry excuse for a man up there; he's in it somehow." I couldn't help but feel if I'd taken out that warrior, our Uncle would be fine. I searched Billy's eyes but he wouldn't look me straight.

The men gathered around us, forgetting about the Indian in the brush who must have taken the opportunity to slip away on foot—his mustang long gone with all the noise. The fight had lasted only minutes. We wrapped Moses-Smith's wounds as best we could, but his right arm was torn bad at the elbow and he'd lost a lot of blood. Infection, what they called the "green rot," would be on that arm in hours. Once it gets to his blood, he'll be dead in a day.

MUUTSI BEGGED ME NOT TO GO. I PROMISED only to ride as far as half a sun would take me each day, and then head back to camp before dark. I had seen a vision in my dreams. My brother was getting closer and closer to a great danger and I would find him before it could happen.

I wouldn't have to ride in all directions. I was sure that Wowoki would never head west, where the sun passed each day. I was sure he had ridden to face the Taiboo wherever they were, but that was still in three directions.

I would cover them all.

Each morning Muutsi packed food for me. On my third day as I was preparing to leave, Tasiwóo approached. He handed me his best rifle and offered any of his best horses for future rides. He would not look me in the eyes, but he spoke firmly, "Wʉkʉbuu, this hunt of yours cannot last a lifetime, we should move camp as soon as you say, but we will wait for your signal."

AUGUST 13. WE BUILT A TRAVOIS TO PULL Uncle behind Billy's horse and retraced our trail south for a mile or two before camping along a creek. It was now or never; to save our father's brother we'd have to take that arm right away, but Uncle would have nothin' of it. Covered in blood and dust from the trail, face all twisted with pain, he was hardly recognizable.

Billy tried to be firm. "Uncle, me and Mal be with you the whole of it. You aren't making any sense. Maybe that's the fever talking, but if Pa were here he'd say the same. You got to let the colonel take that arm before the rot set in." Uncle refused. He asked us how a man with one arm would do his farming or protect his family. He reminded us that he was still helping our pa send money to grandpa. Then I said words that felt strange to me, cold. "Man ought to make up his own thoughts in something like this. Don't you reckon?" Billy stared at me for a long time, as if he was studying a stranger, then he nodded his head.

We stayed up with our uncle through the whole night, kept the fire going, and gave him water. By next morning, the arm had turned for the worse. It was black all around the wound and smelled. Moses-Smith reached for my hand and motioned for Billy's. Our uncle's face was pale, ghost-like, his voice just above a whisper, but I heard him as if nature herself had quieted to listen. "Boys, well, you're men now. I've always been right proud of you both. I expect you to do right by your pa and ma. Stay out of trouble and look after the little ones, you hear?"

Billy pounded the dirt with his fist. "Uncle, we ain't given up on you. Mal, would you say something. You're the smart one." I squeezed my uncle's hand. Moses-Smith squeezed back. He looked me in the eyes like he was searching with his last bit of strength, then he asked me a question. "We've made a bold crossin' into this here country, ain't we, Malcolm?"

A last raspy breath slipped out of Moses-Smith. I felt his grip fall loose and watched his lips pale. Then I turned away so Billy wouldn't see me crying and tried to keep my voice calm. "What'll we tell Pa, Billy? It ain't right for a man to die out here so far from family. I should have shot that Indian clear through. This is on me, plain seeing."

Billy didn't push, didn't let on that he knew I was crying. "Mal, Pa will understand that we couldn't bring him home. Our uncle has gone to be with our baby brothers, God bless 'em. I'll do the talking back home if it helps you feel better about it."

Colonel Moore did two things for us Hornsby boys. He sent Boucher home right away with another volunteer—mostly to save Boucher from us—and he prepared our uncle's body for burial. He placed a coin over each of Moses-Smith's eyes, tied a cloth around the dead man's jaw, and carefully folded his arms across his chest. Other militia members helped him wrap Moses-Smith in his own blanket, but before they did, I slipped my clock gear into the watch pocket of his trousers.

Don't seem to be much good luck in it anymore.

We buried our uncle facing east as Ma would have insisted and covered the grave in hundreds of smooth round stones from the river to keep the bears and coyotes from digging at it. As the Colonel tapped a little wooden cross into the ground at the head of the grave, all the other men in the militia stepped away. I stared at the cross and then asked Billy for a favor, one of our uncle's jokes.

Billy obliged.

"A father going into his barn one day found his son with a slate and pencil in his hand, sitting in the saddle on his horse. 'Why son, what are you doin'?' 'Writing a comp-o-sition, Pa.' the boy replied. 'Well, why don't you write it in the house?' 'Cause, the master told me to write my comp-o-sition on a horse.'"

I RODE WITH TASIWÓO'S RIFLE STRAPPED across my back, nearly blinded by the sun as it rose before me. There was a thin trail of smoke ahead but as I got closer, it disappeared as if someone had quickly extinguished a campfire. Only Taiboo would be so careless.

To stay out of sight, I tried to circle where the fire had been. It might be good to trail the Taiboo. Perhaps Wowoki would be near, looking for a chance to attack. However, without knowing their intended direction, I was just guessing and I guessed wrong.

Luckily, it was a rocky terrain. I heard the white men's horses and their metal shoes on the rocks before they saw me. I dismounted, tied my horse among some brush and eased up a small hill for a look. They were at the bottom of the very same hill, two Taiboo, and one of them had a familiar and terrible smell. They looked a little lost. Each was gesturing with his hands, as if he knew which way to go, only they weren't the same directions.

I could barely breathe. My heart pounded. My stomach twisted. I wanted to run as far and as fast as possible or ease a little higher and shoot that terrible bear of a Taiboo, but I had to stay still and perfectly quiet. If I missed, they would outnumber me and from very close. I would not live to find my brother.

Then I thought what if they climbed my hill to see their trail better? They argued for what seemed like an eternity, then the other man got off his horse and started up toward me on foot. I had no choice, noise or not, I had to run. I scrambled down to my horse and untied him. As I jumped on his back, the man on the hill yelled and took a shot at me from on top of the hill as I rode hard in the other direction.

I don't think Boucher ever knew it was me. I should have stayed there and killed him, but finding my brother had to come first.

I rode hard all the way back to camp, not as much to avoid the bullets, but to get as far away from that smelly Taiboo and the memories as possible. I was sure to ride a crooked path to keep the Taiboo from following, but I didn't slow much. I needed to be in the camp, with those familiar to me, warm and safe.

AUGUST 16. PA HASN'T SAID MORE THAN A handful of words for three days. He won't hold the baby. He walks around the place like a ghost. Yesterday, Ma had arranged for a circuit preacher to perform Uncle's wake but he showed up at the cabin smelling of drink. In front of all the guests, Ma sent him off with a few choice words and no pay. It was just as well, Ma conducted the service and spoke from her heart in the prayer when she said:

> *"Lord, we are not perfect Christians. You have made us of your clay and have great hope for us all, but far too often, we fail to heed your teachings. Our brother, Moses-Smith, however, was of a purer cloth than most. His heart was his guide, his love for his family his compass. He was devoted to his brother and to his brother's children. May he rest in peace and in our hearts for all eternity. Amen."*

After the meal, as neighbors and friends began to leave, Billy and me quietly slipped pieces of molasses candy into the hands of the younger children. Ma watched and smiled through her tears. Pa didn't notice. Losing his brother wasn't all that was weighing on Pa's mind. Ma was the one who had to tell us. Pa had accepted a good offer on selling Tom to a man who was just getting his farm started east of Bastrop. He'd been considering the offer for three weeks now, mostly while we's away with the militia. He didn't have the heart to tell me 'bout it, but I figured when I seen all of Tom's things gone from his cabin. The harsh words, my last words really, that I'd had with my old friend stuck in my throat like dry bread.

I couldn't get my head around it—losin' my uncle and one of my best friends—all in the blink of an eye. This morning, I tried walking the worry off, but that just made me tired from my cough. I could feel the anger building. It seems anger and hurt is all the Hornsby men have to hang on to just now. We's all heated up inside one way or another. I wonder how long before the pot boils clean over.

Alonso and his ma were here for the wake and he spent some time with me after. I told him I was full of everything dark. He said I'd seen my share of loss long before I was due and that in the end it would make me stronger, make me a better husband, father, and friend. I asked him how he figured that. He put his hand on my shoulder and said when a man comes to understand life through losing, he can chose one of two paths—anger and resentment or care in knowing life is a blessing—and Alonso figured I was leaning more on the care side.

I'm not sure about that.

All I wanted to do was break something, hit something or someone, or run until I couldn't stand. I figure Pa's blood is boiling too. When he talks, all he talks about is getting back at old man Boucher.

It's all spinning in my head, that injun, the blood, uncle's face, Boucher. I started working the hay in the barn like a mad man this morning, but the dust and my cough got the worst of me. I was hanging on to a post trying to catch my breath when Miss Mattie came into the barn with a cup of tea. She didn't say a word at first, just handed me the warm cup.

Then, she said words I'll never forget. "Malcolm Hornsby, I have raised you since you were a pup. I know Tom was like another brother for you, maybe a better brother. We live in a time when lives can be short and the loss of a friend can happen in a single minute, but your Tom ain't lost, not like your uncle, God rest his soul. I know things been rough between ya. That's just what growing up black and white do to your hearts once you're grown. Tom is still your brother and he's just down the road a bit. Maybe he'd appreciate a visit, and maybe he'd prefer to hear the news of your uncle from you. You make that trip, Malcolm. Get your head and your heart straight. Then it's time you started a new chapter in your life."

Sounded like good advice, so I rode down the road a bit through town to Tom's farm. He was out in the field in the sun working with the other Blacks. I watched from a distance for quite a long time. Tom never saw me. Them men never spoke to one another, they never stopped to look at the clouds or blue sky, never stopped to eat or drink a little; they just worked, with their heads down and in the shadow of the foreman up on his horse above them, watching as if on his throne.

Then I noticed my shadow on the ground below me, same as that foreman's, same as every white foreman across this country up on his high horse. I shivered at the sight.

I never want to be a slave

I never want to own a slave.

Reckon I ain't man enough for it.

WHEN WE MOVED CAMPS, IT WAS USUALLY toward places we knew, places the People had been before, or near them. This move was different. We were going farther from the great clear river than we had ever gone. We knew that groups of Taiboo men with their guns and dogs were everywhere. We divided into three groups to keep our tracks more difficult to follow. The rains helped as well. It seemed to work. We had very little trouble in our journey north. After three suns, we rejoined and chose a place to set camp.

The new camp on the river the Taiboo called Blanco was not complete when the news came from our hunting parties: the nɨmɨ kutsu were more plentiful here. We had made a good decision. The hunting season should be fruitful. Still, I could not help but worry about my brother. If he was alive, he would find us, but what if his anger had gotten him killed?

Muutsi and I were in our teepee and had not greeted the new sun when Dog barked. It was not just any bark. I listened closely. He barked again. Could it be? I tore open our flap and Wowoki collapsed at my feet.

He was a mess, scratched from head to toe. He had a wound on his head that reached to the bone and there was swelling. One of his eyes was so badly swollen he could not open it. It looked beyond the help of any medicine. He was hot to the touch and shivered with chill. We had no idea how far he had walked or ran; his feet cut so badly that he could barely let us clean them.

For days, he slept, talking and yelling in his dreams, always with anger or alarm. In the mornings, we slowly forced broth into his mouth. At one point, the pain in his head was so bad that Muutsi had me tie his hands and feet to stakes to keep him from clawing at his wounds.

The elders came, sang warrior songs, passed the pipe, waved the smoke over Wowoki, and then left. The young warriors came. Tasiwóo came too, though he did not speak. I tried to return his rifle. He shook his head and pushed it back at me. It was his sign.

The visitors only stayed a short time, each touching Wowoki's arm as he left. Pukutsi visited often. She would sing to Wowoki and rub his head with the medicine we gave her. Sometimes, she would fall asleep sitting beside him.

Muutsi too sat beside Wowoki and sang or waved the sage smoke for most of the day. She would shake her head and mumble about the Taiboo or speak directly to her nephew as if he could hear her. "You are no good as a warrior with all this sleep. You must wake. Your horses are with us, but they need their master. Your weapons are with us, but they need repair and to be made ready. The young women of the People are with us, but they need a warrior to hunt for them and give them children. Your sister and paha take care of the People, but these other things we cannot do."

Wowoki did not wake. His fever grew worse. I washed him with a cold wet cloth every few minutes.

I was losing hope.

OCTOBER 27. HARD TO WRITE. HANDS STILL shaking. Town folk said what I did took a grown man's courage. Maybe. And maybe a grown man doesn't need to write all this down no more. Mattie said I needed to start a new chapter in my life after all my losses.

Reckon I've started.

We rose early to be in Bastrop for the council meeting. A letter had come from Colonel Austin to Mr. Sam Williams. The colonel's words from his Mexican prison cell were dark and without hope for his release. The talk of a revolt was growing. The council was meeting to choose representatives. Pa said he even heard a few touched folks was talking of storming the prison in Mexico City.

The big smoky room stunk of men. Every man of fighting age from around these parts packed into the town council house to argue two things: Mexico and Comanche. My cough was something awful, but I wouldn't have missed this for the world.

As was the custom, especially when there was drinking and politicking, everyone was meant to leave their pistols and rifles on a table near the door. Some didn't follow that rule.

Shortly after we arrived, Jacques Boucher took to the speakers' box in the middle. The minute he stood to speak, me and Billy turned to leave, but Pa grabbed us both and with a firm look and said, "Hear him out boys. Maybe he'll give us more reason to shoot him." Pa patted his coat pocket and I seen the lump of his gun. I'd never know my pa to skirt local rules like this. It didn't set well with me. I could see worry in Billy's face.

Boucher spit on the floor and bellowed at the crowd about how the Mexicans weren't the problem. He said the Comanche are like horseflies. Brush them off one side of the horse, they settle on the other. He said, "If we just get rid of dem Comanch, our lands would increase in value tenfold. Take Hornsby for example. Reuben Hornsby, you der?" The room went quiet. Everyone knew about the death of our uncle and the circumstances. The crowd nervously shuffled to make space for my pa to answer the speaker, face to face.

Boucher went on. "Reuben Hornsby wit yer lots in Bastrop, dat in de bend, and now yeh poor brother's land, ain't a bank in Louisiana would turn ya'll down fer a loan on ten times de value. Am I right? Heck, yeh could sell off yeh brother's land and make fine profit. We just gotta clear out dem injuns."

Billy noticed first: Pa had reached for his small pistol. I looked at Pa's face. It was fiery red. Billy grabbed Pa's right arm, I grabbed his left. The words exploded out of Pa as he leaned forward fighting against us. "Well if that don't take the biscuit. Damn you, Jacques Boucher! He was the finest man I ever knew. I ain't making money off my little brother being in the grave, you son-of-a-dog, but I'm gonna send you to hell for sayin' it."

Some of the other men stepped in front of Pa to help hold him back. Billy grabbed Pa's gun, twisted it loose real quick, and handed it to me. I stuck it in my back pocket as far from Pa's reach as I could find.

With each word, Pa's volume grew. He spit the words out as if they was the bullets he intended for Boucher. "He wouldn't be dead no how if it weren't for your cowardliness, and everyone in this country knows that to be the truth. My boys saved your mangy hide out in that prairie!" Pa paused, as if the boiling had reached its peak. He rose up on his toes to look Boucher in the eyes and slowly thundered one more threat. "I'm gonna fix your flint, mister!"

I felt the heat in my face as I held my pa back. It was upsetting to see him so out of sorts. Boucher stepped off the box and moved toward us, his voice shaking. "God rest his soul, Reuben Hornsby. God rest yeh brother's soul, but we all know dat hunting injuns is dangerous. I just doing my part. Maybe if yeh boy der killed dat injun instead of shootin' up de trees, we'd be celebrating wit de Moses-Smith rather dan puttin' him in de ground."

Pa broke from our hold. He was like a wildcat and no one could have stopped him.

MUUTSI WAS READY TO PUSH A KNIFE INTO Wowoki's head to relieve the pressure. It was risky but she was sure we would lose him if we did not. She heated the knife and brought it close to my brother's head. Wowoki surprised us both by grabbing Muutsi's arm before she could make the cut. Then, after days of nonsense, he finally spoke words we understood. "Paha, you will kill me with your old eyes. Give it to Wukʉbuu." Muutsi fell back with a gasp and a smile. "I was only saving you from your sister. She stays mad a long time."

My brother mended slowly, too slowly. His wounds would not close, even with all the medicine we knew. He was so weak we had to feed him every meal and bathe his body each day. Still he tried to be a warrior, a leader. He would ask me about the hunt. I told him we would eat well this cold season and there would be plenty of blankets. He surprised me by saying my blankets were the best, but then he tried to stand, saying the People will not have them this season unless he hunted. He could not stand.

He said he heard I had urged the elders to move the camp. I tried to apologize for making it harder for his return, but he cut me off and said it was the right decision. Then I asked him what he, an obvious imposter, had done with my brother.

Wowoki said, "You are a warrior in your way, sister, and kaheeka. Father saw this." I hushed him. He should not have spoken of our father. He hushed me back. "Huutsúu Kwanaru, you know that I am not afraid of ghosts." I squeezed his arm. "You will be afraid of me if you call me stinky bird again. Brother, if you are well enough to insult your host, you are well enough to sleep in your own teepee with your wife and get your own meals."

He laughed a little and confessed, "My mistake, Wɨkɨbuu."

IN TWO STEPS, PA WAS FACING A SURPRISED Boucher. He hit the big man in the nose with his right fist, causing blood to fly, then followed with a punch to Boucher's gut with his left. Bent over by the punch, the big man grabbed his long knife from his boot.

Pa didn't see the knife through his fury. He lunged at Boucher to take him down, but the man was so big he just stepped back and raised the knife into the air with Pa hanging on.

I seen Pa was about to get the worse of it. That's when I fired his pistol. The bullet caught Boucher right below his chin. He dropped the knife and grabbed his neck. Pa dropped his hold and rested on his knees as the big man staggered backwards trying to catch his breath. His eyes rolled a bit and he collapsed over the speaker's box.

I don't even remember aiming the gun.

Billy and Pa pushed me out the door quick. I threw up and coughed my fool head off outside on the steps to the council house. It felt like I was going to be sick to my stomach for the rest of my life. Billy tried to talk me through. "Mal, you had to do it. It was him or Pa. You did the right thing. It's just the first time. I hear it can be hard for every man to take another life. Ma's gonna read you the commandments, I'm sure of that, but she will be thankful to ya for saving Pa's hide."

I couldn't get the blood out of my mind. Eyes open or closed, I could still see Boucher's ashen face. His eyes rolling back his head and the noises he was making trying to catch his breath. They were horrible noises. He was a horrible sight.

I'll never forget it, never.

OUR LIVES, OUR LONG PATHS, MOVE IN BIG
circles. Yes, we travel across the land to hunt. We walk across
our teepees to be nearer the fire or a loved one. We ride our
horses to cross a river, but the longer paths of our lives stay the
same. We are born, we live—with one family or, if adopted,
with another—we take care of our People, and we die.

Wowoki was improving. He had carved me a new
charm, a full-grown buffalo bull with a scar on his face. He had
moved back into his own teepee with Pukutsi, was spending
more time with his horses, and had even tried to ride a bit. His
life was moving into its autumn cycle. Muutsi seemed to miss
taking care of him but something else had changed for her. She
slept past the sunrise, ate very little, and rarely spoke to
anyone, even me. Except for Wowoki, of course. She pestered
him like a fly. So much so, he often hid from her.

She was also upset that the elders had been spending
more time trading with another band of the People, the Nokoni,
the wanderers. They had welcomed us to the area, for they too
had lost many members to disease and war with the Taiboo.
Our bands were spending more time together. Women and men
from both sides were talking, testing, wondering—it was the
long path, the circle.

HEADING HOME FROM THAT FATEFUL DAY IN
Bastrop last week, me and Billy rode behind Pa. I still felt
awfully sick like. Shooting Boucher had taken all the salt out of
me. Sure didn't make me feel any more a man.

It was mostly quiet 'til Billy couldn't stand it no more.
He asked Pa, what if the Mexican army did invade and there's
war? Pa thought on it awhile then answered. "Well, I'll tell
you, son. I don't care if I farm under the Mexican, Texian, or
American flag as long as I'm free to keep my family safe and
sound. Leavin' the farm for a fight I didn't ask for, well, it
don't sound safe to me, but you're a man." He turned to look

me straight in the eyes. "You're both men now. You have to make up your own minds, you hear? Still, I reckon the eligible young girls around these parts would miss you both somethin' terrible."

Billy had to be a wise butt and joke. "It's the hogs that would miss Malcolm, Pa."

I tried to smile but couldn't get the darkness out of my head and my cough was plaguing me. Pa pulled on the reins to slow his horse and slip between us. He stretched and reached toward each of us with his hands. We took Pa's hands in ours as he spoke. "I do miss your uncle, boys. I miss him something fierce, but I still have you. There's a bit of his humor, goodness, and good sense in the both of you. You're men now. Make up your own minds on things, you hear? There is likely two wars coming, sooner or later."

I frowned and shook my head, wishing his words away, wishing that day away. It didn't work. "Pa, seems the Comanche and them politicians in Mexico are like two gates to hell and we're stuck betwixt 'em like dry prairie grass in a lightning storm." Pa looked me square in the eye and smiled sort of sad like.

I told Pa that people make a plague of this place. Machines don't cause such a stir. The iron and steel, the pulleys and gears, they just go about their tasks, needing oil sometimes, maybe adjustments or repairs. That's why I want to work with machines. I don't want to shoot another soul, ever.

Pa just nodded. I could see he was thinking it all over for himself.

MUUTSI WANTED NOTHING OF THE NOKONI. She would not say why, but she would spit and grunt anytime their names came up. Most days, if I didn't bring her back, she would sit in one place on a large rock and watch the river all day long. I would have to beg her or drag her back to camp. I would tell her that she could not sit in the sun and wind for so long with no water or food. She would tell me to "stop bothering the dead, child." Then I would ask her, if she was dead, how was it that I held her arm and lifted her to walk? She would answer, "My ghost is not ready."

I would plead with her. "I am still learning the ways, the medicines you have not shared. Who will look after my brother? I will not. It was enough that I had to mother him for so long already." She did not answer. She tried to pull from my grasp but was so weak it was of no use. I would not leave her out there—it was getting dark and there were plenty of wolves and mountain lions to take her and leave us only the ghost she was promising.

Before long, the leaves of many trees along this new river turned a bright red in the yubani season. The hunt was more difficult, the game more hidden. The winds blew harder from the north and it grew colder. She would struggle against me, but I would make sure to wrap Muutsi warmly for her daily river watch. There was talk of moving camp for the winter, perhaps even combining camps with the Nokoni. Each time she heard this talk, Muutsi spit until her mouth was dry.

One morning the wind pushed hard against our teepee. The cold air came through the flap and the smoke hole. I woke before Muutsi and hoped that she'd not want to go out. I kept the fire low and made sure I moved about quietly but I could not stay inside all morning. I had work to do. The elders of our band and the Nokoni had decided to move down the river a short distance to a site better suited for a winter camp. I had to prepare our food stores and help others do the same. We would need the berries, roots, and plants that the coldest season would hide from us.

When I returned to the teepee later that day, Muutsi was gone. I went to the rock where she would sit and watch her river. She was not there but her boots and blanket were. I ran back to the camp for my brother. Wowoki and Pukutsi helped me track our father's sister. With bare feet, she had walked upstream along the edge of the river, away from our camp. She had walked a great distance for one so old.

We found her floating face down in a quiet pool at the edge of the water. The People do not swim. She had walked herself to exhaustion then stepped into the cold deep water to find her ghost, to finish her circle. Wowoki, Pukutsi, and I burned our Paha's belongings. We sang the death songs and buried her beside the river near the large rock. The next day, we moved camp with the strangers.

Our world was turning upside down.

IT TOOK TWO HOURS FOR US TO GET HOME afterwards. Billy and me brushed, watered, and fed the horses. While we was at it, I asked Billy if he reckoned there'd be a Mexican judge coming for me. He said likely not. He said that half the territory seen me saving Pa's life and ain't nobody gonna miss that smelly Frenchman.

That's when I had another coughing fit. When I spit, I seen the blood spots in the dirt. Billy seen it too. He grabbed my arm, not hard, not to wrestle, but firm and said, "Mal, we need you here. You ain't thinkin' of goin' off to no war with the Mexicans is you? Besides, that cough ain't getting no better unless you rest a bit." I put my hand on his shoulder and said, "I ain't going nowhere, brother, 'cept to gather some daisies for Ma. I reckon it will help settle her nerves."

Billy didn't let go. He held on tighter and said, "You done a man's job in Bastrop, brother, and I'm right proud." Then he slipped in what was really on his mind. "Ma know you're bleeding inside?" I didn't want to answer, didn't want to think on it. I told him that I thought Ma worries enough over all of us.

I slipped out of the barn and walked down the trail pulling flowers along the way. Each wave of coughing made my chest hurt, but I had a job to do. As the sun settled pink and purple behind me, I found myself at two twisted oaks. They was standing at attention as if guarding their post. I forced my way through the thick brush beneath the oaks and discovered a mound of white stones on top of a rocky crevice in the hillside. Grass and wildflowers was pushing up between them. Someone had buried a loved one there, I was sure of it.

I took off my hat and tried to settle a cough. I apologized for disturbing the poor soul resting there, then set mom's flowers between two rocks and said some words to make it better. In one of my ma's books, there's sort of a poem. Ma calls 'em sonnets. Can't remember it all, but it goes something like this.

> *"In me thou see the twilight of such a day,*
>
> *After that sunset fades in the west;*
>
> *Which by and by black night take away,*
>
> *Death's second self, that seals us up in a rest."*

Maybe I'll have that carved in my stone when I go. I thought back on my uncle and his last words about bold crossings. I figure, just like Moses-Smith, I've made my bold crossing now. This cough, this country, and all the blood and loosin' side of it, has worn me thin.

WOWOKI RODE NEXT TO ME AS WE TRACED the river's path to the new camp. Only once during the quiet ride did he speak. He said, "Our ghosts are not ready, sister. The people will grow strong again, and you and I will lead them or die trying. What do you see, Wʉkʉbuu? What is our path?"

I did not speak right away. I took my time just as my father had taught me. Then I spoke.

"There is a story of a strong warrior among the People long ago. He was separated from his band as they traveled from the mountains to our grasslands. The warrior had injured his leg as he ran on a hunt and could not hope to catch his people as they pulled their camp behind the strongest women and dogs. Every day he would crawl down to the river for a drink and nourishment, and every day the river would say to him, 'Friend, why are you so sad?'

"The warrior would stay with the river and talk all day of everything he loved in his people, of how he hoped one day to lead them down their path. When he finally grew strong enough to leave, the warrior visited the river for what he thought was the last time. The river asked, 'You are stronger, but why are you still so sad?' The warrior explained that he could never hope to catch his people; they would be too far now, and he would never see them again, never become their leader.

"The river knew better. 'Friend, there are logs here wide enough for you to ride on my back. Take one and catch your people.' The warrior did as the river suggested. He laid on a wide log and rode on the river's back, but the journey was long. Soon the warrior grew tired and fell asleep on the log. When he woke, the river was gone and he now rode on the back of a big powerful animal that he had never seen before. It was a horse and he spoke to the warrior with the voice of the river. 'Friend, your people are just ahead, and if you take me into your band, we will show them the path together.' This is your long path, your circle."

Wowoki did not respond to the story for some time, not even with a grunt or a nod. He was quiet for so long that I worried. "Brother, has my story offended you in some way?" He spoke quietly, as if to a sleeping loved one. "No sister, I am speaking quietly now to the river myself and he is telling me to keep good council with a small but wise little bird, and that she will show us all the long path."

I guided my horse to ride nearer my brother. I reached for his hand. He squeezed my fingers and let go. He lifted his head and yelled to the sky in celebration, then kicked his horse just a little and galloped ahead, laughing and daring me to follow.

* * *

This was the last recorded story that Wʉkubʉu (Doris Parker) shared with Anthropology Professor, Harrison J. Stiles, in 1919. He traveled to Lawton whenever he could to capture her voice on dozens of phonograph cylinders. These were then carefully, laboriously transferred to tape decades later. Wʉkubʉu died shortly after this final recording with the professor, her exact age still a mystery, but estimated at somewhere near 105 years.

EPILOGUE

At Peace in the Bend

William Hornsby, in his rough handwriting made this last entry in his brother's journal, dated December 24, 1840.

* * *

Dear Malcolm, my brother, I'm writing in your book-o'-pages. Hope you don't mind.

Today, as soon as Ma returned to our farm, she and me walked to see you. She fell to her knees at the fresh mound of dirt and new limestone marker. I thought she might pray 'till dark, but she let up and we headed back to the house, with her full of questions.

She asked me again if folks turned out for the service. She asked about the new preacher. She asked if you was in much pain. I told her a whole bushel of neighbors attended the service from all around. That the new preacher came out with plenty more from town. That the Wilbargers stayed over for a couple of days to see that we's all right. Then I told her what you said, brother, about reading and you liking my whistle playing, but that I was sure that was your fever talking.

Ma stopped and held on to my shoulder for support. She said, "Thank you, William. I'm sure that if Malcolm said he fancied your playing he was sincere." So you know what I did, little brother? I walked back down the hill, slipped my penny whistle out of my coat pocket, and set it on top of your stone.

Rest in peace, Bookweevil. We will not forget you. I promise that my first-born son will carry your name.

Hope that suits you.

*　*　*

Folded neatly in the back of Malcolm's journal was this letter...

*　*　*

December 7, 1840

Dearest Mother,

I trust that you, Joe, and Miss Mattie are safe with our kin in Mississippi. We have missed you all here. It is with the heaviest of hearts that I write to you with news that will certainly unsettle. Pa has asked me to tell you that on this day, our dear brother, Malcolm Morrison Hornsby, has died from winter fever here in the Bastrop infirmary. He fought well, bravely, but the seasoning with which he has struggled for some years now did not leave him the strength to win the battle. Pa instructed that he be buried near Messrs. Haggert and Williams and is hopeful that you approve. Please be assured that we will say the prayers and prepare Malcolm, as you would have wished. Mother, in his final days, Mal faded in and out of knowing where he was and who was among him, but before that he shared these words: "I ain't gonna know the love of a wife and my own children, but I have known the love of my family and the pride of beginning this adventure we call Texas."

Respectfully your son,

William Watts Hornsby

* * *

Malcolm Morrison Hornsby—1841-1892, first born son of William "Billy" Watts Hornsby, pictured here with his son James, and named after his late uncle, Malcolm…just as his father had promised.

ACKNOWLEDGEMENTS

This book is a piece of fiction but based on the history of individuals and families that helped shape the kingdom of Tejas, the state of Texas, and the southwestern United States in the early 19th century. Plainly said, these protagonists came from different geographies, races, creeds, and principles with many disparate motivations. They saw the world they lived in, they viewed Texas and their place in it, from drastically different points of view. Nevertheless, I intended that the story illustrate just how humanly alike they truly were, and how difficult and challenging life was for all people who populated this vast expanse in those early days.

Yes, we have photos and little written snippets of insight into their actions, their behaviors, and beliefs, but without our imaginations to complete them as whole people, the story would be little more than a sketch and I fear, much less memorable. Just as importantly, without the historical experts and sources mentioned below, the foundation of the story, the canvas, would have started torn and tattered. Thank you to everyone who helped me create as full and rich a painting as possible.

Thank you from the Osborne's to the Hornsby's, especially the family of Lonnie and Rosemary, for both the decades of friendship that you shared with our parents and for regularly sharing the narrative of your family's part in Central Texas history. The friendship was priceless; the history, a seed that perhaps will now bloom for young Americans for decades to come.

Thank you to Dorothy Lacey Landoll, a friend and devoted soldier for her family name and history—and to her sisters at the Daughters of the Republic of Texas - Reuben Hornsby Chapter, for the family history so painstakingly pieced together in the Hornsby Tapestry. I can never repay you for all your patience as a new novelist found his way down the river of fiction, plot, and character to the sea-of-great-respect he found for his subject.

Thank you to several authors of scholarly work regarding the Comanche in early Texas and the surrounding territories: Pekka Hämäläinen for *Comanche Empire*, S. C. Gwynne for *Empire of the Summer Moon*, and Scott Zesch for *The Captured*.

Thank you to Lila Wistrand Robinson and James Armagost for their *Comanche Dictionary and Grammar*, and to my friends at the Comanche Language and Cultural Preservation Committee (CLCPC) in Elgin, Oklahoma for checking my Comanche and teaching me the correct pronunciations—my jaw is still sore from practicing.

When we first leave on a journey, we often have no idea who we will meet and how they might affect the rest of our lives. On this journey, I found a sister that I never knew I had. She was Comanche, smart, funny, passionate and loving. She gave me support as an artist, helped me understand Comanche history and culture, and took me into her family. My love and my gratitude always to my late Penatɨka sister, Juanita Pahdopony. Plus a big thanks to Lee Francis IV, owner and CEO of Native Realities, for introducing us.

Thank you to Stephen L. Hardin for his clear, calm, and detailed assessment of the Texas revolution in *Texian Iliad*; to Jack Gregory and Rennard Strickland for their scholarly work, *Sam Houston with the Cherokees, 1829-1833*; and thank you to Dr. Gregg Cantrell for his *Stephen F. Austin: Empresario of Texas*, a balanced view of one of the patriarchs of our grand state.

Thank you to Edwin Tunis for writing and illustrating an exceptionally fun book, *Frontier Living* and in the same vein, thank you to Jack Larkin for *The Reshaping of Everyday Life 1790-1840*, an invaluable reference. If you want to learn more about the weapons and tools of this period, go no further than the late Carl P. Russell's fascinating *Firearms, Traps and Tools of the Mountain Men*.

Thank you to these slavery scholars that dared to travel and share often overlooked paths to more accurate pictures of our African heritage, culture and customs, especially John W. Blassingame for *The Slavery Community, Plantation Life in the Antebellum South* and The American Anthropological Association who included *Survivors from the Cargo of the Negro Slave Yacht Wanderer*, by Charles J. Montgomery in their 1908 omnibus, *American Anthropologist.*

Steamboat travel was more than what we saw in old movies. It was both wonderful and terrifying to those who depended on it. For details, I depended on *Steamboats on the Western Rivers an Economic and Technological History* by Louis C. Hunter.

What was New Orleans like in 1830? It was a dynamic time for the crescent city. Snapshots of the day come to us through various sources, but the most telling are those stories that cling to the city's buildings themselves. For this, we have Edith Elliott Long and Rolland Golden's *Along the Banquette* and the folks from the Friends of the Cabildo, 1850 House Museum Store to thank.

Also, in New Orleans, goes my gratitude to James H. Cohen and Sons for help with the antique weapons. Who knew a Kentucky rifle was so barrel heavy? And, if you want some historical education and fun, visit the LSU's Rural Life Museum up river in Baton Rouge, and say hello to Buck the ox (he loves a good rub between the ears.)

Thank you to the smiling, helpful folks at the Austin History Center, the Eugene C. Barker Texas History Collection—a division of the Center for American History at the University of Texas at Austin, and the staff at the Laura Bush branch of the Westbank Community Library.

Thank you to our eternal friends, the faculty and staff at Valley View Elementary, Eanes I.S.D. in Austin for begging and pleading for "more stories of Texas history." Sometimes, a man whose art has bloomed from global historical travels just needs to hear, "welcome home, son.'

It is nearly impossible to imagine the Texas, Mississippi, and Louisiana geography in the early to mid-1800s based on what we see today through the windshield of our cars. So much has changed. To help us stay oriented in the era, we relied on the work of cartographers and map publishers from the day. These artists have long ago passed from this earth, but their work and its value will infinitely reprove itself.

Thank you to Marshall Lardon, an old wise soul in a young man's body, who did such a fine job copywriting and making suggestions for improving an early manuscript. And thanks to Joe Blanda, my dear friend from days long past, for your incredibly kind words of encouragement and the most perfect edits to this latest version.

Thank you to cover designer and original artist, Steve Willgren, native Texan, musician, graphic designer, and dear friend.

For you educators who are using this book to help young Texans understand the diverse reality of our state history with less of the fanfare and more of the true grit, please join me in thanking my niece, Erica B. Hutchison—elementary school teacher, mother, and always in my corner—for her expert help with the teacher's guide.

Finally, I send all my love, devotion and gratitude to Katherine, Ian, Cali, Sabrina, Olivia and Aiden for believing in my art and me, even when I had my doubts.

Lance Elliot Osborne

* * *

The cover art, Lone Buffalo, and the cover design are by Steve Willgren, born in Houston and raised in Austin, Steve attended the University of Texas and received a BFA in Fine Art in 1981. Afterward, Steve worked as an art teacher while continuing to paint and exhibit his work in small art festivals around central Texas. He took decades off to earn a living as a graphic designer, and now has returned to enlivening the canvas with color. Southwestern artists, John Nieto and Jeff Ham's dynamic style and bold colors are big influences. See all of his work and purchase prints at: http://www.stevewillgren.com.

Vintage compass illustration by Jenny at BackLaneArtist (www.Etsy.com)

GLOSSARY OF TRANSLATIONS

Comanche Words and Phrases

1. Ahpʉ – Father
2. Ekapo – Mescal bean from Mountain Laurel
3. Huuna – Badger
4. Huutsúu Kwanaru – Stinky bird
5. Kaheeka – Leader
6. Kohtoo wapi – Fire builder
7. Kooipʉ – Dead people
8. Kʉtseena – Coyote
9. Kwaharu – Comanche band, the antelope people
10. Kwasinaboo - Snake
11. Kwihne – Winter
12. Kwitapu – Feces
13. Marʉa – Herd

14. Nokoni – Comanche band, the wanderers
15. Nakuyaarʉ – Grass fire
16. Namʉsohitʉ – Hurry
17. Naseeka – Persimmon
18. Nʉmʉ kutsu – Buffalo, bison
19. Nʉmʉ tenahpʉ – Comanche man
20. Nʉmʉnʉʉ – Comanche
21. Paha – Aunt
22. Pahabitu – Bathe
23. Paaka and eetʉ – Bow and arrow
24. Pitsaka – travois for dragging loads over land
25. Penatʉka – Comanche band, the honey eaters, quick striking
26. Pia – Mother
27. Pitsi – Breasts
28. Sʉhʉ mupitsi – Screech owl
29. Taiboo – White person
30. Taka – Brother
31. Tami – Little brother
32. Tahmaroi – Spring
33. Tsihabukatu – Menstrual
34. Tuibitsi – Handsome
35. Tʉkʉ ahwerʉ – Edible roots
36. Tʉmakupa – Mountain lion
37. Yubani – Autumn
38. Wasápe – Bear
39. Wowoki – Barking dog
40. Wukubuu – Hummingbird
41. Wutui – Wait

Spanish Words and Phrases

1. Amiguita, estás libre. Vamos – Little friend, you are free. Go.
2. Amigo – Friend
3. Brindemos por México! – Let's toast to Mexico!
4. Ciertamente – Certainly
5. Colibri – Hummingbird
6. ¿Cómo estás? – How are you?
7. Cómo va a trabajar en eso – How will you work like that?
8. En privado – In private
9. Hacienda – Estate
10. Hola – Hello
11. Imposible – Impossible
12. La paz sea con vosotros – Peace be with you
13. Lo siento – I'm sorry
14. Medicina – Medicine
15. Niñas, lento, lento – Girls, slow, slow
16. Niñas, rápida, rápida – Girls, quick, quick
17. No entiendo – I do not understand
18. Nombre – Name
19. No perteneces aqu – You do not belong here
20. Pollos – Chickens
21. ¿Quién eres? – Who are you?
22. Señor – Mister
23. Señor, lo siento – Sir, I'm sorry
24. Señora – Misses
25. Señorita, cree como yo – Miss, you believe like me?

26. Tejas – Texas

27. Todos – Everyone

28. Un hombre del abrigo – A man's coat

29. Vamos a ir por la medicina – Let's go for the medicine

30. Vamos, mi amiga – Come on, my friend

French Words and Phrases

1. Allez-vous – Are you going?

2. Bienvenue – Welcome

3. Bonjour – Good day

4. Comment – How? or What?

5. Des – Of

6. Et – And

7. Étrangers – Foreigners

8. Homme – Man

9. Hôte – Host

10. Je – I

11. Le – The

12. Libre – Free

13. Merde – Manure

14. Mon frère – My brother

15. Monsieur – Mister

16. Nabekukatu – Suicide

17. Oui – Yes

18. Propriétaire.Suis – Owner

19. Puis-je vous faire – Can I make you?

20. Un – A

21. Votre – Your

Gaelic Words and Phrases

1. An dara Sealladh – The second sight, a perception that something is going to happen before it does
2. Bydded inni gerdded mewn heddwch – May we walk in peace (Welsh blessing)

German Words and Phrases

1. Das is ein gutes maultier, gutes maultier – This is a good mule, good mule
2. Herr – Mister

African Slave Words and Phrases

1. Yālä käyāla! Yālä käyāla! – He is very sick

Scottish Words and Phrases

1. Mickle – Large amount